For my nana, Maidie

HERE FOR YOU

NORA VALTERS

INKUBATOR
BOOKS

Published by Inkubator Books
www.inkubatorbooks.com

Copyright © 2021 by Nora Valters

ISBN (Paperback): 978-1-915275-06-6
ISBN (eBook): 978-1-915275-07-3

Nora Valters has asserted her right to be identified as the author of this work.

PROLOGUE

Of course it's going to end in murder. All good plans do, don't they?

That money belongs to me. Just imagine what I'll do with it. Everything I'll buy. Everything I'll have. The house, the car, the perfect life.

You've had a blessed life up until now. You've done whatever the hell you liked. But I've struggled. For years, I've struggled. You don't deserve it like I deserve it. You've never appreciated it. I want it more. And I want it now.

This'll be a piece of cake, a walk in the park, as easy as taking sweets off a baby.

I've got my eyes on the prize. I've got my eyes on all that lovely cash. Nothing and no one will stop me. You'll be throwing your pot of gold at me by the time I'm done. And I'll catch it, of course. Take all that money, put it in my pocket and walk away with a carefree smile on my face and a spring in my step.

You've lost your mind before. You're about to lose it again.

And then goodbye, forever. But first, a hello.

1

"Hi, I'm Jessica... er... Donovan." I stumble over my new surname, my third, and hope no one notices.

I scan the thirty or so eager faces for frowns or narrowing eyes, but everyone looks on with interest. I take a swig of my beer and smile. You'd think I'd be used to these by now, having done more than I can count in the past two years. But no, these introductions still make me nervous – especially because I'm so keen to make a good first impression this time.

Taking a deep breath, I continue, "I'm new in town, only moved here last week. Before, I was a digital nomad, working and travelling all over the world. But after two years away, I thought it was time to return to the UK."

There are some nods and whispers across the crowd.

I push on, keen to get this over with, keen to not be the centre of attention anymore. "I'm a remote freelance LinkedIn advertising and content specialist with international clients, predominantly B2B."

Movement to my left catches my eye. It's the co-working space's manager, hovering on the sidelines. He's the one who positioned me against the windows and ushered in everyone else to sit and stand and mill about in a semicircle in front of me, hemming me in so there's no easy escape. The quickest route to the exit is through at least six bodies and over or around various obstacles. Funny how I still think like that – in terms of escape.

I sense it's time to wrap things up. "I'm looking forward to meeting you all and working alongside you all in this great co-working space." I plaster on my biggest grin and lift up my beer bottle. "Cheers!"

There are a few cheers and encouraging murmurs. The manager steps up next to me.

"Thanks, Jessica. I'll be putting all of Jessica's details on the contacts page of the member portal if anyone has any potential client link-ups or projects. And do please come and introduce yourselves tonight." He turns to me and asks, "You'll be staying for a couple more?"

"Definitely."

"Great," he says and turns back to those gathered. "So, everyone, enjoy your Friday Social drinks! As usual, there's free beer or soft drinks in the fridge. Whether you've had a great week or a crap week, let's let off some steam." He lifts his beer, and everyone breaks off into their own conversations, their attention on the front of the room, on me, gone in an instant.

The manager turns to me, and I welcome the conversation. Networking and talking to people who already know one another is always awkward. But before he can say anything, another man comes up to him and takes his arm, leading him to one side with an ominous, "Can I have a quick word?"

So here I am, billy-no-mates, in a room full of creative, cool, freelance types. *It doesn't matter that I'm thirty-nine; I'm one of these types*, I remind myself for the umpteenth time. But it never quite sinks in. Going freelance wasn't really a choice; it was a necessity. I had to get out of Oxford two years ago. To escape. To hide in countries that weren't England. But that's all over now.

This is my chance to make some new friends, to find someone in this sleepy seaside town of Weston-super-Mare who isn't my aunt and uncle's deaf dog to talk to. Who, I must say, is a great listener, so I can't complain, really.

As the buzz of chatting and laughter continues around me, I feel more and more self-conscious stood on my own. Some people are naturals at talking to strangers. Like my husband, Blake... *ex-husband*. I feel a painful stab remembering how our relationship terminated so miserably, so irrevocably.

I haven't thought about him in a long time. I've moved on. What was it that counsellor said? *Focus on the present and don't dwell on the past.* I slide my fingers into my long, brown, wavy hair and lift it off my scalp. It always feels inexplicably heavy when I'm stressed. I flip it back to reveal my weird pointy ears and then pull it forward again to cover them.

While I was in Buenos Aires, with my hair up in a ponytail, a well-meaning Argentinian told me I looked like a plump Liv Tyler as Arwen in the *Lord of the Rings* movies. I didn't take offence. I was immensely flattered. I do have paler than pale skin that fries in the sun, with similar hair and elflike ears. But I'm not tall and slender like the actor. I'm on the heavier side, a pear shape with wide hips but decent boobs. And I have thick, naturally red lips and hazel eyes. But my nose is definitely not as neat as Liv's. It's round like my round face. I readjust my burgundy cat-eye glasses. I've had them for years, the angular shape perfectly balancing out my round features. I got them at a little optician's shop in a backstreet in Oxford.

I take a deep breath. *Get back to the present, Jess.* I've reset with two years away, and I am ready. I'm excited. Now's my chance to start afresh, to live a quiet, drama-free life. Nobody in this town knows me. And nobody – apart from my aunt and uncle, who are off on a world cruise – knows I'm here, thank goodness.

I look around subtly for an opening, for another lone person to casually sidle up to and naturally start a conversation with. But there's no one.

Everyone is in full swing, clumped already with their people, lounging on the comfy velvet sofas, sat along the shabby-chic wooden benches or perched on the vintage-looking barstools around the high tables.

A swirl of anxiety scoops out my insides. That's just the worst – forcing yourself into groups that have already gathered together, who are already talking merrily. But that's precisely what I'm going to have to do.

The beer bottle feels cold and slimy in my hand. The condensation on the outside rolls in fat drops onto my fingers. I take a swig for Dutch courage but discover it's empty. Dammit. I haven't had a drink in a while, and it went down way too fast. Plus, it's stuffy in this room. The heating is cranked right up against the chilly, grey March weather outside. I feel uncomfortably hot in my chunky roll-neck jumper. Perfectly fine attire all day, but now too much, too thick, too suffocating. With my spare hand, I pull the roll off my neck to get some air to my overheating chest.

The room is brightly lit, and I feel as if I'm squinting at everybody. I swallow, and it tastes like the tuna sandwich I had at lunch. I should've brought some mints. The idea of talking to new people with fishy breath heightens my nerves.

I shake it off and gee myself up. I scan for a suitable target. My eyes fall on two people on beanbags. They look promising. And there's a spare beanbag nearby. But I'm held back by my keen knowledge that I can never – and I mean never – get on and off beanbags with any kind of grace. So I decide to spare them the performance and find an easier mark.

There. A group of three near the windows, one propped against the window ledge. All are holding beers, all looking around at the room while talking, and not so immersed in a conversation that it would be jarring for me to interrupt. And all with easy-going demeanours that look open to another attaching themselves to their unit.

Right, let's do this.

I plaster on a let's-get-to-know-one-another look and set my sights on the trio, but before I can head in that direction, I feel a light touch on my forearm.

"Hi, Jessica. I'm Ashley."

A petite, smiley woman stands next to me. Bags of energy and enthusiasm roll off her. She's a good three or four inches shorter than me at perhaps five foot three with a slim, almost scrawny build. Her heart-shaped face is framed with mid-length, wispy blonde hair that is wavy at the roots but straighter at the ends. A growing-out fringe is swept to one side, tucked behind an ear. Fine baby hairs stick up from her side parting and along her hairline.

All her features are delicate: small green eyes, a slim nose tipped with an ever-so-slight upturn, a dainty mouth with thin lips, and rosy cheeks. All except her harsh eyebrows – a bit too dark and a bit too thin for the dinki-ness of her face – and her square chin, the masculine shape in stark contrast to the rest of her pretty features. She has an unassuming and sweet half-smile, her bottom lip catching on her top teeth and jutting out. What she lacks in stature, she definitely makes up for with a confident, bubbly vibe.

Sweet relief. She's saved me by coming up to me first. "Oh, hi, Ashley. Please call me Jess."

"Jess, I brought you another beer. We might as well take

advantage, seeing as they're free." She hands me the beer, and I take it gratefully.

"Perfect timing," I say and hold up my empty. "Just finished this one."

I look around for somewhere to place it, but she saves me again by taking it from me and, with two steps, placing it easily on a nearby high table surrounded by people. They part with friendly nods to let her deposit it. She moves back to me.

"So you're a LinkedIn expert?" Ashley asks.

"Yes. Been doing it for the past two years."

"That's cool. It always amazes me that I still meet freelancers with jobs I've not heard of before."

"Yeah, it is quite niche. I used to work in recruitment for a big firm, and it was a small part of the job. But it was really in demand, so I decided to drill down and learn all about it. And then I left the firm to offer it to clients. It took off massively."

"Good for you. I love to hear freelance success stories like that."

Her genuine praise makes my heart sing. I wonder if she might be someone I could hang out with outside of the co-working place. A new friend. Well, my only friend, really. "Thanks. What do you do?" I ask.

"I'm a marketing freelancer for SMEs. Quite generic stuff, really. I used to work in a small London agency and went out on my own a few years ago. Business ticks along just fine, you know."

"In London?" My soaring heart sinks. Perhaps she's only visiting, and after tonight, I'll never see her again. Disappointment rears up, but I keep it out of my voice and keep my tone light. "What are you doing in Weston?"

"Well, believe it or not, I'm actually new in town too. That's why I thought I'd come and say hello. I only moved here two weeks ago. And I only started at this place last

Monday. I had to do the dreaded introduction this time last week, so I know how it feels." She laughs.

"Yay, another newbie," I reply. "What made you move here?"

"The property in London is so ridiculously expensive, and I'm fed up with renting. And the pace is just insane. I want to buy a nice, affordable house by the sea and live a more chilled, healthy lifestyle. And you? What are you doing in this quiet town after all your gallivanting around the world?"

"It was definitely time to come back. There's only so much sleeping in a different bed every few days that I could handle." I laugh, and she nods in understanding. "My aunt and uncle live here. They're my only family, so I thought why not?"

I don't tell her that I can't go back to where I was living. That I sold my house before I left and cut all ties. That it's better that way.

"Why not, indeed," she replies.

I say, "Here's to our new lives in Weston-super-Mare!"

She clinks her bottle to mine. "To a quiet life by the sea!" We both sip our beer.

After a few gulps, I say, "I'm looking forward to exploring the town."

"Ooh, me too," she replies enthusiastically.

"Perhaps we could do some exploring together?" I say before I can stop myself. I definitely don't want to come across as too desperate.

But I needn't have worried. Her face lights up.

"That's a wonderful idea," she exclaims and squeezes my forearm.

"I need to hit up the arcade at the end of the pier and try to win an ugly teddy or some sweets or a pencil sharpener or something."

She laughs. "OMG, yes!"

The manager appears before us with a tray of drinks. "More beer for you two?"

"Sounds good," I say and down the last of my second beer before placing it on the tray and taking another bottle.

Ashley does the same, and I think: *A girl after my own heart, can't leave even a drop. Excellent.*

The manager heads off to the next group.

Ashley pulls a lip balm from her jeans pocket and applies it to her delicate mouth.

"Mmm, that smells nice," I say as the fragrance hits me.

Ashley shows me the tube using two hands as if she's presenting the product on a TV advert. "It's peach flavoured, peach tinted and peach scented. It's my absolute favourite. I swear I get through one a month, I love it so much."

My eyes linger on her hands. They are inexplicably attractive with long, perfect fingers, expertly manicured fingernails and unblemished skin.

Ashley asks, "Are you looking at my hands?"

I've been totally rumbled, and I'm not entirely sure what to say. "Er... yeah... sorry."

"Ha, don't worry. They're strangely elegant, aren't they? In another life, I'd be a hand model." She flounces her hands about, and we both laugh.

"Come on," Ashley says and links her arm through mine, "let's go and socialise. I'll introduce you to everyone. I want to see if I can remember everybody's names. It'll be like a game."

"Sounds good," I say. And it does sound like the best idea anyone has ever had – I'm shy at first and terrible at introducing myself to strangers, but if I have a wingwoman to do the introductions, I'm naturally a social creature, naturally a talker. Especially now that I'm a couple of beers down and feeling a tad tipsy. This is going to be a great night, I can tell.

.   .   .

"SEE YOU ON MONDAY. Have a great weekend," the manager says as he lets Ashley and me out the front door of The Hive co-working space and locks up. Ashley shoulders her backpack with her laptop and slings her small handbag across her body. I hitch my heavy bag up and attempt not to knock my laptop.

We were the last two there, chatting with everyone and with each other all night. Ashley remembered everyone's names, which is a feat in itself, and we took full advantage of the well-stocked fridge.

The manager heads off on his bike in the opposite direction to where I live, and we wave him off.

"Whereabouts do you live? I'm in this direction," I say, pointing down the street.

A group of lads spill out of a pub a few doors down and make a racket, hollering football chants and play-fighting with one another before disappearing up a side alley. It's late and dark, and I realise I've never been out in town on a Friday night before. My walk to The Hive from my aunt and uncle's house is only fifteen minutes. Too close to call a taxi, but almost too far as a lone woman at night.

It'll be fine, I reassure myself. I've travelled to some far-flung places and never had an issue. What's going to happen in an old Victorian seaside resort in the off season?

"I'm that way too," Ashley replies and stumbles into me as she marches off down the street.

We fall in line, knocking elbows and bumping shoulders as we struggle to walk straight.

"I've had so much fun," I say.

"Me too. That's been the best night out I've had since I moved here," Ashley replies. "Let's do it again soon."

"Ab-so-lutely," I slur.

We turn a few corners, dodge some Friday-night revellers, make our way around a long, rowdy queue for a kebab shop and skirt round some sick. But Ashley misjudges it and steps in a big puddle that splashes up her legs.

"Oh," Ashley says, staring at her submerged shoe.

I burst into a fit of giggles, and Ashley joins in. We walk further away from the town centre down a deserted street.

"I'm up this way," Ashley says and indicates a road on the right.

I hug her. "So lovely to meet you. You've got my number. Let's get together soon."

She bear-hugs me back, salutes, and turns up her road. I continue on.

Almost immediately, my good mood evaporates. The street is empty and dark. It's a pleasant route during the day, but now it feels sinister. A chill dances up my spine and spreads across the back of my neck. I feel as if I have a spotlight on me and an arrow pointing above me for all to see that says 'lone woman, ripe for the picking'.

Don't be daft, Jess. This is a quiet seaside town in North Somerset. I'm not in one of the most dangerous cities in the world. I pause to shake out the paranoia from my limbs but hear footsteps. They immediately stop. Oh my God, there's someone behind me. I pick up my pace. The slapping of feet on the damp pavement picks up too. My breath catches, and fear rubs against my ribcage. Screw this, it could just be a woman wanting to walk close to another for safety. I stop and look. Big mistake. I get bundled by a hooded figure – clearly a man – into some large wheelie bins down a narrow alley between two buildings.

He's strong, and my mind is dulled by the alcohol, but the sudden pain of slamming against the bins momentarily knocks me sober. I scream at the top of my lungs. He pushes me in between the bins and face first up against the brick wall. It knocks the breath out of me, and my scream fizzles to nothing. He wrangles with my hands to pin them behind my back and uses his chest to press my torso into the wall.

I thrash and jerk, shouting for help. My bag slips off my shoulder and falls to the ground. Beer and bile launch up my throat, but I swallow them back. Then a small voice in my booze-addled brain says, *You should've vomited. That stops attackers.* But that thought disappears faster than it arrived and is replaced by all the terrible things that are about to happen to me flashing through my mind.

The man's breathing is heavy in my ear. "I've got a knife," he hisses.

Oh shit. My pulse hammers, and my legs turn to jelly.

But his grip loosens.

"Get the fuck away from her!" a woman yells.

He steps away from me and holds up his arms to fend off the swinging handbag the woman smacks against his body and head.

I peel myself off the wall and see red – just like I did with *her*. I lash out at the attacker with my fists, then my feet. "That's right, get the fuck away from me," I shout.

The man backs away and sprints up the alley.

I go to charge after him, but a hand on my arm holds me back.

"Oh, Jess, are you okay?" the woman says, and I realise it's Ashley.

The fury clears, and I put the memory of *her* back in the box marked 'The Past' in my mind. I look at Ashley open-mouthed. Gratitude, relief, shock and fear all ooze out of my pores, but words can't find their way out of my mouth. I blink at her.

She continues, "I heard a scream..."

She picks up my bag, puts her arm around me, and leads me out of the alley back onto the main road. At that moment, the heavens decide to open.

"It was him," I blurt before I can stop myself. "It has to be him."

"Him? You know who that was?" Ashley asks while holding up her handbag – moments ago used as a weapon – to shield her face from the downpour.

"My brother."

2

_____

"Your brother?" Ashley asks uncertainly.

"No. No, it can't be," I backtrack.

"Jeez, Jess, if you know who that was... you need to tell the police."

The shock of the attack jolts it all loose. I know I should hold my tongue, but I can't. I babble almost incoherently, "He stalked me once before, but a very long time ago, when he was angry."

"Fuck," Ashley replies. "Are you sure it was him?"

"No. It must be a stranger. He doesn't know I'm here. I've kept my whereabouts secret for years. I'm careful not to post on social media and that sort of thing. He can't possibly know."

"Right," Ashley says, confusion flashing across her face. I can see she wants to help me but doesn't know how.

I'm making no sense. I know I'm not. I need to bottle everything up again, put a stopper on it so it doesn't spill out. I thought two years away making new memories had chased away the bad ones once and for all. But they're still there, lurking. Being back in England has made them bubble up to the surface again. I need to get a handle on it. It's all done now. I know it's all done now. I'm safe – from my brother, from Blake, from *her*.

Rain slaps my face, and I take in Ashley. She's just as shaken up as me, her face ashen and her bottom lip quivering. Her eyes are so wide they're almost popping out of her skull. I channel the adrenaline coursing about my body to think practically.

"Let's head back to mine," I say in a voice much steadier than I was expecting. "Neither of us should be walking home alone right now. And then you can call a taxi back from mine. I'll call the police on the way."

"Sounds like a plan."

I grab her arm. "Just forget I mentioned anything about my brother."

"Sure," she replies with a shrug, as if she's already forgotten.

We hurry through the puddles, clutching each other. My shaking fingers fumble in my bag for my phone.

I LEAVE Ashley dripping by the front door to sprint upstairs, grab a wedge of towels from the airing cupboard, and run back, attempting not to get too much water on my aunt's carpet.

"Here." I hand her two large towels.

We're both absolutely drenched from the rain. I peel off my coat and hang it in the hallway, putting a towel on the floor to catch the drips. Then I pull off my boots and leave them on the towel. Ashley follows suit.

She wraps a towel around her hair like a turban. She pinches her sopping wet jeans. "Do you mind if I take these off?"

"Go for it," I say as I dry off my long hair with a towel and wrap it in the same way as Ashley. My long coat and knee-high boots kept most of the rain off my skirt and tights. And the hood did a good job, but I feel damp all over.

Ashley puts the second towel around her waist and legs like a sarong. "That's better."

"The police should be here any minute. I need to let the dog out. Do you want a tea?"

"Or something stronger?" she suggests.

I look at her, and she waggles her eyebrows. I smirk. We're both still inebriated. In shock, yes, but still full of beer.

She continues, "Just kidding. A tea would be perfect, thanks."

I guide her through to the large open-plan kitchen-diner at the back of the house. The Victorian terrace is deceptively large, looking narrow from the front but going back a long way. It has three floors, the roof converted into an en-suite bedroom and a further four bedrooms and two bathrooms on the first floor. It had been a bed and breakfast when my aunt and uncle first moved in twenty years ago.

The décor is solely my aunt's responsibility, and the place is homely and comfortable but with a quirky vibe. My aunt lives for patterns and colours. Each room has a theme and invariably one too many colours or patterns that ever-so-slightly clash. The walls are predominantly adorned with Aunt Alice's watercolour paintings of shells, Highland cattle, or their dog, Doug.

Doug is fast asleep in his bed next to the radiator and under the dining table. I kneel down and tap on the floor and blow gently on the little dog's fur, something Aunt Alice told me to do to wake him up without startling him.

His eyes ping open, and he jumps up in his bed and stretches. I stand.

"He's old and completely deaf now," I explain to Ashley.

"He's gorgeous," she gushes and bends over to fuss him. "What is he?"

"A border terrier," I reply.

"And what's he called?"

"Doug."

"Doug the dog! I love it."

She lifts him up into her arms and nuzzles her face into his. Doug laps it up.

"He lives for fuss and attention. Don't you, Doug?" I say and tickle behind his ears.

He squirms, and Ashley sets him down. He runs through the kitchen to the back door, pawing at the glass to be let out. I follow him, unlock the door and open it for him. He dashes out. I leave the door ajar and head back into the kitchen to put the kettle on.

As I'm reaching for two mugs from the cupboard, the doorbell rings.

"The police," Ashley says.

I open the door to the two police officers and invite them into the large lounge at the front with a big bay window that overlooks the street. It has a nautical theme with two brown leather sofas, a window seat covered in a sand-coloured fabric dotted with starfish, wood flooring and a dark-blue rug with a sailboat pattern. To set off the marine feel, there are three bright-blue lifebuoy prints across one wall and a mirror above the fireplace adorned with thick knotted white rope. I offer the officers a drink, which they decline. I offer them a seat. One sits on a sofa, and the other stands. I sit on the window seat. Ashley comes to sit next to me.

It's comforting and reassuring to have her so close. I take her hand. She squeezes mine in return.

We sit there, hand in hand, attempting to be sober but actually propping each other up, as the police introduce themselves. Their names go in one ear and out the other, and I've forgotten within seconds.

"So, you're Jessica Donovan?" the seated police officer asks while taking out his notepad and jotting notes.

"Yes," I reply.

He turns his attention to Ashley. "And you're Ashley...?" He gestures in a way that asks her to confirm her surname.

"Ashley Brown," she replies.

He looks around the room, and his eyes catch on the in-your-face lifebuoy prints for a second before falling back on me. "And this is your house, Jessica?"

"It belongs to my aunt and uncle. Edwin and Alice Donovan. They won some money on the lottery and have gone on a ten-month world cruise, the lucky things, and I'm here house- and dog-sitting for them while they're away."

"I see. And how long have you been here?"

"Only a week. I can't believe this has happened. Such bad luck."

"Yes, it is." The police officer flips a page on his notepad and pauses to write something.

"I'm a Gemini. They're one of the unluckiest zodiac signs, apparently. Bad luck just seems to follow me around. Do you read your horoscope? I always read mine. Bit obsessed..." I fill the silence, having an inexplicable urge to talk.

The police in the house are making me twitchy rather than reassured. The skin across my back itches. They can't possibly know what happened three years ago, when I made a deal not to tell them what *she'd* done. What I'd done. I rabbit on, "In fact, my horoscope did say that I was going to have a bad day when I read it yesterday morning—"

"Can you give a description of the attacker?" the officer cuts in, clearly not impressed with my chatter.

"It was definitely a man. Tall, broad, strong. But the hood of his coat was up, and he had a black scarf wrapped around his face. His eyes were in shadow, so I couldn't see them. He was wearing a black coat, blue jeans, black trainers – I think – and black gloves."

"Did he have any distinguishing features like tattoos or a limp? Was he wearing anything unusual or different?"

I glance at Ashley, and she chews the side of her lip, thinking.

My earlier outburst that it was my brother seems ridiculous now. So I don't mention it. "No," I reply. "I can't think of anything."

"Neither can I," Ashley says, respecting the fact that I asked her earlier to forget my outburst too. I like her even more for that.

"Do you have any other family nearby, Jessica? Just to look in on you over the next few days? You've had a shock. Your parents, perhaps?"

"No, my parents are no longer with us," I reply.

Ashley squeezes my hand.

"And what about you, Ashley?"

"My parents are no longer with us, either," she says and gives me a knowing, supportive look.

"Does either of you know anyone else in town?"

"Just my boyfriend," Ashley answers. "But he's away this weekend. We're new here too."

After a few more questions, the seated police officer, who's done most of the talking, stands and gives a look to his colleague. She makes a move, and we all follow her to the front door.

The officer talks as he walks. "Jessica, Ashley, thanks for your time. We'll have a look to see if there's any CCTV of that area and put a call out for any witnesses. We'll also check our database for any previous attacks of a similar nature and see if there was a perpetrator identified. But otherwise, without a clear description, we don't really have much to go on. We'll be in touch if we find anything."

"Thank you, Officer," I say.

Before he leaves, he says, "Look after each other, especially since you don't know anyone else in town yet. Sounds like you're lucky to have met one another."

I close the door and turn back to Ashley.

"That was intense," she says.

"Sure was a shite end to the evening."

"Are Geminis really unlucky, then?" she asks.

"Uh-huh."

"What about Scorpios?"

"You're a Scorpio?"

"Yep."

I give her a sad look. "Unfortunately, Scorpios are pretty unlucky too."

"Ha, well, that figures."

"But one good thing has come of today."

"Oh yeah? What's that?"

I poke her playfully. "We met each other!"

"Yes, we did. Hurrah for that." She opens her arms wide to me.

We hug, then wander back into the lounge and sprawl on the sofas.

"So, um, you're an orphan too?" she asks.

"Yes. My mum died when I was fourteen and then my dad at sixteen."

She nods. "I'm sorry."

"Yes, it was horrendous. I came to live with my aunt and uncle. But they lived in Exeter at the time. And you?"

"Mine died in a car crash when I was eight. My, um, dad was drunk driving."

"That's awful. I'm so sorry."

"Yeah, it was. I was carted off to my godparents. And then

after some unpleasant drama at fifteen, I moved in with my nearly-always-drunk grandad. It wasn't the best childhood. But that's in the past now."

"Sounds tough. I had a pretty rotten time growing up too. But we make our own way now. Thank goodness we're adults, ha."

"Thank goodness," she agrees. "You know, it's nice to meet someone whose parents died when they were younger. It's not an easy thing to try to explain to people. That feeling of such immense loss. But you get it."

"Yes, I do." There's a deep, deep well inside me marked 'Crushing Grief for Parents'. It will always be there, but I've got better at not falling down it, and I rarely visit it anymore. But talking about them with Ashley makes it pull at me. I do my best to ignore it. I don't want to plummet down that hole.

Ashley smiles at me before slapping her thighs. "Right, I should put my soggy jeans back on and get home. Might call a taxi first though."

She picks her handbag up from the floor. She finds her phone and fumbles with it. "Can't flipping remember the name of the taxi firm. It's in my contacts somewhere..." She scrolls.

A huge crash rattles through the house from the back door.

Startled, Ashley drops her phone. And my heart leaps into my mouth.

3

"What the hell was that?" Ashley whispers.

I freeze, waiting for the sound to come again. When it doesn't, I look around. "Doug? Where's Doug? Oh shit, did I leave him outside all this time?"

I jog through to the kitchen. Ashley picks up her phone and follows hot on my heels.

The back door is no longer ajar. It's wide open. Rain falls in sheets outside, splattering the wood-effect lino flooring.

"Doug," I call from the doorway and then realise that's pointless. I have to go and find him; he can't hear me calling.

I switch the garden light on and slip on a pair of garden shoes by the back door. They're huge, so they probably belong to my uncle. I unwrap the towel on my head and hold it above me.

"There was an umbrella by the front door. I'll go and get it," Ashley says and dashes off.

I step out into the night, the large bath towel keeping off most of the rain. The well-maintained garden is an odd shape, an upside-down L, long and thin with an extra bit at the top, which is around a corner. It used to belong to a neighbour. The extra bit is grassed with an area for the rubbish bins.

The outdoor light doesn't reach quite this far, and I curse myself for not bringing a torch. But it's just about bright enough to see.

I stop dead in my tracks at what I see when I turn the corner.

It's not the dog. It's the bins.

They've been tipped over, rubbish strewn everywhere. All three are on their sides. And all three are empty, the contents spewed over the grass. It looks like they've been... searched through?

"Did Doug do this?" Ashley's voice comes from behind me, and I'm relieved she's there.

"He must've done," I reply.

"Stupid dog," she says, but with affection.

"Yeah," I reply.

But could a little, old dog cause this much carnage? Even his running full tilt at the bins might not tip them over. But to topple them *and* make them vomit their insides up everywhere?

My gut twinges. There's something not right about this.

"Where is he?" Ashley asks. She's hunkered under a big golf umbrella and with one hand turns on the flashlight app on her phone, shining it around the garden in all the dark nooks and crannies.

I also look around, but not for Doug. The extra bit of garden is surrounded by low fences and vegetation. It's not exactly private, and it's not exactly intruder-proof. A cold droplet of water soaks through the towel and plops on my forehead.

"Let's get inside," I say and gently shove Ashley ahead of me in the direction of the back door.

"Oh, look," she exclaims as we get closer.

There, sat in the dry kitchen, observing us like we're barmy, is Doug.

She fusses him as we get into the kitchen, and I lock the back door. I debate whether to turn off the back light and then decide to leave it on to be on the safe side. As a deterrent.

"Is that the bathroom?" Ashley asks, pointing to a door that leads off the kitchen to the utility area and downstairs loo.

"Yes," I reply. "Help yourself."

"Won't be a sec. I'm bursting."

While she's in the bathroom, I stand in the middle of the empty kitchen, in the middle of the big, empty house, and I shudder. It's a violent full-body jerk. I'm spooked. I've been happily living here this past week on my own. I craved my own space, some quiet, some alone time after two years of staying in bustling hostels or lively hotels or in apartments in large, busy blocks.

That had been a choice then: I'd wanted the company, as I hated to be alone in a building and needed to have people all around. But I'd got that out of my system and felt strong enough to be the only person in a house again. I couldn't wait to have my aunt and uncle's place all to myself. That's how I knew it was time to return to England. But, for the first time in the week that I've been back, I don't want to be here on my own.

It rises to the surface – what *she* did to me in my own home when she knew I was alone. And my hatred of being there solo afterwards. I had loved that Oxford house, bought it when I was just eighteen and lived in it until I went off travelling. A pang in my chest tells me I still miss it. I feel silly for missing bricks and mortar. The attack and now this bin weirdness are shaking free feelings that I thought were well behind me after two years away.

Ashley joins me in the kitchen. "Right, I'd better book that taxi."

"Do you think that was weird?"

"What was weird?"

"All the bins tipped over like that? Do you really think Doug did all that?"

"How else did it happen? It must've been the daft dog."

I smile at her, tamping down my uneasiness. Doug's the culprit. Of course he is. My teeth grind and chatter, whether from being cold and damp or from feeling out of sorts, I can't be sure. Although I suspect it's the latter. No matter how much I try to contain it, I can feel the anxiety of being in the house on my own growing.

Ashley dials the number and then hangs up. "Wait, what's the address here? That might help."

"I've got it written down in the other room. I haven't memorised the postcode yet."

We head back into the lounge, and I hand Ashley the notepad where I've written the full address. She rummages in her handbag as she dials the taxi firm and holds the phone to her ear. As it rings, she frowns.

"That's not good," she mumbles. Her search becomes more frantic.

I hear someone answer her call on the other end, but she hangs up the phone. She drops to her knees on the rug and tips her bag upside down, separating the contents – wallet, peach lip balm, tissues, a dog-eared paperback of Jane Austen's *Pride and Prejudice* – and turning things upside down.

"Everything okay?" I ask.

"No, my keys aren't there."

"Might they be in your backpack?"

"I never usually put them in there," she says, but she

grabs her backpack and rummages in all the pockets and in the compartment holding her laptop. "Nope. They must've fallen out when I was hitting the attacker. Bollocks. I can't get in my apartment."

"Does anyone else have a set of keys?"

"Yeah, my boyfriend. But he's away this weekend in London until Sunday. Or my landlord. But he's an arsehole, and I doubt he'll appreciate me calling him at"—she checks the time on her phone—"almost two in the morning. Urgh."

She goes through her things another time. She looks up at me. "I'm really sorry to ask this. But is there any chance I can crash here? I can stay on the sofa, you don't need to sort me a bed or anything, and in the morning I can retrace my steps and see if the keys are still in that alleyway. Or call my landlord. Or get my boyfriend to come home early. I know it's not your house, so I don't want to impose..." She trails off.

"Of course you can stay here," I say immediately, a little too eagerly. "It's a four-bedroom house; there's plenty of room. And my aunt and uncle told me I could have guests over and visitors to stay. And to treat the place as my own while I'm here. So no problem at all."

Ashley stands and hugs me. "Thank you so, so much."

"To be honest, you're doing me a favour. After everything that's happened tonight, I really don't feel like being on my own in the house anyway."

"It's been one stressful evening," Ashley agrees.

My anxiousness dissolves at the knowledge I won't be alone tonight.

"Welcome to Weston-super-Mare!" I declare, and Ashley laughs. "Come on, I'll put you in the back bedroom. Everything in it is blue with a bit of a jazzy Aztec theme. And you'll have your own bathroom just outside. Not quite an en-suite, but right next door."

"Sounds perfect," Ashley replies.

"And you can borrow some of my PJs."

"That's so kind of you."

"It's the least I can do for you, honey, after you saved me."

"What are friends for?" she says.

4

"Morning," I mumble as Ashley appears in the kitchen-diner. "How's the head?"

She groans and rubs a palm over her forehead. Her blonde wispy hair sticks out at all angles, and the back is one big muss. She's drowning in my pyjamas, which are a good few sizes too big for her, and she has to hold up the legs of the trousers so they don't drag along the floor.

I heave myself up from the dining chair and have to steady myself as my hangover reels precariously. "Fancy a coffee?"

"Yes, please. What time is it?" Ashley peers up at the clock on the wall. "Gosh, it's nearly midday," she exclaims. "I can't believe I slept so late. Sorry, have you been up for a while?"

"Goodness, no. I literally just dragged myself out of bed." I wander into the kitchen and put the kettle on. "How do you take it?" I ask as I find the coffee jar.

"Black, strong and with one sweetener if you have any, or one sugar if not."

My aunt likes to keep a very well-stocked kitchen, and I

hunt in the cupboards for sweeteners, sure she'll have some somewhere. The kitchen has a country-cottage vibe with jars, plants and teapots everywhere and a big sage-green range cooker. The concentration of the search makes my head pound at twice the intensity as before. "Ah, here we go."

As I make her drink, Ashley takes a seat at the dining table. "I didn't quite realise how drunk I was last night. But I'm hanging this morning."

"Same."

"How you doing after the attack?"

I put her steaming mug down on a coaster in front of her and sit back down. "I'm feeling fine. Just rotten luck. I was in the wrong place at the wrong time. Thank goodness you heard me scream. I'll know now not to walk home alone at night."

"Yeah, I will too. I thought it would be really safe here, but I suppose you can't be too careful anywhere." She blows on her coffee and then takes a sip. "Oh, that tastes good."

"Have you got any plans today? Looks a bit miserable out there, but I think the rain's going to hold off."

"No plans. The boyfriend is away until tomorrow night, so I was just going to potter about. Maybe retrace my steps to see if I can find my house keys or just bite the bullet and call the landlord. You?"

"Well, first I have to clear up that mess outside."

"What mess outside?"

"The bins."

"Oh, yeah." She scans the room. "Where is that toerag of a dog?"

"Watching the world go by from the lounge window. If he's not in his bed, that's his second favourite spot."

"Aww."

"I'm not looking forward to it. It's going to be gross."

Ashley takes a sip of her coffee. "Yeah, bin juice, yuck."

My swirling, crazy thoughts last night – that the attacker was my brother and that someone had gone through my bins – seem ridiculous now in the cold light of day. I haven't heard from my brother in ten years, and nobody knows I'm here. Everyone has moved on. I'd moved on too; that's why I knew it was time to come home. *Right, from now on, Jess, keep the past in the past.*

"I tell you what," Ashley says brightly. "I'll help you with the bins, and then we can go and grab some lunch at that pub down the end of the road. It's meant to be really nice in there, and I've not been yet. What do you reckon?"

"You want to help me clear up a load of stinky rubbish? You're mad."

"Ha, yeah, that bit I'm not looking forward to, but I've got a bad case of the hungover munchies, and the quicker that crap outside gets sorted, the quicker you'll be ready to join me for a good feed. C'mon. Let's go." Ashley launches herself up, groans a little and massages her forehead again, and then heads for the back door.

Her enthusiasm for clearing up rubbish makes me chuckle. The crazy woman. But her enthusiasm for lunch I can get behind. I'm ravenous too. I follow her to the back door, picking up a roll of black bin bags from the utility area on the way. We both find a pair of garden clogs in the box of shoes. I dig around and find a pair of tatty gardening gloves.

I don the gloves, then open the back door and look at Ashley. "Let's do this." She gives me a nod.

At the end of the garden and around the corner, Ashley holds open a black bag while I scoop up litter. Together, we make short work of it.

About thirty minutes later, we're both showered, dressed, and ready to head out, deciding to forgo make-up and scraping our unwashed hair into ponytails to get to the pub quicker for lunch.

"Are you okay if I leave my laptop bag here and pick it up later rather than lug it to the pub?" Ashley asks.

"Yeah, feel free." I grab the house keys. "Ready?"

We leave the house and walk the few steps to the pub. Aunt Alice had said it did great food and that I should give it a go, so I'm delighted to be here. And as I look around the bustling restaurant area, I'm pleased that I'm not here on my own.

"I know what I'm having," Ashley says after scanning the menu for all of two seconds.

"What's that?"

"The steak and French fries. With pepper sauce. And mayo for the fries. That's my favourite meal of all time. There's no way I'm eating anything else."

"Yum. I'm going to have fish and chips with mushy peas and tartare sauce. That's my favourite."

"Perfect! Thank goodness we came here." Ashley claps her hands.

"And... I know this is all kinds of wrong, but I think I'm going to get a shandy."

"Ha, I was literally just thinking the same thing – hair of the dog might sort us out." She turns and calls over a server, who comes to take our order.

Ashley pops to the toilet and arrives back as our drinks do: two shandies and two pints of lemonade and orange juice to rehydrate.

I take a few gulps of the soft drink, followed by a long swig of the shandy. "Ah, that tastes good. I can't wait for food."

"Me neither. So, tell me about your travels. Where did you go?"

"I went all over, really. It's a long story."

"Tell me everything. I have all the time in the world today."

"Well, I started in Bali in Indonesia and stayed at this surf and yoga place."

"Wow, so cool. How did that work with your job?"

"I surfed first thing in the morning. Came back to my little bungalow to eat breakfast and worked for a few hours. Then I did a yoga class before lunch and spent the afternoon working before perhaps going for a swim in the pool or for a walk along the beach before dinner. Then dinner and evening yoga or drinks at the bar. It really was an incredible experience. I was there for six weeks."

Ashley leans into me, eyes wide. "Jealous! What did you do next?"

"After, I went to Dubai, then spent a while hopping around Asia before heading over to South America and hanging out in Buenos Aires for a few months. I loved it there. Then to Peru, Colombia and Mexico. After that I went to New York because I thought it would be cool to live in that buzzy city. And it was cool, but it was super expensive, and I'd already blown my budget."

"Were you not earning while you were there?"

"Oh yes, I was still working pretty much full time remotely. But I still wanted to do all the touristy things and not deny myself anything. Plus, the flights were a big expense, so I had to dig into my savings a bit."

The food arrives, and Ashley rubs her hands together and then stretches across the table to squeeze my shoulders in delight. We tuck in. After a few mouthfuls, I ask, "How about you? Have you travelled anywhere?"

"No. I've not really left the UK. I'm not a massive fan of flying. I've been to France once on the ferry, but that's pretty much it. Living in London has been so expensive, so I've never really had the funds. Any spare cash has gone into savings for a house deposit. But one day, I'll go. I want to go everywhere."

"Where would you go if you could go anywhere right now?"

"Oh, definitely South America. I've got a bit of a thing about ancient civilisations like the Mayans and the Incas."

"Really?"

"Yeah, geeky I know, but I watched a TV programme about it, and it was fascinating."

"I went to a few Mayan ruins when I was in Mexico. It is absolutely fascinating."

"Ooh, tell me more."

A couple of hours later, after eating and drinking and talking about all sorts, we head back to mine so Ashley can grab her laptop from the lounge.

"Gosh. I'm stuffed," I say as I plonk myself on the sofa and reach for the telly remote while Ashley sorts out her backpack.

"Same," she replies. "That was amazing food, so pleased we went there. All I want to do now is to lie on a sofa and watch movies all afternoon. In fact, that's probably exactly what I'll do when I get home."

"That's exactly my plan! Do you fancy staying and watching one here?"

"Yeah, why not? That sofa has my name on it." She melts into the sofa on the other side of the room. "OMG, I'm sooooo comfy right now."

"What shall we watch? What are you into?"

"Anything, really. But I do love a bit of action comedy or funny superhero stuff. Like..." She trails off as she thinks of a movie.

"*Deadpool*? *Guardians of the Galaxy*? *Thor: Ragnarok*?"

"Yes! All of the above. I guess we need to decide on Ryan Reynolds, Chris Pratt or Chris Hemsworth?"

I pretend to ponder this with hand to chin. "Hmm, tough choice."

"Chris Hemsworth," Ashley says.

"*Thor: Ragnarok* it is."

"Or why not all three?"

"Ha. That's some kind of movie marathon right there."

She shrugs. "I'm not doing anything else today – you?"

"What? Apart from watching superhero movies? Nope."

"Good times," she says and grins at me.

We settle in as I find the first movie on a streaming platform.

HOURS LATER, after the credits roll on our third movie – *Deadpool* – my stomach grumbles.

"I can't believe I'm saying this after our massive lunch, but... are you hungry?"

Ashley wriggles around on the sofa to look at me. "Yeah. I am, actually."

"I'm not sure what I have in the fridge. And I'm not sure I can be arsed to cook. Shall we get a takeaway?"

"A takeaway sounds amazing. But I don't think I can afford to eat out twice in one day, to be honest. Have to be careful not to spend too much at the moment because of trying to buy a house."

"Oh, it's on me. To say thank you for last night."

"Really? Wow, that's so kind."

"And I owe you for helping me clear up the rubbish this morning."

Ashley waves her hand at me. "Oh, that was nothing, really."

"Seriously, it's on me. What do you fancy?"

She pauses to think for a moment and pats her stomach as if asking its opinion. "Thai?"

"Done."

AFTER EATING ourselves stupid and watching *Deadpool 2*, I know it's time for bed. I check the time on my phone. It's late, nearly midnight. Ashley is almost asleep on the sofa opposite, cuddling Doug under one arm. The dog snores contentedly. Ashley's eyes flicker as she attempts to keep them open.

"Why don't you stay here another night?" I suggest. "I don't want you walking home after last night, and there's a bed for you here. And pyjamas."

"You don't mind?"

"Not in the slightest. I'm enjoying having a friend to stay." And it's true. Last night I didn't want to be in the house on my own, but tonight is different. That freak-out has passed, and it feels like a lovely, normal girly evening and sleepover. "Plus, you don't have your keys, and it's too late to call your landlord."

"Oh, crap, you're right. I'd totally forgotten about that. Thank you." She tumbles herself off the sofa, and I haul myself up.

As we head up the stairs to the bedrooms, Ashley says, "I'd much rather stay here than the teeny studio flat that I'm renting at the moment. Kevin and I are trying to save as much as possible, so we didn't want to fork out on rent while we get to know the area and suss out what's on the market. I swear your front room is bigger than my entire apartment."

"There's plenty of room here. Consider that your bedroom now, for whenever you come to stay."

"You're the best."

She gives me a hug as we part in the hallway, her going off to the bedroom at the back and me heading towards the one at the side of the house. It's known as the 'pink room' and has bedsheets, carpets, curtains and wallpaper in various shades, from fuchsia to pastel, as well as patterns including cherry blossoms and polka dots.

The biggest bedroom by far is in the loft conversion, but that's my aunt and uncle's room, and they moved lots of 'odds and sods' up there before they headed off, to declutter the rest of the house for me. I've never been up there, and I wonder briefly what the décor theme is.

THE NEXT MORNING, we're up at a relatively decent hour for a Sunday and compared to the late start we had yesterday. Ashley drinks a black coffee and gets ready to head off home.

"I've had a great couple of days, babe. Thank you. But I need to go and call the landlord to let me in and sort out the flat before Kevin gets home. And do some laundry. And various other bits of boring life admin. Will I see you tomorrow at The Hive?"

"You certainly will."

"Are you sure you're okay after Friday night?"

"Yeah, I'm fine. Forgotten all about it."

And it's true. I have. Just a minor blip. I file it away with all the other blips in my head and vow to focus on the present. And on my new friend, who has made my weekend.

We hug, and she heads out the door with a look back over her shoulder and a wave.

"Come on then, Doug, the weather looks half-decent out there. Let's go for a walk," I say.

Doug cocks his head at me and blinks, having zero comprehension of what I've just said. Even though I know he's deaf, I still talk to him. Hard habit to break, talking to dogs. Then I reach for his lead by the front door, and he bounces up and down, whining. He's so excited about walkies that I struggle to get him to stay still long enough to get his harness over his head and fasten the lead to it.

I take him for an hour-long walk to the seafront and along the beach. It's bracing by the sea, the wind kicking up sand in my face. The tide is out, and Doug sniffs longingly at the water in the distance – too far and too muddy for us to get to. He likes a paddle, according to my uncle.

"It'll be too cold for you anyway, boy," I say out loud before chuckling inwardly and looking around to make sure no one noticed me not only talking to a dog but talking to a dog who has a neon orange bandana on his harness that says 'I'm Deaf'.

We turn and head home, walking the ten minutes to my aunt and uncle's Victorian terrace. It's not Bali, but it's perfect. The fresh air lifts my spirits, and the cold energises me. I'm pleased to be back in England. There's no place like home, as they say.

I open the gate to the little paved front garden, and Doug pulls on the lead to get to the front door. I let his lead go as I shut the gate. I know he can't get out, as the wall that surrounds the garden is waist-high on me.

He snuffles intently at something on the square of black-and-white Victorian-style tiles by the front door. Not the originals, as my uncle told me sadly. They couldn't be saved.

"What is it, Doug?" I say and attempt to shoo him off with my foot.

The dog continues to fuss, so I grab his harness and pull him away.

"Oh, my!" I blurt. Then I hold my other hand to my mouth.

It's a dead mouse. Its insides spill onto the tile, and there's the tiniest pool of blood. I retch and take a step back. What the hell is a butchered mouse doing on my doorstep?

I immediately look around me, into my neighbours' front gardens, down the street, up at the house. There's no one about. But movement catches my eye from across the road. A ginger cat jumps from a fence into a garden.

A cat. Of course. It's been dropped by a cat. Or a bird. It's nothing sinister. Just like the attack on Friday night and the toppled bins were nothing sinister. I'm a Gemini, aren't I? It's just bad luck.

It's nothing.

I pick up Doug so he doesn't try to eat the thing, carefully step over it and unlock the front door. Once inside, Doug goes immediately to his water bowl for a drink. I grab the garden gloves and some kitchen roll and steady myself.

Opening the door with a grimace on my face, I lean out with a gloved hand and scoop up the remains with a wad of kitchen roll. I can feel the squishiness through the paper sheets and dry-heave. I do my best to cover the body so I can't see it and then kick shut the door and dash through the house, open the back door and run down the garden, putting the mouse in one of the black bags already inside a bin.

Job done.

Doug follows me out, sniffing in the garden; then he trots behind me as I head back inside. I wash my hands vigorously in the sink with three pumps of soap. The dog presses his nose against my legs.

"Think it's time for a cup of tea, don't you, Doug?"

He looks up at me.

"No, it's not time yet for your dinner. That's another two hours away."

I crouch to give him a big fuss. He rolls onto his back.

"Who's a soppy boy, then? Who's a—"

Banging on the front door startles me into silence. *Thump. Thump. Thump.* Whoever it is really wants to make themselves known. It's not a polite knock.

I'm rooted to the spot. The dead mouse has unnerved me, and my mind immediately jumps to the worst possible conclusion. It's my past catching up with me. Doug, oblivious to the sound, paws at me for more belly scratches. His touch breaks the spell, and I stand. No, it's just a delivery or a neighbour. Or perhaps someone for my aunt and uncle who doesn't know they're away. I need to stop being so nervy and go answer the front door.

Then someone presses the doorbell. Again and again and again.

5

I tiptoe towards the front door, holding my breath. The shrill bell screeches in my ears. I can see the shadow of a figure through the stained-glass window in the top part of the door.

The figure bends, and the metal flap of the letterbox flips up.

Oh shit, can they see my feet? I should've stayed back. Whoever this is will know there's someone in the house now.

"Jess? Jess! Are you there?" Ashley's voice echoes through the hallway. Then quieter, as if to herself, "Oh, please, please be in."

I spring forward, relieved, and open the front door. "Ashley?"

Ashley's leaning on the door and, not expecting it to open so suddenly, falls through the doorway into me.

"Oh!" she exclaims.

I catch her and hold her steady. "Are you okay?"

She finds her feet and looks at me. Her eyes are red-rimmed, and her cheeks look raw. The happy, bubbly woman I said goodbye to a couple of hours earlier has been transformed into someone the complete opposite. Sadness billows off her in great plumes.

"No," she splutters, and tears well in the corners of her eyes.

"What's happened?"

"It's... it's..." Her chest heaves, and a great sob erupts. The floodgates open, and she can't get her words out.

"Come on, come in and through to the lounge." I close the front door and guide her into the hallway. I take her backpack and the large suitcase she's pulling and put them to one side. Ushering her into the lounge, I sit her on a sofa and place myself next to her, an arm around her shoulders. She smells strongly of peach.

She leans forward and holds her head in her hands, crying noisily.

"It's okay," I say soothingly, feeling daft for getting scared by the doorbell earlier and channelling my focus into comforting my friend.

"It's Kevin..." she manages through sobs.

"Your boyfriend?" Although we chatted the entire time we were together, we never quite broached the boyfriend subject. Ashley mentioned his name a few times, but not much else about him. Not because she was being secretive – I'm sure if I'd have asked, she would've told me – but because we didn't quite make it onto that topic.

"He's... he's dumped me."

"Oh no. I'm sorry, babe." I rub her back.

She takes a long inhale through her nose and sits up. She stares out the bay window opposite as if reliving the moment in her mind. "He got back from London before me and was sat waiting for me. We had a massive row. He noticed I was still wearing the same clothes as I went to work in on Friday and asked me where I'd been. I said I'd stayed with you for two nights, but he didn't believe me. He accused me of lying. Said I'd been with another man."

"That's shit. Why didn't he believe you?"

She glances at her fingernails, and I notice her manicure is chipped. She must notice too, for she tucks her hands under her thighs. "He can get like this sometimes. Jealous and a bit possessive. And he can be quite controlling. He's been doing so well keeping it in check, but sometimes it just explodes. But this time was worse, way worse. He said he didn't want to be with me anymore. That our relationship is over..." She trails off as the tears come again.

I think of my ex-husband, Blake. "I know exactly the kind of behaviour you're talking about. It's not cool, not cool at all."

"I packed a bag and grabbed my stuff and left. I thought about trying to find a hotel, but then I thought I'd see if you were in. You're the only other person I know in this town."

"I'm glad you came here and not to some crappy hotel. You're always welcome here."

She sniffs and wipes her eyes with the corner of her jumper. "Thank you."

"Let me get you a tissue." I grab the tissue box off the side table and offer it to her.

She plucks one out of the box and blows her nose. Then she takes another and dabs at her eyes.

"I just can't believe he dumped me..." she says and shakes her head sadly.

"How long were you together?"

"A few years now. We met in London and were going to buy a house together here. Start a family and raise them by the seaside. That's all over now."

She chokes back a sob.

I know I should say sympathetic things and hint that perhaps they'll get back together, but I see the warning signs from personal experience, and I don't want my friend – or any woman, for that matter – to go through what I went through. I wish I'd left earlier, when Blake had first become controlling. I'm sure Kevin is nothing like Blake – but if he's even a smidgen like him, then I need to try to make Ashley see things from a different perspective. "Maybe it's for the best... if you say he was controlling?"

"I love him so much. I don't know why he would suddenly do this now."

"Perhaps it's a power trip?"

Ashley shifts so she can turn and face me on the sofa. My arm around her shoulder slips away. "In what way?"

"Well, if he likes to be in control, then perhaps he gets a thrill from manipulating your feelings?"

"I... I don't know. He never used to be like this, not at first. It seems to have got worse recently. I don't know why."

I pick up a cushion and hug it to me. It has an embroidered anchor on the front, in keeping with the nautical theme. I trace my fingers over it. "People can change."

"What do you mean?"

"I mean, people you fall in love with can become completely different people over the years."

She shakes her head at me, uncomprehending.

I continue, "I'm divorced."

"Oh, I didn't realise."

"It's okay, but I don't want to make this about me."

Ashley settles back on the sofa, reorganising the matching embroidered seagull cushion behind her to get comfortable. "No, please tell me."

"It was a messy one. The divorce came through shortly before I went off travelling. But we were separated for a year or so before that. But he, well, he was not the same man at the end as the man I fell in love with. He... he became a monster."

Ashley's mouth falls open. "Eek. How?" she asks with a voice full of horrified curiosity.

I chew my top lip.

She continues, "You don't need to tell me if you don't want to."

I clutch the cushion tighter to my chest like a protective shield, bracing against the charging emotions that always attack when I think back to that time. "We suffered some... grief... and he became obsessed with controlling everything, with controlling me. I was no longer a person to him, no longer someone with my own desires, but a possession."

"How long were you together?"

"We met at uni when I was twenty-two and he was twenty-four. We got married when I was twenty-seven and divorced ten years later. So, all in all, together for fifteen years."

"Some time, then."

"Anyway, let's just say that I can relate to what you're going through."

She nods.

My armour wins out, and the threatening emotional over-whelm retreats. I'm left with practical thoughts of self-preser-vation. I continue, "Did you give him this address?"

"No, why?"

"I don't know him, but is he the kind of guy to... well... follow you here? Show up or hang around outside?"

"Goodness, no, I don't think so. Is that what your ex did?"

I give a noncommittal half-shrug. *Not every man is as screwed up as Blake*, I remind myself. "Well, that's good."

A thought blares in my head. *Was the attacker Blake? Did he go through my bins and leave that dead mouse on my doorstep?* I shudder. It can't be. Although, I wouldn't put it past him.

I continue, "Stay as long as you like. It's no problem."

"You're so kind. It'll just be tonight, and then I'll sort something out. I don't want to impose."

"Honestly, you'd be doing me a favour. I've realised I don't like living on my own. Not after two years of being around people all the time."

And if it was Blake, then it's safer for me to have someone else in the house, but I don't mention that out loud. Instead, I continue, "I really wanted to cook a Sunday roast. Not had one in ages. But it always seems a bit extravagant for one person. So now you're here, do you fancy it? We can pop to the shop and pick up all the bits. What do you reckon?"

"Sounds like a brilliant idea." She scrutinises her nails and picks at a chip in the polish. "And then I'm going to paint my nails. It always calms me down."

6

My alarm buzzes at 6.30 a.m. I groan, roll over in bed and switch it off. Mondays always suck. Even if you love your job like I do.

I heave myself out of bed and into the bathroom next door. I have a shower and get ready for work. I listen out for Ashley but don't hear anything. Perhaps she's a late riser and gets ready in record time. I take ages to get ready, especially when I wash my long, thick hair, which takes forever to dry. Usually, I leave it to air-dry because my waves look better that way, but it's too cold at the moment.

I head downstairs and sort myself a tea and some cereal. Still no sign of Ashley. Will I need to go and wake her up? I finish breakfast and put my things in the dishwasher. Ashley filled it and emptied it last night – her way of saying thanks for my cooking the roast dinner. She also cleaned the entire kitchen, which was totally unnecessary but very generous of her.

As I straighten up, I notice Doug's bowl. *Crap, he needs his breakfast.* I realise then that I've not seen him this morning. He's not in his bed under the dining table or in his usual spot on the window seat in the lounge. I scour the downstairs, look in all the nooks and crannies. Then I look out the back door. I'm not sure why because I didn't let him out in the night. I head upstairs and look in all the rooms apart from Ashley's. The door is still shut. Perhaps he's snuck in to sleep with her?

I'm about to tentatively knock when the front door opens. I run to the top of the stairs. No one else has keys apart from me and my aunt and uncle, who, according to their latest email, are currently somewhere in the Caribbean.

"Morning!" Ashley calls cheerfully up the stairs. "Thought I'd take this little monkey for a walk around the block. He did *three* poos, can you believe it? Thank goodness I brought loads of poo bags with me."

Relief surges through my veins that it's not some stranger bursting in. "Oh, morning. Thank you. I thought you were still in bed."

"Ha, no, I'm an early riser during the week. Helped myself to a bit of toast, I hope you don't mind? I did call to you, but I think you were drying your hair, so you didn't hear me over the hairdryer."

I head down the stairs. "Help yourself to anything. *Mi casa, su casa*. Thanks so much for taking Doug for a walk. Are you all set to head to The Hive?"

"Just about. Need to grab my laptop from upstairs."

"Right, well, I'll give Doug his breakfast, and we'll head off."

"Perfect. It's so nice having someone to walk to work with."

"I know, isn't it just?"

We pass each other on the stairs as Ashley jogs up to her room.

I head into the kitchen to feed Doug. He greedily eats. I

grab my laptop from the dining table and stuff it in my bag, heading back to the hallway.

Ashley comes bouncing down the stairs, looking a million times brighter than yesterday.

"How are you feeling today, about Kevin?" I ask.

She opens her mouth to answer, but her face twists and contorts. She drops her bag at the bottom of the stairs and clutches her belly.

"Oh my God," she wails.

She doubles over and then collapses to the floor.

"Ashley?" I drop my bag and bend over her.

"I need to get to the toilet. Now!" She claws herself up using the banister as I grab her elbow to help.

She skirts past me and hurries to the downstairs toilet. I follow close behind. She closes the door behind her, and I hear the lock slide across and then the toilet seat go up. She groans.

I knock gently on the door. "Are you okay in there, babe?"

"I'm sorry, don't suppose you have any sanitary pads or tampons? Think I'm having a super heavy period."

"Nothing to be sorry for. I'll grab some from upstairs. Won't be a sec." I dash upstairs and grab a handful of supplies from my bathroom cabinet, then jog back down. I knock gently on the door again. "Here you are."

"Could you give me one minute... I'm bleeding so heavily... and... fuck... having some serious cramps... and feel so weak... can't get off the toilet quite yet to open the door..." Her voice trails off.

"Have you ever had a period like this before?"

"No..."

"When was your last one?"

"Oh... now I come to think about it, it was probably a couple of months ago. And now it's hit me with a vengeance."

Concern hits as all the pieces fit together. "Ashley, is there any chance you could've been pregnant?"

There's a pause before another groan escapes from behind the door. "There's a chance. I'm not on the pill, and Kevin and I use condoms, but sometimes when we've run out... or if we're drunk..."

Memories flood back. Memories that haunted me for years and were finally put to rest emerge from the dead to fly around like ghosts circling a medium. "I think you might be having a miscarriage."

I hear a great sob and then silence.

"Ashley?"

In a faint, small voice, she says, "How do you know?"

"Because I've had miscarriages."

"More than one?"

"Yes. Seven."

"Shit, seven? Really?"

I don't want to go into it. I don't want to dredge up that trauma. "It was a while ago," I say, attempting to sound stronger than I feel. I need to be here for Ashley.

"Oh, I think I see something." And then the sobbing starts. "I shouldn't have looked... stupid... stupid... that could've been my baby..."

All I hear is the sound of Ashley's desperate crying. And it breaks my heart. I lean my forehead on the cool wood of the door frame, wanting to help my friend and understanding her pain.

There's a sound of shuffling, and the door opens a crack. "Do you have those pads?"

I pass through the supplies, and moments later, Ashley emerges. Her face is crumpled and slick from tears. There's blood on her pale-blue jeans.

"I need to go to bed," she says, her voice hitching. "Can you... I can't bring myself to..." She nods towards the toilet, and a wail rumbles up and out of her throat from somewhere deep inside.

The toilet seat is down, but I understand what she's asking of me. "Yes. You go and get into bed."

She shuffles away from me, head hung, shoulders slumped, and back heaving as she cries, and slowly goes up the stairs. I hear the door to her bedroom shut.

I rally myself and step into the downstairs toilet. The sooner I do this, the sooner it's done. I reach for the flush button but can't press. It hits me then. I collapse to the floor. My vision goes fuzzy, and my surroundings shift and move, as if they are separating themselves from me and moving away at a great speed. Nausea spirals in my gut. My sweat glands go into overdrive, and I feel clammy all over. Every part of me trembles.

When I open my eyes, I see my bathroom in Oxford. I see Blake standing over me. I see the bloody, watery mess on the floor, with the fully formed foetus and umbilical cord. Right there. My baby. I reach out to it, but Blake kicks my hand away.

He's furious. I hear him shouting, but I'm cocooned in a grief bubble, and it sounds distant. "You killed our baby again. You fucking bitch. I thought this was our time. You made it to sixteen weeks this time, and then you fucked it up. For the seventh time. You do this on purpose, don't you? You want to ruin my life. All I want is to be a father, and you keep denying me. You're one sick, twisted woman, you know that? Denying a man his desire to have a child. I hate you. You're despicable."

He slaps me then, and I feel the sting. "Clean this fucking mess up. And then clean yourself up. I know that fertility doctor said to wait two weeks before having sex again, but fuck that. We try again immediately. Now and every fucking day until you're pregnant again. You hear me, bitch? You'll open those legs for me until I plant another baby in your damn belly."

He storms out of the bathroom and slams the door. I vomit down myself and shake with the grief and the shame. As I grab a towel off the rail to cover the remains of my seventh baby, a boy, I vow to never go through this again. Blake will force himself on me, but I can't let him. I can't do it for an eighth time. I can't. I'd rather die. He's broken me down over the years, got steadily more abusive, but enough is enough. I can't let him treat me like this anymore.

Something cold chills my cheek, but that's wrong. That's not part of the scene. I come back to myself and realise I'm lying on the cold tiles in the downstairs toilet at my aunt and uncle's Weston-super-Mare terrace. It's quiet in the house, and I'm very still. Blake is not here. I had a waking nightmare, that's all, a flashback. I relived that traumatic experience, but it's in the past.

I'm safe.

And I have a friend upstairs who needs my help. I ball up my emotions and tuck the memory in a pocket and immediately feel numb. It's what I learnt to do when I was away. And for the most part, it works, but Ashley's miscarriage has set all that alight again. But I can fight fires. I've done it before, and I'll do it again.

Slowly, as if on autopilot, I prop myself up and then kneel and then stand. Devoid of emotion, I flush the toilet. I go through to the kitchen and pour myself a glass of water. I drink it all to steady myself before heading upstairs.

I knock on Ashley's bedroom door. "Can I come in?"

"Uh-huh."

Ashley is all tucked up in bed, her clothes discarded on the floor, covering most of the blue geometric-patterned rug. The crying has stopped, but her face is pallid. Everything about her is... deflated.

"You'll probably bleed for a good few days. Possibly longer," I say, switching into nurse mode and sitting on the edge of her bed.

She grimaces. "I just can't believe I was pregnant. But it makes sense. We weren't trying. We wanted to get settled in a house first. But now I know I was very nearly a mother, I feel so... empty. So full of grief. And disappointment and... anger at myself."

Recalling all the words from the nurses and doctors, all the advice and recommendations, I say, "You need to be kind to yourself. It is a horrific thing, and it's very normal to feel emotional and upset. Your body and your mind need to heal."

"All I want to do is stay in bed."

"And that is absolutely fine. You can stay right here for as long as you like. There's zero judgement from me. It's going to take time. And I'm going to be right here for you. I know what it's like to not have support."

"Thank you. What happened with you?"

I hesitate. Worry that I might have another flashback spikes but then wanes. I'm safe here with Ashley. "We tried for a baby for ten years, from the moment we got married. And after seven miscarriages, I knew it wasn't going to happen. I didn't want to try again. Blake did. He was desperate to be a father. The never-ending excitement-grief-excitement-grief cycle wore him down until he decided to try to control everything. My diet, what exercise I did, how much I worked. And when I got pregnant, he would wrap me up in cotton wool and not let me do anything. But when that didn't work, he was overwhelmed by fury at the whole situation, by the endless visits to fertility experts, by the fact that we were both perfectly normal and healthy and it should've happened for us. And eventually, he directed that anger at me."

"What a bastard."

"Yes. At the end."

Ashley touches her hand to her chest. "My heart won't stop hammering."

"You're probably in shock."

She rubs small circles under her collarbone as if massaging her heart beneath. "It definitely was – and still is – a shock."

Although Blake was unsupportive, the father of Ashley's baby might be different. "Do you want me to get in touch with Kevin?"

Ashley shakes her head on the pillow. "No, thank you. I need to tell him in my own time. We're not together anymore. It just feels weird right now. It's too soon."

"I understand. You need time to process it all. There's no rush." I pat her leg through the navy-blue duvet. "But you need to go and see a doctor. I can drive you—"

Ashley sits bolt upright in bed, her movement so quick it makes me jump. "No! No doctors!"

"It'll be fine, honestly. They know what they're doing," I say in a reassuring tone.

"Absolutely no way am I going to see a doctor. I hate doctors and surgeries and hospitals." She shudders and wraps the duvet around her.

"But you need to make sure everything's okay. You don't want to get an infection, and you need to make sure it's all out, if you know what I mean."

"I'll be fine," she says adamantly.

I frown, not understanding where this vehement refusal to look after her own health is coming from.

She continues, softer, "Sorry, I need to explain. I have a crippling fear of doctors and hospitals. It's been diagnosed, and I've had it since childhood. The fear of doctors bit is called iatrophobia, and the fear of hospitals bit is nosocome-phobia. I know it sounds utterly ridiculous with big, silly words, but just the idea brings me out in a cold sweat, and I have panic attacks."

I study her. Her entire body is tense, her knuckles white from clutching the duvet and her jaw clenched so tight it pulses through her cheeks. "I didn't know that was a thing."

"The absolute worst times of my life have been in hospitals, and the absolute worst news I've ever received has always been delivered by doctors. It scarred me in a big way."

"Your parents?"

"Yes, they both died in hospital after suffering horrific injuries, and I was there. When I was five, my younger brother died at three after a long struggle with a heart condition, and I spent a lot of time visiting him. And when I broke my arm at twelve, they messed up my treatment, and look." She holds out her arms. Her delicate hands and pristinely painted fingernails almost touch me. "See the left one is slightly bent at a weird angle at the elbow? It didn't heal properly."

I see the difference immediately. "That's terrible."

"When my grandad was dying, I couldn't go and see him, although I wanted to. I made it to the hospital car park but couldn't get out of my car. It was awful. He died without me seeing him." She wipes a tear away. "Look, I'm sure I'll be fine. My body will heal. If anything's not right, anything at all, we'll go to a doctor, okay?"

"Sounds good."

She lies back in bed. "I'm definitely not going into the co-working place today. But you go if you want to. I'll be fine here on my own. I just want to sleep."

Although those words come out of her mouth, I can tell by the worried crease in her forehead that she doesn't mean it. "I'll stay here with you. I can work from anywhere. That way, I'll just be downstairs if you need me. There's loads more sanitary pads in my bathroom if you need any more."

She relaxes. "Thank you. I'm still bleeding and still have insane cramping."

"You might do for a while."

She turns onto her side and readjusts her pillow. "I think I'm going to email my clients and let them know I'm off sick today. Maybe for the week. I can't face work right now."

"That's a good idea. You need some time to take care of yourself. It's a massive blow."

"Oh, I left my bag downstairs." Ashley moves to get out of bed, but I stand.

"I'll bring it up. You stay there. Do you need anything else?"

After I've taken up Ashley's bag, a cup of tea and a hot water bottle, I open my laptop on the dining room table. But I can't concentrate. I stare at the screen for what feels like hours and fight to stop my head slumping. The flashback has taken it out of me. I succumb to the exhaustion and head to the sofa to nap. I'll catch up on work this afternoon.

7

Two days later on Wednesday, I decide to work from home for the rest of the week. Ashley is still traumatised and hasn't left her bed or changed out of her pyjamas since Monday morning, and I still don't want to leave her on her own – especially because she refused to see a doctor, and there might be complications. The desk at the co-working place is a minimal outlay in the grand scheme of things and will still be there next week.

She's been easy to care for, and I've not minded it at all. I know it's what she needs – her own space but with a supportive friend to bring cups of tea and make sure she eats. And I know it's what I needed all those years ago but never received.

But I'm going to need to leave her for a bit to head to the supermarket because we're running low on food, and I finished my toothpaste this morning.

I call up the stairs, "Ashley, I'm popping to Tesco. Do you want anything?"

"No, can't think of anything," comes the weak reply.

"Chocolate, sweets, ice cream, crisps, or any other comfort food?"

"Umm. I don't know. Yeah, maybe."

I understand that decisions are still hard for her. Her head is somewhere else. "I'll get a bit of everything."

"Amazing. Thanks."

"Doug's asleep on the windowsill in the lounge. Be back in a bit. I'm driving Edwin and Alice's old car for the first time – wish me luck."

"Ha, good luck," she replies half-heartedly.

I grab the car keys and head out the door, looking up and down the street for the car. I spot it; it's hard to miss. It's a mint-green Honda Jazz with a big 'Border Terrier on Board' sticker across the rear window. The back seat has a pile of old towels for Doug to sit on after a muddy walk on one side and a pile of reusable shopping bags on the other.

As I carefully let myself into the car, avoiding the grime that's settled after a couple of weeks of not being used, I'm hit with the fuggy scent of wet dog. There's a small border terrier soft toy propped on the dashboard, angled to look at the driver.

Alice and Edwin insisted they insure me on their car, even though most places in town are walkable, for this exact purpose – to go to the big Tesco to do a big shop. They didn't quite comprehend when I told them I'd set up food deliveries. But I've not quite got round to doing that just yet, so it's off to the shop I go. I put my GPS on to find the big Tesco, this being the first time I've headed there, and see it's a seven-minute drive away. The little hatchback starts first time, and I edge out of the tight parking space, hoping I won't have to reverse park when I get back and that there'll be a nice, easy-to-get-into space right outside my front door.

"I wonder what your name is?" I ask the plush toy as I follow the directions to the supermarket, not daring to turn on the radio in case I miss an instruction. "I think I'm going to call you Maisie. And you can be Doug's girlfriend. Doug and Maisie. Cute."

I park up, grab the shopping bags off the back seat, and head into the supermarket.

After about an hour, I push the trolley laden with healthy food and, way more than was necessary, junk food back to the car. I pop it all in the boot and drop the trolley off in the nearest bay. I walk around to the driver's side and notice something in the dirt on the bonnet.

It's words.

I wander around to the front of the car and read what is written:

This car is as soiled as your soul.

Air expels forcibly through my teeth as if I've been punched between the shoulder blades. I lose my centre of gravity and wobble, momentarily forgetting how to stand. I hold onto a nearby bollard to stay upright. I'm clearly still jittery from the flashback a few days ago. I look around. There's nobody nearby.

Who the hell wrote that?

A yell comes from the front of the store, and my attention zooms there. It's an unkempt man who stumbles and sings and holds out his hand for spare change to people going into the shop. Was he there when I went in, and I just didn't notice? He spots me staring and points a finger at me. It's surprisingly steady for a man who is clearly intoxicated.

"Retribution," he yells at me before turning his attention to a mother with a pram and cooing over the baby. He breaks out into a rendition of 'Baby One More Time' by Britney Spears.

Did the local lunatic write that on my car? Why? What

did he mean by shouting that at me? He doesn't even know me. I've never seen him before in my life.

Suddenly, I feel exposed, out in the open with no cover and nothing between me and harm. I open the driver's door and jump in the car, slamming it closed. I hunch down out of sight. Is someone out there watching me? Gleefully observing my reaction to their message? I feel small and jumpy and watched like a flea in a glass jar.

Was that writing there before, but I just didn't see it? Perhaps it was written ages ago? Although the lines do look fresh, it could've been something Uncle Edwin wrote to Aunt Alice as a joke? He has a bit of a unique sense of humour.

Perhaps it was just kids playing a prank. But surely, that's too serious a statement for kids – they'd draw a smiley face or a penis, wouldn't they?

Or maybe someone recognised the car and left a note for my aunt or uncle. But why write that – was it a hint to get the car cleaned? *As soiled as your soul* isn't exactly a light-hearted reminder to wash the car. Dirty cars and vans usually sported the innocuous 'Clean me' scribed into the dirt.

But could it be Blake? Or my brother, Tim? Or *her*... Toni?

She went super weird when she found out. All the people I'm trying to hide from, all the people I don't want to know that I'm back. Has one of them finally caught up with me? Is this message somehow related to the attack, the bins and the dead mouse?

No. Get a grip, Jess. Don't catastrophize.

All three of those people are out of my life now. This is my fresh start. It's just a coincidence.

It was probably the local lunatic. I glance at him. He's sat cross-legged now, outside the shop, leaning against the wall. He's no longer singing, he's sermonising. I catch words including Noah, ark, and animals. I can imagine him thinking about soiled souls.

A group of three walk past. An elderly woman, a middle-aged man and a teenage girl. They get into the car next to mine, chattering amiably. There are people everywhere. Nothing is going to happen at a busy car park in the middle of the day.

Bolstered by two women chatting a few paces away from me, I pull a tissue from my handbag, get out of the car, and wipe the bonnet. The words come away to be replaced with a smear. I chuck the filthy tissue in a nearby bin and then head home, forcing myself to be strong, to forget all about the meaningless words in the dirt.

Instead, I turn my attention to the ice cream I purchased earlier, hoping it hasn't melted.

8

"Morning," Ashley says at 11 a.m. on Friday.

I look up from my laptop on the dining room table to see her showered, dressed, and fresh-faced.

"Morning," I reply with a smile. "You look better. How are you feeling?"

Ashley pulls out a dining chair and sits opposite me. "I feel a bit better. The bleeding and cramping have eased off. And I think I've had time to process it and come to terms with it a little."

"That's good."

"Thank you so much for having me to stay and for taking care of me. Honestly, I can't even begin to imagine what I would've done if it hadn't been for you and your generosity."

"You're very welcome. I've not done much, really, just been a supportive friend. And I've enjoyed you staying. You've been a great house guest, no bother at all."

"I should probably look at sorting myself out somewhere to rent, though. I'm not sure I'll be able to afford to buy somewhere on my own without Kevin. He really screwed up my future home ownership plans. I'll probably have to flat share again…"

She sighs, and a sad look comes over her face.

I wave away her concerns. "No rush for you to go anywhere, seriously."

"You're too kind." She looks out the window. "It's a lovely day out there. I've not been outside all week. Do you fancy doing something? I know you're working, so no worries if you're busy. Just feel like some fresh air."

I shut the lid of my laptop and push it away from me. "Do you know what? I've actually finished all my urgent work for the week and was just doing some admin stuff that can wait. I've not really been out all week either."

It's true. I went to the supermarket on Wednesday and found that creepy message written in the dirt of the car and haven't been out again since. But that was nothing, I tell myself for the umpteenth time. A coincidence. A random event. Just my Gemini bad luck striking again.

I continue, "Shall we play tourists in our own town and go and check out the seafront and all it has to offer?"

Ashley claps her hands in excitement. "That sounds like a brilliant idea. And we can grab some fish and chips for lunch and a Mr Whippy ice cream."

"Perfect. I've got a wallet full of loose change to burn in the arcades."

Ashley laughs. "And I really want to win some pointless crap."

"And we could buy a stick of rock each."

"And maybe go for a ride on a donkey!"

I laugh at that. "Now that might be taking it a bit far."

"True. Well, I'm ready when you are."

"I'm pretty much ready too. Let's head out."

We wrap up warm for the chilly March weather and head towards the beach. It's only a ten-minute walk, and both of us are pleased we've remembered our scarves as the brisk wind coming off the sea hits us full pelt in the face.

Ashley attempts to tame her wild hair as blonde locks fly everywhere in the wind and slap her in the face. "Wish I'd put my hair up now. I'm going to have some crazy frizz later."

I'm wearing a beanie hat, and my long brown hair is under control in a plait that hangs down my back under my scarf. "Hang on, I think I have a spare hair band. I usually have a few floating around in the bottom of my bag." I rummage in my handbag and pull one out. "Here you go."

"Amazing," Ashley squeals. "I've never been so happy to see a hair band."

She tussles with her hair as we walk along the promenade towards the Grand Pier, Weston's famous pier that first opened in the early 1900s.

We walk up to the barriers, and I get my wallet out to pay the pound to enter.

Ashley searches in her handbag. "Oh, crap, I've left my wallet at home. I'll run back and get it."

"No, don't worry. I'll shout you. It's only a few quid. I don't mind at all."

"Are you sure?"

"Absolutely fine." I ask the ticket attendant for two and pay us in.

We stroll along the deck. Although it's a sunny day, there aren't that many people about. It's a weekday in the off season, so pretty quiet, but there's still enough of a buzz for a fun atmosphere. We pause at the railings to look at the beach. The tide is right out, and muddy sand stretches off into the distance.

"I've not seen the tide in yet," I say.

"Ha, no, I don't think I have either. We'll have to consult a tide chart and come down when it's in."

"Good plan. Shall we hit up the arcade? I'll cover it. I've

got plenty of change; don't worry about that. As long as you promise to share all winnings with me."

"Hell yeah!"

We enter the arcade building, and the whoosh of the wind and squawking of the seagulls is replaced by electronic bleeps and music and flashing lights and that slightly musty smell of too many machines in one place.

"Right, first things first, we need to find a shooting game," I say.

"There it is," Ashley replies and heads off towards the back.

After playing the shooting game four times and then having a go on numerous others, including driving, air hockey, penny-pushers and a hilarious turn on a dance machine, we decide we've had enough of games.

"OMG, are you up for this?" Ashley points at a ride.

I read the sign. "Britain's Smallest Rollercoaster? Yep, let's go."

Buzzed from the rollercoaster, we then take a turn around all the rides, including the spooky house of horrors and one called 'Freefall'. We then howl with laughter on the dodgems, bumping into each other.

We exit the arcade exhilarated and happy.

"That was bloomin' awesome," Ashley exclaims as she links her arm through mine.

"I had so much fun," I say and notice the tension from the past couple of weeks that had been sitting heavily around my shoulders has lifted. "Is it time for fish and chips?"

"I reckon so."

We head towards the food concessions along the deck of the pier. As we do, a ginger-haired, ginger-bearded man ducks behind one of the food outlets onto the other side of the pier.

My gut leaps up into my mouth – more forcefully than on the rollercoaster earlier. I gasp and stop dead in my tracks.

Ashley, arm linked through mine, is jerked back, like a dog running to the end of its lead. "Jess, what's up? You look like you've seen a ghost."

"I... I think that was..." I stutter. I can't get my words out through the shock that's lodged behind my teeth. I duck behind her. *Please, please don't let it be him.*

"You saw someone you know?" Ashley looks around us.

"Come on, let's get lunch," I say and lead her quickly to the nearest chippy to hide amongst the queue of people waiting to be served.

I buy us two portions of cod and chips, and we sit on one of the benches on the deck looking towards Brean Down, the bit of rock that sticks out into the Bristol Channel like a natural pier.

Ashley wolfs hers down, but I pick at mine. I'm no longer hungry; a sour knot fills my stomach. It can't have been him. What would Blake be doing in Weston? He has no reason to be here.

I take in my surroundings. The pier is busier now, with people strolling and milling about. My eyes search for a redhead. Blake is hard to miss, his flaming hair like a beacon on his head.

"Are you going to eat that?" Ashley says and points at my half-eaten bit of fish.

"You have it. I'm done."

Ashley grins and picks up the cod from the tray on my lap. "Yum," she says as she proceeds to eat it.

I can't see anyone who looks like Blake. It was probably my imagination. I rally. "Do you want to do the Museum of Memories now?"

"Yup," Ashley replies. She pats her stomach. "That was delicious."

She reapplies peach lip balm as we head into the museum. There are rows and rows of black cabinets filled with quirky old memorabilia, including old breakfast cereal boxes and TV shows. We follow the narrow trail through the tall cabinets. Ashley jabbers on excitedly and points things out, but I feel hemmed in, claustrophobic in the dark, stuffy space.

Ashley leads the way, turning corners at random. I follow but then realise I'm lost. If I needed to, I couldn't find my way out. Couldn't escape.

My skin crawls. Jitters race around my neck and down my back. I can't catch my breath. I spin around to try to get my bearings, and that's when I see the man with the ginger hair again. He turns a corner and is lost from my view. He was behind us. He was following us.

Anger rankles.

"Blake!" I yell and chase after the man.

"Jess?" I hear Ashley's voice from behind me.

I veer around the corner and grab Blake's arm.

"What the hell are you doing here?" I shout. "Why are you following me? It was you, wasn't it, leaving that message on my car—"

My words curdle in my throat as the man turns around, his eyes wide and a look of shock on his face.

It's not Blake.

It's a man with the same build, the same colouring, the same walk as my ex-husband. But it isn't him. Ashley catches up to us.

"Oh God, I'm so, so sorry. I thought you were someone else," I grovel at the man.

He still looks stunned.

I double over, woozy, and I think I might faint. I feel Ashley's protective arm around my shoulder.

"Is your friend all right?" the man says. "Should I get someone?"

"It's okay," Ashley replies. "She's just had a fright, that's all. She thought you were someone else."

A constrictor snake tightens around my lungs. "Air," I utter. "Can't... breathe."

Ashley fans my face with the museum leaflet. "Come on, let's get you out of here." She heaves me up with the help of a member of staff who has materialised from somewhere. The man who isn't Blake fades into the background.

I can hardly walk, can hardly see. I realise I'm outside when the cool breeze hits me.

"Breathe," Ashley is saying. "Just breathe. In and out. That's it."

"Let's sit her here," a young male voice that I don't recognise says. It must be the member of staff.

I'm sat on a bench, and I place my head between my knees. Ashley thanks the staff member.

"Thank you," I mumble. "Sorry to cause a scene. I'll be okay now."

The staff member and Ashley talk for a little longer. She reassures him that she'll look after me from here, and he goes.

She sits next to me and places her hand flat on my back. She doesn't say anything. She just breathes calmly next to me and allows me to come round at my own pace.

Eventually, I sit up. I get an immediate head rush. When the dizziness passes, I say, "I'm so sorry."

"Don't worry. What happened?"

"I got really claustrophobic in that place, and then I thought my ex-husband was following us. I feel so silly. That poor man."

"Yeah, you proper yelled at him," Ashley says, but she's

not having a dig. She's trying to lighten the mood, and I appreciate that.

I give a small snort and attempt a smile.

She continues, "I think that red hair of his will turn white before the day's up."

"Ha," I reply.

"Are you up to walking home? Or do you need some more time? We have all the time in the world, so no rush."

"Yeah, let's head home. I'm sorry you won't get your Mr Whippy."

"Oh, another time. Don't worry about that. Besides, I think you said there's some ice cream in the freezer from your Wednesday shop."

"There certainly is."

We walk slowly back to Alice and Edwin's house in amicable silence. I need to stop thinking everyone is out to get me. It's getting ridiculous now. I just ruined a perfectly lovely day by being so paranoid. I got that police injunction against Blake when he bothered me before. He won't do it again. He can't risk having a police record. I'm sure he's moved on with his life now. Like I have.

I fish my keys out of my bag as we get close to the house.

"After you," Ashley says and pauses to let me go through the gate first so I can let us in.

I step up to the front door, and something white catches my eye.

There's a piece of paper folded in half and attached to the door. No, nailed to the door. Who the hell nails something to someone else's front door? The rusty nail has been hammered straight through the piece of paper. I pull at the nail, but it doesn't budge.

"What's that?" Ashley says from behind me.

I attempt to shift the nail from side to side to get it out.

But it's no use. I'll have to find some of Edwin's pliers to get that out.

"Is that a nail?" Ashley asks incredulously.

I yank the paper down. It rips as it comes free. With shaking hands, I open it. There's a handwritten message. It reads:

I've found you, Jess.

"Oh fuck," I say and stuff the note in my coat pocket as I scrabble to open the door as fast as possible. I get inside and yank Ashley in, slamming the door behind her.

I shakily hand her the note from my pocket. "Look."

She opens the note and reads aloud, "'I've found you, Jess.' Who's found you? What is this?"

"I'm being targeted. There's no mistake now. Someone is out to get me." I thought it was all random coincidences. Bad luck. But it's not. My breathing hitches again, and I take the few steps through the hallway to sit on the stairs.

"Who?"

"Blake."

"Blake? But that wasn't him at the museum?"

I concentrate on taking a few deep breaths before I reply, "I wouldn't put it past him to hire someone who looked like him just to freak me out."

"*Seriously?*"

I hold onto the stairs as a feeling like I'm dropping from a great height comes over me – it's how I felt on the Freefall ride, but this time I'm not strapped in. I feel the panic rising as it did earlier and attempt to quash it. I'm safe in the house. I'm safe here. There's no one here who can hurt me.

Ashley considers for a moment, then says, "What about your brother? Didn't you think the attacker was him initially?"

"Yes. Or Toni."

"Toni? Who's that?"

Talking about *her* means talking about Marcus. And I'm not ready to open that can of worms yet. "That's a story for another time."

"Sure, yeah, another time," Ashley says, her eyebrows scrunched.

She must think I'm bonkers, having all these people who might want to target me in this way. It's not normal, I know. But I had some serious bad luck before I left Oxford. But she'll understand, I know she will.

I reach out for her hand. "I know you mentioned earlier about moving out and finding somewhere to live. But please stay here a little while longer. There's plenty of room. I really don't want to be on my own right now. I just want to be around people I trust. Is that okay with you?"

She kneels in front of me and gives me a big hug. "I'm not going anywhere. I'm right here for you."

Doug nudges my knee and whimpers. Ashley stands. I pick up the dog and put him on my knee, scratching under his ears.

"Well, I don't suppose you saw who did this from your spot in the window?" I ask and hug the border terrier into me.

Ashley waves the note. "What do you want to do with this? Should I bin it?"

I sigh. I know what I need to do from dealing with the police in Oxford. "No, I need to start a diary and keep hold of it. I need to build a case, as such, before I can go to the police. Otherwise, they won't take it seriously. I've got a new note-book upstairs. I'm going to do it now."

"Sure." She hands me the note. "Dougeeee, do you need wee-wees? Come on, then." She heads off towards the back door, and Doug jumps from my knee to trot after her.

I heave myself up, find my keys, and put the deadlock on and slide the security chain across the front door. I head upstairs and call to Ashley, "Can you make sure the back door is definitely locked when he's done?"

"Of course," she calls back. "No problemo."

In my room, I fish out a new notebook. It came from Singapore and has a photo of the stunning Gardens by the Bay on the front. I smile as I remember the brilliant few days I spent there exploring and sightseeing. And eating some incredible food.

Why did I ever come back?

But I know why. I couldn't have travelled forever. It was fun for two years, but I needed to return, to have a home again. Towards the end, I began to crave a quiet, settled life. I thought two years would be long enough for everyone to move on. But I was wrong.

I jot down the various events that have happened and the dates: the alleyway attack, the bins, the dead mouse, the message in the dirt on my car, the Blake lookalike at the museum, and now this note. I reread it before stuffing it between the pages near the back of the notebook. I don't recognise the writing.

Someone has found me. But who?

9

After a fitful night's sleep going over and over the past, I drag myself out of bed at midday and head downstairs. Ashley is busy cleaning the oven hob.

"Hey," she says. "Woke up in the mood to clean. That doesn't happen often, so I thought I'd make the most of it."

"I'm not sure I'm ever in the mood to clean." Doug spots me and trots over for a fuss. "I'll take you for a walk in a bit, boy. Just going to have a coffee."

She sprays cleaner on the rings. "Not to worry, I've already taken him out this morning."

"Oh cool, thank you."

"I started dwelling on the whole Kevin thing and miscarriage and whatnot and needed some fresh air to clear my head. It was pissing it down, so we got soaked." She pauses her scrubbing to take a look out the window. "It's eased off a little now."

"How are you doing now?"

"I'm still bleeding a little, but I think the worst has passed. And I keep thinking that if we'd still been together and I'd stayed pregnant, then we might have been a little family in our new home. But everything has changed now. I need to consider a new future."

She returns to scrubbing with a determination to remove the burnt-on scum that impresses me.

"We've both had pretty rough weeks, haven't we?"

"Hmm," Ashley replies distractedly, her attention on wiping down the oven knobs.

I take off my glasses and polish the lenses on my dressing gown. I pop them back on and chew the inside of my cheeks. I can't let this person targeting me stop me from living my life. I can't crumple and stay at home like last time. I need to be strong. What did that counsellor say? That they've won if they prevent me from doing what I want to do with my life. It's a rainy Saturday. What do I want to do? What will distract me and entertain me and be in a busy place around lots of people where nothing and no one can hurt me?

An idea darts into my head. "Once you've got all the cleaning out of your system, do you fancy going to the cinema this afternoon? And then grabbing dinner, maybe? That new Marvel movie is out."

Ashley looks up. "That sounds fab. Oh... wait. I'm a bit low on funds at the moment. I'm still paying for that studio with Kevin. We haven't quite sorted that out yet. He's not been in touch since he dumped me, and I've not messaged him. I need a bit more time before I do that. It all seems so final if we start splitting our things and I stop paying towards rent. But I need to do it soon. Anyway, I also need to start saving for my own deposit now I won't be buying with him. So the cinema would be lovely, but I really need to be strict with my spending. Boring, I know."

Now I have the idea in my head, though, I really want to go. And I definitely don't fancy going on my own. "I'll pay. My treat."

"That's really lovely of you, but absolutely not. You paid

for everything yesterday, which I still need to pay you back for."

I wave my hand in a gesture that says not to worry. "That was a few quid. It's nothing, really. You can return the favour at some point in the future. No rush. I have funds."

"Only if you're sure?"

"I'm sure. It's already a done deal."

Ashley grins. "I bloody love Marvel."

WE COME out of the cinema screen, and Ashley nips to the loo. While I wait for her, I take my time to look all around me. But I don't see anyone I know, and I don't notice anyone looking at me or acting suspiciously.

"What do you fancy eating?" Ashley says as she rejoins me.

"What about that pizza place we passed on the way here?"

"Perfect."

As we walk to the Italian, grateful for a break in the rain, I keep looking over my shoulder as Ashley details her confusion over a couple of the questionable moments in the superhero movie we've just watched. I can't see anyone following us.

It's a quaint little restaurant with red-checked tablecloths, and we're seated in the window, which initially I think is brilliant, because I love to people-watch, but then I soon realise everyone can see in and see us. It's dark outside, and we're lit up under the spotlights in the restaurant.

I attempt to keep it cool as I order a mushroom pizza, and Ashley orders a spicy pasta dish with extra spice. "Don't be shy with the spice," she tells the server as they walk away from us.

"I love spicy food – the spicier, the better. Can't wait for this. I'm starving. Must be all that cleaning earlier. It's pretty good exercise, I think."

"Ashley? Hi!" A male voice comes from over my shoulder.

"Oh, hi!" Ashley replies.

A man comes to stand over our table. I look up at him, and my insides quiver deliciously. He's very handsome, standing about six feet tall, wearing a tight, grey-marl fine-knit sweater that hugs his muscular torso and arms and well-cut jeans that skim his toned thighs. His mesmerising light-brown eyes are almost feminine, framed by long, dark eyelashes. His eyebrows are neatly trimmed, as is his black beard stubble, which shows off his masculine square jaw. He has a small yet proud nose and carved-out cheekbones. His black hair is thinning slightly at the hairline, but there are no visible greys. It's long on top and slicked up and over. His thicker bottom lip protrudes slightly in a sensual, kissable way. He's groomed to perfection and clearly takes very good care of his appearance and his body.

He's more attractive than the male lead in the movie we've just watched. If I were an emoji right now, I'd be the drooling face one.

"I thought it was you," the man says with an accent. He smiles at Ashley and then looks at me. His head is slightly cocked, and he holds eye contact. His lavish gaze seeps deep inside and unearths all my hidden desires. I feel sexy with him looking at me. How is that even possible? I'm not sure a man has ever looked at me so intently before. I'm beyond pleased that I wore a nice dress and put some make-up on.

He licks his lips almost imperceptibly, but enough for me to notice. "And who is this?"

"Jess, this is Jamal," Ashley says. "Jamal, this is Jess. Jamal is also from The Hive, but I don't think he was in the week you joined."

"Ah, no, I can't have been. I would've remembered *you*,"

Jamal says without taking his eyes off me. He smiles warmly, and it lights up his stunning face.

My cheeks redden, and I can't think of anything to say in return.

"Have you had dinner? Or are you about to?" Ashley says.

And for a moment, I think she might ask him to join us. And I know I'll be tongue-tied for the next few hours.

He tears his eyes away from me to look at Ashley. "Just finished. Was here with a friend, but he had to dash off to pick his wife up from a party, so I stayed to settle the bill. Sometimes, it's nice to be the single one. No chasing around needed."

"We've just ordered," Ashley says.

"Ah, yes, what did you order?"

"I got the spicy pasta." Ashley pauses for me to speak, but when I don't, she continues, "And Jess got the mushroom pizza."

He looks at me. "I just had the mushroom pizza. It was delicious. You'll enjoy it."

"Can't wait," I squeak. The sexiness of this man has well and truly floored me.

"Well, I'll leave you two ladies to it. I hope to see you both at The Hive soon. And, Jess, I especially look forward to seeing you again soon."

He pulls on his leather jacket in one smooth movement and sweeps out of the restaurant, leaving a god-shaped hole where he was stood.

"He was fit," I say when I know he's well and truly out of earshot.

"He was *soooo* into you," Ashley replies.

"No."

She circles her index fingers at me. "Hell yeah! He couldn't take his eyes off you."

"Why would he be interested in me?"

"Babe, you're beautiful."

I shake my head, batting away the compliment. The server arrives with a bottle of red wine and two glasses. He pours a glass for both of us.

Ashley waits for him to go and pushes on, "Yes. You are beautiful. You've got a kind of Liv Tyler vibe about you. And I say you should meet up with Jamal. He mentioned he's single. And so are you. Why not?"

I take a sip of wine. "It's been a while…"

"A while since what? Since you dated?"

"Yes. I mean, I had a few short-term flings while I was a digital nomad. But nothing serious."

"So your last relationship was with that arsehole, Blake?"

"Umm, well, no, not exactly."

The server returns with a bowl of olives, and Ashley watches him impatiently. "Spill," she insists once he's moved away.

I eat an olive. Do I want to get into this now? I chew around the olive pit and think, *Why not?* Ashley is my friend, and it'll be good to talk about this and hear another point of view. I've not spoken about him in two years. I remove the olive pit and put it on my side plate. "I had an affair. Well, I say an affair, but Blake and I were separated by that point and waiting for the divorce to come through, and he'd moved out of the house. And the guy told me that he was divorced and single, and I believed him. So it was a relationship, I suppose."

"What was his name?"

His name really suited him. I roll it around my mouth for a while, savouring it, savouring the memory of him before it all went sour. "Marcus."

"And I'm guessing he wasn't divorced or single?"

I'd trusted him so completely. What an idiot I'd been. "Nope."

"How long did it go on for?"

"Three months."

"Until the wife found out?"

"Bingo."

"Yikes. Messy. Were you really into him?"

My lips tingle with the memory of his passionate kisses. My hair aches for the times he ran his fingers through it, and my nose reaches into the air for just a hint of his perfect scent.

I take a gulp of wine and nod at my friend. "Yes. I really fell hard for him. It was when I'd returned to work after my... er... after I had some time off. I met him at a LinkedIn event in Birmingham. I told him I was going through a divorce, and he told me he was recently divorced. It was so refreshing to have a relationship with a man who wasn't driven by making babies or control. It felt healthy. I felt sexy and desired again. He lived in Reading, and we would meet up in hotels between Reading and Oxford. Or he would come to my house in Oxford. Blake found out and wasn't happy. But I never went to Marcus' place in Reading."

"I bet that made you suspicious."

"Not especially. I was so wrapped up in this caring, kind, generous man that I didn't really think about it. Anyway, she followed us to a hotel and caught us in the act. It was horrendous. Such a scene."

"Toni?"

"Yep. Toni. I was horrified that he was not only still very much married but had two young kids."

Ashley shakes her head and slaps the table. "What a dickhead. I hate men who cheat."

"Anyway, Toni went mental at me. She didn't believe that I didn't know. Accused me of trying to steal her man, of deliberately trying to wreck her marriage. She welcomed Marcus back. It was a bit bizarre, really, how fast she forgave him. Then she decided to teach me a lesson."

The server interrupts our conversation by bringing our food and places the plates down in front of us.

Ashley takes a mouthful of pasta and then flaps her perfectly proportioned hand in front of her mouth. "Wow, that is spicy."

"Too much?" I ask as her cheeks go red, and I see sweat breaking out on the tip of her nose.

"Nope. Perfect." She continues to tuck in, and I get started on my pizza.

After a few mouthfuls, Ashley asks, "What lesson?"

I let her question hang in the air. I don't feel like reliving that awfulness right now. "Oh, nothing."

Ashley's phone dings. She fishes it out of her handbag and looks at the message. She looks up at me with a cheeky twinkle in her eye.

"It's Jamal. He got my mobile number off my profile on the co-working member directory. Have you set yours up yet? Am guessing not. Anyhow, he's asked if I could pass on his number to you."

"What? No way. Why?"

She rolls her eyes at me. "Why'd you think? To organise a date."

I squirm in my seat. "He's way too attractive for me."

"That's absolute nonsense. He clearly fancies you. And I can tell you fancied him. You should totally go on a date with him. Just one. What have you got to lose?"

"I guess..."

"Look, if nothing else, it'll be a massive confidence boost for you. Or if it all goes tits up, then it'll be a funny bad-first-date story. Amiright?"

I laugh. "Go on then, give me his number." I get my phone

out and add Jamal's number to my contacts. I put my phone back down and continue eating my mushroom pizza.

"Well?" Ashley says after a while.

"Oh, the pizza is delicious."

"No, not that! Send him a message."

"Right now? Won't that look a bit keen?"

"Who cares about all that? There's no time like the present, I say."

"Fine." I pick up my phone and tap out a message.

Hi Jamal, it's Jess. Ashley passed on your number. Pleasure to meet you earlier.

I put my phone down on the table. "There, done. Happy now?"

Ashley claps her hands together. "Oh yes, I'm happy! He seems like a really lovely guy. And you deserve a really lovely guy."

My phone lights up with a message. "It's from him."

"Ooh. What does it say?"

I read the message out loud. "'Hi Jess, the pleasure was all mine. Fancy meeting up tomorrow? I'm free all day, so whenever is good for you.'"

I feel an electrified crackling under my skin. A date. Tomorrow.

Ashley practically vibrates with excitement. "Are you free?"

"Yeah. All day."

She grins a huge cheeky grin and then flicks her eyes down to my phone and back.

Screw it. I need something good to think about after that note nailed to my door. I can't let whoever is targeting me stop me from living my life. I can't let them win.

I pick my phone up and tap back a message.

10

"One latte," Jamal says as he hands me a mug of coffee, then eases himself into the chair opposite me, holding his super-frothy cappuccino.

The coffee shop is busy for a Sunday, and I'm pleased. It was my choice to come here, thinking a mid-morning coffee date would be best in case we didn't get on. Casual and not too romantic. And with plenty of people around to deter whoever left me that handwritten note from doing anything else.

"Thank you," I reply and resist the urge to take a long inhale of his incredible scent that follows him like a cloud. A woody, spicy cologne with a hint of nutmeg that suits him perfectly.

"They asked me if you wanted chocolate sprinkles on your latte, and I said yes. I hope that's okay? The chocolate sprinkles are the best bit of the cappuccino, in my opinion. But I can get you a new drink if you're not keen."

"Ha, I'm very happy you said yes to chocolate sprinkles. I'm all for chocolate sprinkles."

"*Très bien*," he replies.

"You speak French?"

"Yes, I'm fluent in English, French and Arabic. I'm originally from Lebanon. Moved here when I was fifteen. My father died when I was young, and at thirteen, my mother married an Englishman."

"And you moved to Weston?"

"To Bristol originally. But I went off to London, and they moved here to be by the seaside. Then, sadly, my stepfather died last year, and it's just me and my mother because I have no siblings. So I moved here to be close to her. She is my whole world, you know."

"My parents both passed away when I was younger."

"Oh, my sympathies." He reaches across the table and gently squeezes my forearm. It's a sincere, easy gesture, and the touch sends shivers up my spine. Just as naturally, he pulls his hand away.

"I'm very close to my aunt and uncle. They live here in Weston. In fact, I'm staying at their house."

"Oh, lovely. Family is very important. Perhaps because I'm an Arab, but family always comes first." He leans in close to me. "I must tell you, because some find this weird, but I live with my mother now. I know, I know, I'm a thirty-four-year-old man, and I don't need to live with her, but I'm pleased to be with her. Does that worry you?"

"Absolutely not. To tell you the truth, I'm more worried that you're five years younger than me." I chuckle nervously and wonder why I just brought that up.

Jamal's eyes go wide. "You are thirty-nine?"

"Uh-huh."

He gazes at me. "I thought you were younger than me. Your skin is so... flawless. So pale and blemish-free. You remind me of Botticelli's painting *Venus*, voluptuous and divine, except with long brunette waves rather than ginger."

I blush hard. "Er, wow, thanks."

"No, thank you. It is a joy to behold you."

And he does just that, beholds me, his attention squarely on me as if he's taking me all in and savouring every detail. My cheeks catch on fire, and I fidget and play with the ends of my hair. But I realise I like it, his attention. It's not lecherous, it's loving. I lap it up greedily.

I take a sip of my coffee and then ask, "So what do you do for a living?"

His eyes snap back into focus, and he takes a drink before answering. "I'm a freelance English-Arabic translator. Been doing it for years."

"Oh, that's cool."

"Yes. I have plenty of work. I sometimes go to The Hive when I want to be around people, but mostly I work at home for the quiet. Although my mother insists on feeding me all day when I'm at home. She believes I am eternally hungry." He laughs, and like his scent, it wholly suits him – smooth and rich, like the perfect piece of chocolate melting on your tongue. "And what do you do?"

"I'm a self-employed LinkedIn advertising and content specialist. I've got a healthy number of clients and work coming in."

"Intriguing. I do not know much about social media or advertising. But I do know a lot of interesting words." He waves his hand self-deprecatingly. "Useless knowledge, really."

"Oh, do tell! I'm a bit addicted to this Scrabble app on my phone. I'm always after new words."

He thinks for a moment, stroking his precisely trimmed black beard stubble with a beautifully shaped masculine hand – in another life, he could be a hand model with Ashley. "One I came across in a legal document the other day was 'recuse'." He spells it out for me. "It means when a judge or juror must excuse themselves from a case or legal duties due to a conflict of interest or lack of impartiality."

"Oh, that's a good one. I'll have to remember that. And not too many letters."

"Yes. It's a good word. Another word I came across recently which I like saying is succubus. It feels good on the tongue. Suc-cu-bus."

I watch his sensual, luscious mouth move as he forms the word. My voice hitches slightly as I ask, "And what does it mean?"

"A succubus is a female demon who likes to have sex with sleeping men."

"Seriously? Well, I've never heard of that before."

"Neither had I until I was translating a nonfiction novel recently. I had to find the right way in Arabic to explain it. But what a word. So, tell me more about you."

He rests his elbows on the table, in close proximity to me, while I tell him about my two years away and my dog- and house-sitting for my aunt and uncle. I don't go any further back than that, not yet. I don't want to scare the poor man off. He listens attentively and asks questions that prove he's interested and wants to keep the conversation going.

After a good hour or so of chat, I say, "I'm just going to pop to the bathroom. And then we can talk about you."

He leans back and makes a shy, humble gesture with one hand. "Oh, I'm not nearly as interesting as you, my dear."

"I'm sure you are." I stand and head across the coffee shop to the toilet in the back. I glance back over my shoulder and see he's watching me with a smile on his face.

I freshen up my make-up in the toilet mirror and flick my hair over to the other side of my head. I readjust my glasses and head back to the table.

He looks at me for a moment when I sit. "Your hair. It's different. It was to this side, and now it's to the other."

I'm amazed he's picked up on such a small detail. "Yes, that's right. I wear it both ways. All ways, really."

"It is beautiful either way. I love the length. So natural with gorgeous waves."

"Shall we get another coffee?" Our drinks are long since finished, and my stomach is grumbling for lunch.

Either Jamal is also hungry, or he hears my belly gurgling, for he says, "Or a bite to eat? They do sandwiches and salads here. Or we could find somewhere else?"

"A sarnie sounds perfect."

"I shall go and see what they have and report back."

Before I can stop him, he stands and heads over to the counter, looking at the display of packaged food there. Trying not to be too obvious, I watch him. He's well dressed in jeans and a chunky jumper, but they're just a tiny bit too tight and hug his muscular figure. He's sexy and funny and intelligent. This first date couldn't be going any better. Butterflies flutter in my stomach.

He returns and relays the information efficiently, counting off the options on his fingers.

"Chicken Caesar sandwich for me, I think." I bend down to pick up my handbag. "What do you want? I'll get it. You got the coffees."

"No, no, I insist. This is my treat. I cannot let a lady pay on the first date. And besides, you will feel obliged to return the favour, so I shall hopefully have a second date." He winks at me and then heads back to order our food.

AFTER ANOTHER TWO hours chatting over lunch, Jamal asks if he can walk me home. I agree. He walks me right up to the front gate. I turn to him.

"Well, this is me," I say as I indicate the house.

He looks up at it and then at me. The chemistry sizzles between us.

"Jess, this may be very forward of me, and please do say if I'm completely overstepping the mark, but I'd like to kiss you goodbye. Would that be agreeable to you, my dear?"

I would very much like to kiss him. I've literally been thinking about it since he said the word *succubus*. I move closer and lift my face to his, standing on tiptoes. He closes the gap between us, reading my body language. He brings his hands up to cup my face and gives me an exquisitely gentle kiss. I feel as if I might float off.

He pulls away at the perfect moment, leaving me wanting more.

"Jess, I'd like to see you again. You set me on fire."

"Likewise."

"I will message you." He strokes my hair, and when he reaches the end, he gives it a gentle rub between his fingers. Then he takes a step back, gives me a gentlemanly bow and walks away. I swear if he were wearing a top hat, he would have tipped it at me.

I head inside, thrilled.

"Well?" Ashley's voice comes from the dining room. I head through, and she puts down her laptop lid. "Thought I'd get a head start on work for next week, seeing as I took last week off," she says by way of explanation. "Tell me everything!"

"It was an excellent first date. He's so... exotic and sexy," I say in a swoon.

Ashley jumps up and high-fives me. "Yay," she exclaims.

A WEEK PASSES, and I cook a beef roast for Sunday dinner. I'm in a state of bliss after more wonderful dates with Jamal, including one last night where he stayed over and we had sex for the first time, and no more messages were nailed to my door or other weird happenings. I'm sure the person who was targeting me has given up. Maybe they just wanted to freak me out once, for some sick reason, and then leave me alone.

Ashley and I walked together to and from the co-working place every day and have been getting on like a house on fire. I'm so pleased I met her.

"Babe, dinner's ready," I call up the stairs.

Ashley has been in the bath. She loves to lounge in the bath for ages and read. I'm definitely more of a shower person. But I'm also a big reader. As is my aunt Alice, and we've both been raiding her overflowing bookshelves in the lounge.

I put everything on the table as Ashley settles herself.

"This looks amazing, Jess. Thank you so much! I'm starving."

"Dig in," I say.

We help ourselves to roasties, beef, veg, stuffing, Yorkshire puddings and gravy. For such a petite woman, Ashley has a huge appetite. She piles her plate high and licks her lips.

"So Jamal stayed over last night, then? I heard him leave this morning," Ashley says, attempting not to sound too nosey but failing miserably.

"Yep."

"And... did you...?" She waggles her head playfully and whistles.

I brighten at the thought of Jamal in my bed as if someone has lit a candle inside me, and I'm glowing from within. "Yep," I reply demurely.

"And..." Ashley probes, not buying my fake modesty. "How was it?"

I pantomime an explosion from my forehead and make a sound like a blast. "It was mind-blowing. I've never had sex so good. He is the best lover. Just wow."

"Woohoo!" Ashley singsongs and raises her glass of water at me. "To great sex."

"We're getting on so well. I honestly think he might be a contender for a serious relationship. I don't want to get too ahead of myself, but he could even be *The One*."

Ashley gives me a look. "You think that after a week of dating?"

"I know, that sounds ridiculous. I need to rein it in, but I'm a hopeless romantic. I always fall head over heels too fast."

She loads up her fork with beef and stuffing and eats it before replying, "Well, I say go for it if he makes you feel good and he's treating you with respect. But also, look after yourself. Don't get too attached if he's not feeling the same way. That's only asking for heartbreak."

"Yeah, I know. But we've talked a lot about everything. He has a six-year-old daughter from a previous relationship. She lives in London with her mother. Her name's Kayla, and he wants me to meet her. I've seen photos of her, and she looks just like him. It's uncanny. I don't think he'd want that if he didn't think we were going somewhere."

"Very true. Sounds like you guys are on the same page."

"We are. I don't think it's infatuation. I really feel like we're connecting on a deeper level."

"That's incredible. It sounds like Kevin and me. We just knew we were meant to be together. But... well... I probably shouldn't have brought that up. Seeing as it didn't work out in the end. Sorry." Ashley's good mood evaporates.

"Have you heard from him?"

"No. And I haven't messaged him either. I know it's been weeks, but I just don't feel ready to speak to him yet to sort out the flat and everything. That all feels so final. I'll do it soon. Or he'll give in and message me. We're both stubborn, so I guess we're probably waiting for the other to crack first."

· · ·

A FEW HOURS LATER, after Ashley insisted on cleaning up the kitchen because I cooked, we're sprawled on the sofas in the lounge, digesting the roast dinner, and both with our noses in books.

Doug is snuggled up on the sofa next to me, looking as cute as ever. I check my phone. No reply yet from Jamal to my last message of a few moments ago. We've settled into a hilarious banter, knowing exactly what to say to keep the conversation rolling. But I notice I've got an email.

I open it and see it's from my aunt. She's written a short note about where they currently are in the world – Honolulu – and forwarded on an electricity bill. We agreed that I would pay half towards the bills while they were away. Nothing for living in the house, as I'm doing them a favour by looking after Doug. But I insisted on contributing to the bills for the ten months I'm here.

I click on the attachment and scroll to the bottom to see the amount. Oh. It's way more than I was expecting. I didn't realise how much it would cost, but I guess it's a big house.

I open my banking app and set up a monthly direct debit to pay a certain amount into my aunt's account, which should cover this bill and any others that come through for the foreseeable. I have enough money, and it saves the hassle of doing a bank transfer every time.

Ashley chuckles at something in her book and turns the page.

Should I ask her to contribute to bills? She's been living here for the past couple of weeks now. She's been eating my food and using the electricity, water, and Wi-Fi. And watching tons of reality TV on Sky, a passion I definitely don't share with her. No, that's a crazy idea. Ashley is my house guest for as long as she wants to be. She's a great friend, and it's been so nice to have her in the house. She might not pay, but she cleans and tidies and helps out with Doug. And I feel safer with her here. I don't want to rock the boat by demanding cash from her all of a sudden when I've encouraged her to stay. That would just be rude.

And besides, I can afford it, and I know she's saving for a deposit now she's not buying a house with Kevin, so she's not as well-off as I am. Technically, after selling my house in Oxford, I'm a millionaire. But that money is sat waiting for a rainy day, waiting for when I'm ready to buy my next house. There's no rush on that front.

I won't think about asking Ashley to pay again. The direct debit is set up to cover the bills, and I've finally got the supermarket delivery organised to come weekly, so that's that.

My new life in Weston got off to a rocky start. But it's turned around, I just know it. I live with my best mate in a lovely house by the seaside, and I'm dating a dream man. My work is good, and I'm financially secure. I'm cautiously happy. No, sod it, I'm really happy. Why shouldn't I be?

My phone dings, and I see it's my turn on the Scrabble app against another player in the US. I play the word 'recuse' and smile happily to myself. *Thank you, Jamal.*

11

T he next day, as Ashley and I are in the kitchen after work, deciding what to eat for dinner, the doorbell goes.

"Do you mind going? It's probably my ASOS delivery. Just feeding Doug," I say with Doug's dry food in one hand and bowl in the other. Doug wags his tail so vigorously that his entire behind waggles.

"Sure thing," Ashley says and heads to the front door.

I hear the door open, and then there are murmurs.

"Hon," Ashley calls, "it's for you. It's not a delivery."

I put Doug's bowl down and then wander through to the hallway.

"It's Tim," Ashley announces and stands aside so I can see the man in the doorway.

My brother.

I choke and fall like stepping on splintering ice that drops you into the freezing, suffocating water below.

"Jess!" Ashley yells.

"Jess," Tim repeats, concerned.

His voice screeches in my head, the voice of so much woe.

"You stay right there. Do not come in this house," Ashley commands as she comes to assist me.

"That's my brother," I manage in a whisper.

"Your brother?" Ashley says, and she glares at Tim.

It's the first time she's heard his name, and she's not heard anything good about him. I thought the attacker had been him.

"Shall I tell him to fuck off?" she asks me in a voice loud enough for Tim to hear.

From the doorway, Tim pleads, "It's been ten years. I'm not the same man as before. Please, just give me a chance."

As Ashley helps me to my feet, the initial shock subsides, and I take him in. He's certainly changed. Where he was once tall and skinny, he's filled out. He's chunky but in a muscular way, his neck and arms thick but with a slight belly. He's no longer gaunt and pale. He still has freckles, but he's tanned with a healthy glow about him – gone the pallor of a heroin addict. His round face has filled out in the same way as his body, but his little quirks remain – his strong nose with a dimple at the very tip and one nostril slightly lower than the other. And his left ear still sticks out more and is obviously higher than the ear on the other side. His hooded, small eyes are still the same hazel colour as mine.

He always had a strong jaw and chin, but this is now covered with a full beard. When I saw him last, it was a wispy tangle. It's now neatly trimmed and slightly gingery, but with no grey. However, one complete change is his hair – or the lack of. It used to be a light-brown flop, but he's now completely bald, as if all the hair that had been on his head has crept down to his chin. But it didn't stop there, as his beard trails down his neck to meet the chest hair that pokes out his shirt.

The deep frown lines between his eyebrows give away his age. But he's a handsome bald man. He has a great-shaped head and really pulls it off. In short, he looks nothing like the man I last saw ten years ago.

"I'm here to say sorry. For our childhood, for the scene I made at your wedding, for the stalking. I want to make amends. I don't want anything from you. Look." He turns and holds up a key fob. He presses it, and the fancy car parked over the road bleeps. "That's my car. I'm doing well for myself now."

As he presses the key fob again to lock the car, I notice an equally fancy silver watch on his wrist. His stylish clothes are pristine and fit him perfectly – a navy-blue peacoat over a knitted burgundy jumper and dark-blue jeans, topped off with a striped grey scarf and black leather lace-up shoes. He has an undeniable air of wealth about him. He's confident and self-assured, his back straight and posture open. He's no longer hunched into himself in his own dazed, drug-addled world.

Could he really have turned himself around? A decade is a long time. A lot can happen in that time, I know this from experience. My life looks nothing like it did ten years ago. Is it such a stretch to believe he has changed too? But I know his history. And it isn't pretty.

He pockets the key fob. "I don't want that money anymore, Jess. I want to be your brother. I want us to be siblings, to have a relationship. Will you give me a chance, please?"

"Hmm," Ashley sneers at him, her loyal-friend protective instinct kicking in.

He looks pleadingly at me. It's not the angry, bitter face he once sported. His expression is conciliatory, longing even. I decide to give him a chance. "I just need a moment," I say and give Ashley a reassuring nod.

"Okay, well, I'll just be in the kitchen, getting dinner ready. Call for me if you need me." She looks pointedly at

Tim. Although she's much shorter and much thinner than him, she has an if-you-mess-with-my-friend-there'll-be-some-serious-trouble look about her. He scratches his beard, slightly uncomfortable with her manner. She breaks off her intense stare and says, "I'm just a *second* away." Then she heads towards the back of the house.

We look at each other. He smiles and gestures at me. "You look good."

I glance down at my outfit: a smartish but super comfy floral knee-length dress, red cardigan and thick black tights. Standard going-to-The-Hive wear. And then I twig. He's not referring to that. He's referring to my weight. I'm about four stone lighter than when he last saw me. It was just before Blake took control of my diet and exercise regime in a bid to improve our fertility chances. Although I'm not as slim as at my thinnest, putting on some weight once we divorced, I'm still lighter than what I was.

A gust of wind ruffles Tim's clothes and beard. "Are you going to invite me in?"

I cross my arms. Although I'll hear him out, I'm still suspicious of this man, and it overrides my polite nature. "No."

He raises his hands in a friendly, placatory gesture. "Fair enough. I really don't deserve your trust. But I'd like to rebuild it. That's why I'm here."

"Yes. Here you are." I pause to fully process his presence on my doorstep. "How did you know I was here? How did you know Aunt Alice and Uncle Edwin lived here? They lost touch with you years ago."

"I still have my Facebook profile. And although I never posted or used it much, I'm still connected to Aunt Alice. You deleted me after your wedding fiasco, and I totally understand that – I was a complete shit. But one day, I saw that Alice had posted that she and Edwin were off on a world cruise after winning some money on the lottery, and one of her friends had asked what she planned to do with Doug for all that time and recommended some Weston-super-Mare dog kennels. Alice innocently replied that you were coming to dog- and house-sit."

"So you knew I'd be here."

"Yes, I've been wanting to reconnect for a little while. My therapist says it'll be good for me. And well, you are family, and we only have each other and Alice and Edwin. I came to see them before they went away. But I wanted to apologise to you for everything in person. It's taken me a long time to deal with what happened with Mum and Dad. And the drama with the inheritance. I went off the rails, but I understand it all now. I've been clean for eight years."

I scrutinise him for any signs of lying, but he appears genuinely apologetic.

He continues, "Look, here's my business card with my mobile number on it. I don't want to force anything. I know it must be a surprise, me turning up like this. So call me. If you want to, that is. It's all on your terms."

I take the card from him, careful not to brush my fingers against his. I glance down at it and notice the address. "Leeds?" I ask. I haven't known where he's been living for a long time. He always replied 'up north' whenever questioned.

"Yes, that's where I'm based now. I have a property port-folio with rental tenants. And I manage properties for others. I've booked a short-term apartment for a while in Weston because I want to be close if you change your mind and want to see me. I can run my portfolio from anywhere, really. Anyway, I'm going to head off. I hope to see you again soon. But I totally understand if I don't. All the best, sis."

He backs away before turning and closing the gate. I watch as he gets into his fancy car and drives away. Then I close the door.

"You okay?" Ashley asks, coming out of the kitchen.

"Um, yeah. I just need to call my aunt." I point up the stairs and grab my bag off the side cabinet and head up. I find my phone and sit on my bed. I have no idea what time zone my aunt and uncle are in, but I dial my aunt anyway. She told me to call her in an emergency. And my estranged, once-crazed-and-drug-addicted brother showing up on the doorstep is an emergency.

It rings for a while, and then I hear a female voice. It sounds very far away.

"Jess, love, what's up? Is it Doug? Oh, goodness me, Edwin, something's happened to Doug."

I hear Uncle Edwin's voice in the background. "Oh crikey, not Doug."

"It's not Doug. Doug is fine."

"It's not Doug," Alice repeats to Edwin.

"Thank God," he says.

Her voice becomes clearer. "Is it the house? Has it sprung a leak? I knew we shouldn't have gone away for so long—"

I interrupt before she can work herself into an unnecessary tizzy. "Aunt Alice, the house is perfect too. It's Tim. He's just come round."

"Tim. Oh, dear. Yes." Then to Edwin she says, "It's about Tim."

"Ah," Edwin says.

Alice sighs heavily, her breath amplified through the phone and sounding like white noise in my ear. "He got in touch with me on Facebook a few weeks before we went away. I didn't even realise he was still my friend, or whatever you call it. I never mentioned you in any of my posts, just like you asked me not to all those years ago, but I wasn't thinking and mentioned you'd be dog-sitting. I'm sorry. What a pickle I've made of everything."

I know she's made an innocent mistake. My aunt would never do anything to hurt me. She's like a mother to me.

"Don't worry, Aunt Alice, it's done now. What happened after he got in touch?"

"He came across as such a normal young man on the messages. So we agreed to meet him in a cafe in Weston. And, well, he seemed to be a decent fellow. Completely different person. Really regretful about the past and wanting to make amends. I told him that he needed to reach out to you directly, and then it would be your choice. I wasn't going to be the in-between."

"Why didn't you tell me you'd seen him?"

"Oh, I'm so sorry, dear. All the packing and the excitement about the cruise just took hold of us. And then when you arrived, you were so happy, and we didn't want to upset you because we'd not seen you like that for years. And then suddenly, we were off."

"Did you give him this address?"

"Um, well, yes. He asked for it so he could keep in touch. I didn't even think about it. Oh, fiddlesticks, what a mess."

"Aunt Alice, don't worry. He came here, that's all. I just wanted to understand how he knew where you lived when you met him at a cafe."

She sighs again, and I hold the phone away from my ear this time. "Yes, that's my doing."

"He looked so different."

"I know. And he was so warm and kind and genuine. I really believe he's turned a corner. Did you invite him in? Did you talk?"

"No, and not really. I need a bit of time to decide if I want to talk to him."

"You take as much time as you need." Her voice goes faint, and I hear, "No, Edwin, not that shirt, the grey one. You got gravy down that one last night." There's a brief moment before she continues to me, "If Tim's serious about reconnecting, he'll wait. And if you don't want to, then don't. I wouldn't blame you."

"It's literally just happened. So I'm going to have a think. Anyway, how are you both doing?"

Alice proceeds to tell me all about their travels to date, recounting much of what she's already told me in emails and moaning that they've had to buy Edwin more clothes because he seems incapable of eating without dropping something down his front that inevitably stains. I fill her in on dating someone from the co-working place and about Ashley staying for a while.

"Oh, that's lovely news all round," Alice exclaims. "Looks like life in Weston is suiting you."

I don't, however, tell her about the creepy note and the nail sticking out the front door or about the alleyway attack and the other strange things that have happened. That would panic them into returning, and I don't want that. I want them to enjoy their well-deserved holiday.

We say our goodbyes and hang up.

I reach for the business card my brother gave me. It says, 'Tim Salmon, Salmon Properties' and has a website, email, mobile number and address printed underneath. It gives me a pang of nostalgia, seeing my first surname. I'm surprised and also proud that Tim has called his business that. We both used to hate that surname when we were kids – an endless source of teasing and bullying about smelling fishy, looking fishy, being fishy and so on. I couldn't wait to change it when I married Blake. And I couldn't wait to get rid of Blake's surname and take Donovan, my aunt and uncle's surname, when we divorced. I didn't want to go back to Salmon. It felt like going backwards. And I needed to move forward. I needed a new surname for a new chapter of my life.

I open a browser on my phone and type in the website. It loads quickly and is a professional, super-slick site with stunning photography of a number of houses as well as a photo of Tim with a big, warm smile on his face. He looks open and welcoming.

I read the 'About' page and learn he's been doing this for the past eight years, starting with one rental property and growing his portfolio before taking on portfolios for clients and also acting as a consultant for people starting out in the property investment business.

I read through the gushing client testimonials and click on some links. Then I open the 'News' page. There are a few posts, mostly about new properties but also about the charity work that Tim does. He helps troubled youth in Leeds with mentoring and by offering work experience. There are pictures of him with smiling teenagers in front of properties.

It's all perfectly legit.

Then I go onto my aunt's Facebook profile and scroll through the posts until I find the one about the world cruise. I read through the comments and find the one that mentions me. It's in passing, but it says 'Jess'. If Tim had been watching her page for any mention of me, he would've seen it. I find his profile from searching through her friends list and click on it. The profile picture is his professional head shot used on his website, but his profile is private.

My brother and I have had a troubled relationship since Mum got diagnosed with bowel cancer when I was fourteen and he was sixteen. Now that I'm thirty-nine and he's forty-one, could we be friends again? Do I want that?

On the one hand, I'm curious. He does appear to have changed. We had been thick as thieves as children before Mum's illness.

But on the other, there's many years' worth of hurt to unpack, and I don't know if I want to do that. Perhaps it would be better to never see him again. And could he have left that note? Perhaps it wasn't as sinister as I imagined? Or perhaps that's someone else entirely and Tim's arriving now is a complete coincidence.

I continue to pick over his sudden re-entry into my life, his intentions and what to do like Doug with one of his chew toys – worrying at it, pawing and nibbling, flinging it about – until my stomach grumbles and I put it aside, heading downstairs just as Ashley's taking a lasagne out of the oven.

"Perfect timing," she says. "Hope you're hungry. There's tons here."

I sit at the dining table as Ashley dishes up and puts a plate in front of me.

She sits, picks up her knife and fork and says, "Look, I don't want to pry, and I will totally respect if you'd prefer not to tell me, but what's the deal with your brother? You thought it was him who had attacked you."

I take a deep, steadying breath. "That's because he'd done it before."

"Attacked you late at night down an alleyway?"

"Not quite. It was in a deserted multi-storey car park. I was on my own after having dinner with a friend, and he jumped me, shoved me into a wall and threatened me. It was terrifying. I thought I was about to die. But then I realised it was him. That was the last time I saw him, ten years ago now."

Ashley gawps at me. "That's terrible."

"For many years, he followed me and did stuff to scare me to get my attention, to make sure I didn't forget him. He was off his head on drugs. I wouldn't see him for months on end, and then he'd rock up and do something to upset me and hang around for a while like a bad smell and then disappear again. That Friday night down the alleyway, I thought he was back and up to his old tricks again."

"He said something about not wanting any money. Is that

what it was all about? He was trying to get you to fund his drug habit?"

"It's complicated," I reply.

She gets the hint that I don't want to go into it any more than that. "And now he's here claiming to be a changed man."

"Yep."

We both dig into our meals.

After a few mouthfuls, Ashley says, "From what you've mentioned, I think you should be cautious about him. A leopard never changes its spots, after all."

"**G**reat shot, *ma chérie*," Jamal exclaims as my golf ball plops into the hole. "A hole in one!"

I'm surprised. I'm not really paying attention; my mind keeps wandering to other things. I'm trying my hardest to be present, to focus on our Friday night date, but I've been distracted all week. It's been five days since Tim rocked up on my doorstep, and I haven't called him, vacillating between wanting to and not wanting to.

"Wooo," I reply, feigning enthusiasm. "Your turn."

Jamal drops his ball onto the start and wiggles his bum into me to make me move out of the way. I laugh. It's a rainy evening, and it was his genius idea to come to this glow-in-the-dark indoor crazy golf place after dinner at the restaurant next door. I should be having a lot of fun, but I'm distracted.

"There is something on your mind," Jamal says as he lines up his golf club and then putts the ball. It bounces off the back and comes to a halt nowhere near the hole. He tuts, but instead of chasing after it, he looks at me expectantly.

I kiss his cheek. "I'm sorry, it's just my whole brother thing."

"I thought as much. You can talk to me about it."

I've seen Jamal twice already this week and talked to him about it. I'm surprised he's not sick of it. He heads toward his ball and lines up another shot.

"Come on," he encourages. "You are beating me at golf. I need something else to think about."

I tap my golf club against the wooden flooring. "He just came across as so genuine. Like a different person. But I know what he was like, and I can't disassociate the past from the present. Do you think it's possible for people to change?"

Jamal looks at the hole and putts. The ball goes in, and we move to the next hole, a windmill, which happens to be our last, while he considers his reply. I like that about him, that he is very considerate and thoughtful and doesn't just blurt out something to fill the silence. He always takes his time to form a response.

"Yes, I do. I think people are changing all the time. I'm a different man after meeting you. You're a different woman after meeting me – I hope, anyway, ha. We make new experiences every single day. Each morning, I wake up striving to be a better man."

"That's a wonderful life philosophy."

"Your brother was an awful person. Then he grew and evolved. Perhaps think about him as two people. Tim in the past and Tim in the present. Ten years is a long time to amend your ways, to reflect, to shed your skin to reveal a new you."

"I just can't stop linking his sudden reappearance to the note nailed to my door and the attack."

"But why would he do those things and then announce himself? If he wanted to scare you, why show up at your door to apologise for past sins?"

I nod as I line up my shot. I putt, and the ball races all

over the place, travels cleanly between the rotating windmill blades and drops in the hole.

Jamal exclaims, "Another hole in one! And you're not even trying. You should be a professional crazy golfer."

I laugh. "What can I say? Clearly, a natural."

Jamal takes his go quickly. And has to hit the ball five times to get it in. He slaps his forehead. "I'm clearly not a natural."

We take our clubs back to the counter and hang out in the reception area, looking at the pouring rain through the glass doors.

"I won't stay over tonight, *ma chérie*. I have this wedding in the morning in London that I have to be up early for."

"That's fine."

"I will be staying overnight in a hotel room with my mother. She snores like a train of pigs. Wish me luck."

I laugh. "Good luck. Remember your earplugs."

He kisses me. "But I shall be back on Sunday. Shall we do something... romantic?" He sucks gently on my earlobe, and my insides melt. "At your place, of course. It's still too soon for you to meet my mama. She'll hound us about getting engaged and when she can expect her next grandchild. And there's no way you could stay over until we're married. She's very traditional like that."

Until now, I hadn't even considered trying for another baby. Remarrying, maybe. But the idea of getting pregnant with Jamal makes me feel warm and gooey inside. Could it happen between us? It hadn't happened with Blake, but maybe that was for a reason, and it's this man who's destined to be the father of my children. I know I'm jumping way ahead, and it's too soon in our relationship to be considering that, but it pleases me that I think it's a possibility. And it also pleases me that Jamal talks about it without being cagey or cold. He almost speaks as if it's a done deal.

I cup his face in one hand, taking in his sparkling light-brown eyes. "Perhaps I could make us dinner, and then we could have dessert in bed?"

"Yes. I very much like the sound of that." He takes my hand and kisses my palm. "I'm going to call us a taxi. I'm not walking in that rain."

"Good idea."

As he speaks on the phone, I watch the water run in rivulets down the glass.

He puts his arm around me and squeezes me into him. "It's a minute or so away. We'll drop you first, then me. Look, this is what I think about your brother – perhaps give him another chance? Everybody deserves a second chance. If he messes up, then you don't have to see him again. If he turns out to be a nice guy, then you have a potentially wonderful new relationship to experience with your brother."

"True."

"But there is no rush. Take as much time as you need to decide what to do. Let it"—he waves his hands around—"percolate."

"Oh, good word."

"*Merci.* It was in a document I translated earlier today. I vowed to use it. I think that was appropriate."

"Ha, very. My thoughts are percolating right now."

He kisses my forehead as the taxi's lights sweep into the car park.

THE FOLLOWING NIGHT, the shrill ring of the doorbell wakes me. At first, I think it's in my dream. Ashley and I had a quiet Saturday night in with a bottle of wine, a takeaway and a movie. And I went to bed at a decent hour and fell straight asleep. But the piercing noise shatters the silence in the house a second time.

Jeez, someone is ringing the doorbell – I look at my phone's display – at 3 a.m. *What the hell?* I drag myself out of bed and put my dressing gown and slippers on. The bell shrieks out a third time, this time pressed for longer.

I open my bedroom door and meet Ashley in the hallway. She looks exactly as I feel: dishevelled, tired, confused. Her face is scrunched up, still not quite awake. She has her phone in her hand, as I do.

"Who the fuck is that?" she says.

It hits me then, and my stomach somersaults. Could it be the person who left the note? I thought they'd had their fun and were gone. But why would anyone be ringing the door-bell in the middle of the night?

"I don't know," I reply and look at her.

She must sense my apprehension because she takes my hand. We stand together at the top of the stairs.

"We should go down and open it," she says.

The ringing cuts off. We both hold our breath. Then I hear it. The front door handle rattling. Someone is trying to get in.

Ashley continues, "Did you lock the front door? I don't think I did. Oh, shit." She squeezes my hand.

"I did. I *definitely* did. And I put the deadlock and chain on when we came up to bed."

The pressure of her grip relaxes. "Thank goodness."

The rattling stops, and then there's silence.

Ashley continues, "I think we should go and see. We're together, and we both have our phones to call 999 if we need to. But maybe someone needs our help? Maybe there's been a car crash outside or something?"

"Okay," I reply.

Ashley is way braver than I am. I'd prefer to go back to my bed and put the pink polka dot covers over my head. But she's right. It could be someone needing assistance. Someone walking home who needs help.

We creep down the stairs, Ashley leading the way. I clutch her hand tightly.

She reaches out and unlocks the deadlock and then opens the door as wide as the security chain allows. Cold air barges its way in. I shiver uncontrollably, as if I'm riddled with holes and an icy wind is blasting through them all.

"No one there," she says.

My teeth chatter, and before I can get them under control to tell her to shut the door and forget it ever happened, she undoes the chain and opens the door fully.

The dark, chilly night looms large like a snake reared up, fangs bared, ready to strike at two little, unaware mice. A damp earthy tang wafts in, the smell after a heavy downpour. Although the rain has stopped now, there is the distinct current in the air that indicates it will start again at any minute. I raise a trembling finger to switch on the hallway light.

Ashley wraps her dressing gown around her and takes a step onto the front porch. Emboldened by the light, I peer out past the threshold. The street is empty. Quiet. Still. It's eerie. I've never seen it at this time. I can almost hear the houses and the cars sleeping soundly, the trees swaying happily in the midst of sweet dreams.

Ashley points at the front wall. Shivers dance from my ears to my toes. I know what she's trying to tell me. Whoever was ringing the doorbell could be crouched right there on the pavement, hidden behind the wall. We should check, I know we should. It could mean catching the culprit red-handed.

But I'm frozen with fear. I cannot leave the safety of the house to step out into the night, into a street the fabric of which feels so different, so alien, to in the daytime.

"I'll go," Ashley whispers. She grits her teeth and stands

up taller. She jogs the couple of steps to the gate, swings it open and looks behind the wall.

I half expect a giant mouth to snatch her up and suck her down out of sight, but she looks back at me and shakes her head. I beckon her in urgently.

She heads back into the house, and I close the door, putting the deadlock on and the security chain across again.

We both stand there awhile, catching our breath.

"Whew," Ashley says, a hand on her heart. "That was intense."

I puff out my cheeks and huff through my lips, expelling my fear as much as possible.

"Do you think it was the same person who nailed that note to the front door?" I ask as we both head up the stairs towards our bedrooms.

"Maybe," Ashley says. "Or some drunk idiot on their way home from the pub who was ringing doorbells in the middle of the night for fun. We used to get kids doing that all the time on our estate in London."

"Or... Tim?"

She shrugs. "Well, whoever it was is long gone. Bloody bastard waking us up." She gives me a hug, yawns, and heads back to her bedroom. "See you in the morning, babe," she says as she closes her bedroom door.

I get back into my bed. Was that random? Or was it deliberate? I take a few deep breaths to steady my nerves. I'm safe in the house. No one can get in. I've locked up everywhere and double- and triple-checked. I'm not getting caught out by that again.

I must drift off because I wake with a start again to the doorbell ringing. I check my phone: 5.17 a.m. This time, I fly down the stairs, not waiting for Ashley, wanting to catch whoever it is in the act. To know for sure who I'm dealing with. And to make them stop once and for all.

I fumble with the locks and chain and fling open the door. But there's no one there. The gate is wide open. Did Ashley leave it open earlier? Or was that the person targeting me making a quick getaway? It's chucking it down, and I don't step outside. It's still dark, sunrise not for another hour or so, but the street feels like it's coming awake. A van drives past. It's branded with the name of a national newspaper, so it's probably on its way to deliver papers to the corner shop.

I shut the door and head back upstairs. I meet Ashley at the top.

"Was that the doorbell again?" she asks drowsily.

"Yes. Nobody there."

"Not cool," she replies.

"No, not cool at all."

"It's a Sunday. I'm going back to sleep. Until at least midday." She goes back to her room and closes the door.

But I just stand there. I feel wired, and there's no way I'll fall back to sleep. My brain is whirring too much. The adrenaline has spiked and left me wide awake. Once in the night is random, bad luck. But twice is on purpose, designed to disrupt. Whoever is targeting me hasn't gone away. They're still very much out there, and they're still very much after me.

13

A t 11 a.m. I'm on the sofa in the lounge, nursing my third cup of coffee. I'm staring off into space, as I've been doing for the past couple of hours, when Ashley comes bustling in. She's dressed in a pretty skirt and smart sweater, make-up and hair done, and spritzed with perfume. Her nails are freshly painted in a new colour, and her lips glisten with lip balm.

"It's Kevin," she announces as she puts her coat on. "He finally messaged me this morning. He's sorry about everything and wants to give it another go. He's begging for a second chance, for me to forgive him. So we're going to meet up and talk things through."

This news wakes me up. I'd thought he was well out of the picture, Ashley not mentioning him for a while. But clearly not. "Do you think you'll get back together with him?"

"I don't know. I just don't know... but I want to hear him out. Give him a chance to explain himself. I'll be back later. I don't imagine I'll be long. I've got my keys." She pats her handbag.

"Cool," I reply. I gave her the spare set of keys a while ago.

It didn't make sense for me to keep letting her in and out all the time. And I certainly didn't want to have to leave the door on the latch so that anyone off the street could just walk in.

She heads out. I hear the gate clang as she shuts it behind her. Doug jumps up on the sofa next to me and paws at my knee.

"Well, what should we do today? I suppose I'd better take you for walkies."

Although he can't hear me say the W-word, his tail wags eagerly. I can't sit here all day fretting about who rang the doorbell last night and what they might do next. I need to keep living. And I need some fresh air and a bracing walk. Some exercise will do me good. That's what helped me out of the slump last time, just getting out for daily walks.

I stand with purpose. "I know, let's go for a walk at Brean Down."

Doug woofs.

I DRIVE the mint-green Honda the short distance to the Brean Down car park. The drive is difficult. I can't quite focus on what I'm doing, and my vision is slightly blurry. I get beeped by one car on a roundabout because I pull out in front of it without really even seeing it. It's the stress, I know it is. I have a bundle of writhing nerves in my chest that won't stay still. Burning off some nervous energy with a walk is exactly what I need, but the thought of being on my own, outside, churns the anxiety within.

I can handle this.

I park up in the little car park at the bottom of the hill and pay at the machine. It's run by the National Trust, and there's a small cafe and toilets nearby that overlook the beach. There are also a few other buildings dotted around. I get Doug out of the car. He's pulling and fussing, clearly excited to be here.

We get tangled in his lead as I attempt to also put my handbag across my body. Finally, we head towards the steep steps up the side of the cliff to get to the top. Brean Down is essentially a hill that juts out into the sea and has a ruined nineteenth-century fort at the end. It was also the site of a Roman temple, apparently.

Uncle Edwin told me all about it and that it was well worth a visit for its stunning views across to Wales and back inland. Also that Doug was more than happy to walk along the top of the Down but would need carrying up the stairs as 'he gets a bit doddery after one too many steps'.

So I pick him up and start the climb. It's hard work, but it's refreshing. The weather is blustery and overcast but dry. Perfect to blow the cobwebs away. I pause about halfway up and look back to where we've come from. On my right is a long stretch of beach. And on the left, the car park is hidden behind the buildings and a few trees, but beyond is a lovely long stretch of green in the form of farms and a nature reserve.

"Come on then," I say to Doug and keep going. He is perfectly happy in my arms and doesn't wriggle. He's completely relaxed. It's as if I'm carrying the soft toy from the car.

We get to the top, and I put him down. My arms ache slightly. I stop to catch my breath and take in the view. Edwin was right – it is stunning up here. Being out in nature soothes me. It's the middle of the day, and there are people about on walks. I don't feel threatened. The stress from the doorbell ringing seems to lift up and get taken away by the wind. I take Doug off the lead and march towards the tip that juts into the sea. Doug happily trots and sniffs and cocks his leg every few steps beside me. We reach the end and explore the ruined fort.

As we're taking a break, sitting on a mound and looking

across the Bristol Channel, dark, stormy clouds roll in. Everything goes very grey all of a sudden, and the collapsed walls and stairways to nowhere take on a sinister hue. "Let's get back, Doug. And quickly."

When we're a few paces from the head of the stairs, the clouds burst. Heavy droplets splatter my raincoat, and I'm pleased I wore my weatherproof hiking boots rather than trainers. With my hood up, I suddenly feel very alone. As I reach the top of the stairs, I look about. There's a couple a few metres behind me, clutching each other against the weather. But otherwise, most walkers have retreated from the rain already.

I pick up Doug and start my descent. From here I can see the car park over the tops of the buildings. There are only five cars in it now. The mint-green Honda's still there.

But all the blood drains from my body. The back door is open. And – I squint to see – and someone is crawling in the back seat.

Oh my God.

I stumble, lose my footing and trip down a step. I look down to see where I'm going and grab the railing, at the same time keeping my hold on the dog.

"Shit," I exclaim.

A gust of wind blows my hood off, and the rain soaks my hair in an instant.

Readjusting Doug onto my hip, I pull my hood back up and stare at my car. The door is now shut. And I can't see in the back windows.

Did I lock the car? I can't remember. I remember the tussle with Doug, but I have no memory of pressing the button on the key fob. Did I do it as I walked away? Or did I leave the back door open after getting Doug out? I was so concerned with getting my bag over my head I can't recall. And I just happened to see it before the wind blew it shut.

No. I know what I saw. There's someone in the back of my car, lying in wait for me. There's hardly anyone around. What is their plan? To put a knife to my throat and drive me to somewhere remote? Or worse, kill me right there in the car park?

Fuck.

Terror seizes me, and I grip the railing again.

The couple catches up with me.

"Are you okay?" the woman asks. She's about fifty. She looks harmless, reliable. As does the man.

"No," I blurt, petrified.

They stop on the step next to me. The man frowns, pulling his coat closer around him and hunching inside his hood out of the rain.

But the woman's face is full of concern. "Oh, goodness, what can we do to help? Are you scared of heights? It is pretty high up here."

I point a shaky finger towards the car park. "I just saw someone get in my car. I must've left it unlocked. They're going to hurt me."

The couple both turn to look at the car park.

"Are you sure?" the woman says at the same time as the man says, "Which one is your car?"

My voice quivers as I reply, "Yes, I'm sure. It's the mint-green one."

He peers at my car. "Can't see anything."

"I saw the door open and someone getting in. Please, could you come with me? Please?"

But the man grumbles, "We're not parked in that car park." He gives his wife a look as if to say *this woman has clearly got a screw loose. Let's leave her be.*

But the woman dismisses him with a curt, "Of course. It's a couple of minutes out of our way, at most."

My hood blows off again, and I yank it up, blinking rain

out of my eyes. "I'm having issues with this... um... person. It could be them."

"I see. Come on, let's go and check." The woman motions for her husband to lead the way.

He sighs and sets off quickly. She gestures for me to follow, but I can't move. She indicates to Doug. "Do you want me to carry the dog?"

I shake my head no. Clutching Doug to me is giving me strength. I need to stay upright for him, to get him home and into the warm and dry.

"Very well." She gives my elbow a gentle nudge, and I take a shaky step forward.

"That's it," she encourages. "One foot after the other." As I get moving, with her a step behind, she asks, "What's your name?"

My name forms on my lips, but I can't get it out. My mouth is dry. After a few moments of uncomfortable silence, the woman gives up waiting for a reply and doesn't try to talk to me again. I feel bad. She's been so kind, but my voice has retreated into the depths and will take a while to coax out again. Every so often I look up at my car, but the closer to the bottom we get, the more the trees and buildings hide it from view.

At the bottom of the steps, the man is waiting, hands on his hips. "I'm soaked wet through," he complains to the woman. She shushes him with an expression that says *stop your griping in front of this poor woman in need.*

The three of us walk towards my car. I don't put Doug down. I carry him against me like a lucky charm. As we get closer, I stop and reach out and clutch the woman's arm. She pauses with me.

"Can't see anyone," the man says. He glances over his shoulder to see we aren't moving and carries on.

He peers in the back window, then purses his lips. He turns to us. "Nobody there."

I know what I saw. I know I saw someone getting in my car. "Is the door open?" I squeak.

"Is the door open?" the woman repeats, louder.

The man grumbles under his breath but tries the door handle anyway. It's clear he doesn't think it'll open. When it does, his posture changes. He makes a show of looking inside.

"Oh," he says. "Dina, you'd better come and look at this."

The woman glances at me and then goes to the man. I trail behind her. The man moves out of the way so she can see.

"Gosh," she says and then looks at me in confusion – or perhaps fear.

I edge past them to look. The material of the back seat has been slashed multiple times. Wads of white stuffing spill out of the gashes. And there in the middle is a large, generic kitchen knife with a black handle.

I'm transfixed by the guts of the car seat spilling out everywhere. Slashed with a knife. Did whoever do this see I wasn't alone? They'd planned to stab me but saw I was with the couple, so they attacked the seat instead? Or was this meant as a message to me of what's to come? I jerk back as if burnt and bump into the couple, who are mumbling to one another behind me.

The man clears his throat and asks, "Was that there before?"

Does he think I did this to my own car – and not even my car – my aunt and uncle's car? Why would I do that? What would be the point? I get that he thinks I've possibly got a screw loose, but that's insane.

"Of course not," I snap defensively. Then I soften. "I knew I saw someone get in the back seat."

"But why would they do that?" the woman asks gently.

I shake my head.

"You should call the police," the man says in a tone that is more of a demand than a suggestion.

A prickle creeps across my neck as if I'm being watched. I spin around and take in the car park. "They're still here. I can feel them watching me."

"I seriously doubt that," the man says, his patience wearing thin.

"I can't stay here," I blurt. "I need to get out of here. I don't feel safe." I slam the back door closed and open the driver's door. I lean across and put Doug on the front passenger seat, then get in.

"You should really call the police," the woman says.

"I will, when I'm home, when I'm safe. I need to go. Right now. Thank you for all your help."

I turn on the engine. Part of me expects it won't start, as if it has been tampered with in some way. But it comes to life immediately.

I put the car into gear and speed away to the exit, leaving the couple standing in my dust. It's stupid, I know. I should take their details; the police will want witnesses. I should be more thankful for their help, get their address, and pop round a bottle of wine or a card or something. But all my brain is full of is escape. Escape, escape, escape. The great outdoors suddenly feels menacing. All that open space that someone could be hiding in, watching, waiting.

I check my rear-view mirror, but no other cars move from the car park to follow me. But it's a long road away from the car park, with lots of places a car could lie in wait and then follow. I need to get home. The drive is a blur. I speed, jump red lights, pull out onto roundabouts without really looking. I park the car in the disabled space outside the house because

I can't stand the thought of finding a space down the road and having to walk any distance.

I grab Doug and fly into the house, locking and dead-locking the front door and putting the chain across. We're both drenched, and I should rub Doug down with a towel, but first things first. I get my phone out and dial the police.

"You left your car unlocked in a public car park. It was probably kids, Ms Donovan," the officer on the phone repeats for perhaps the fifth time.

He's not getting it. He's not getting the significance.

"I've got a stalker! They're out to get me. This was a warning. My life is in danger. You have to believe me."

"What else has this stalker done?"

"Rang my doorbell in the middle of the night. Twice. Nailed a note to the front door. Hired a lookalike to follow me and freak me out—"

The police officer cuts in, "Hired a lookalike? Of who?"

"My ex-husband!"

"Who is the stalker?"

I grind my teeth in frustration before admitting, "I don't know."

"Do you have any proof that any of these things are connected?"

"What? Of course they are connected."

"Not necessarily. Look, Ms Donovan, I'll make a note of this incident, and I need you to keep a—"

It's my turn to interrupt. "Keep a diary. Yes, yes. I know the drill."

"Good."

"Oh, can you link this incident to the attack a few weeks ago?"

"Attack?"

I tell him about the Friday night attack down the alleyway, the date and that the police came to the house.

He pauses for a moment, and I guess he's finding the details on his system. "Ah, yes. Here it is. You think this is linked to that? The same person who attacked you in the street slashed your car seats?"

"Absolutely."

I hear some typing before he says, "Okay, I've made a note of that. But honestly, I still think it was bored kids having some fun. Kids do strange things around here."

"I will keep a diary and get proof."

"Excellent."

We say our goodbyes, and I realise I'm shivering and can barely feel my toes. I'm freezing, still in my wet clothes. As I lower my phone, I realise I'm all alone in a big house. My shivers turn into full-body quakes until I'm hyperventilating.

I grab my hair and pull it up from the scalp just to feel something. To feel the pain. I don't want the panic to envelop me.

Keep it together, Jess. This can't be happening to me again. I can't fall apart for a second time. I just can't.

14

I call Ashley. As the phone is ringing, I sit in the corner of the lounge in a dark spot between the sofa and the wall. I pull my legs up to my chest and hug them, resting my forehead against my knees. It's comforting, as if I'm hiding, as if no one will be able to find me here.

Ashley's phone rings off, but she doesn't have voicemail set up. I try her a second time and then a third. She must still be with Kevin and have her phone on silent or in her bag.

It's 3 p.m., and I wonder if Jamal will be back from London yet. I call him, but there's no answer. He must still be with his family after the wedding or his mum or travelling back to Weston. But, unlike Ashley, he has voicemail.

I leave a message:

"Oh, Jamal, please, please call me back. Someone's out to get me. They slashed my car seats with a kitchen knife when I was out. I'm at home now, but I'm terrified. It could be Blake or Toni or maybe even Tim. All these people hate me. I know I've not told you about all of them, but they've all got it in for me. It was a warning. A death threat, I'm certain."

I ramble on incoherently, repeating myself until I hear a

robotic voice tell me that I've reached the time limit for a message and can either leave the message or delete it. I leave the message. How long was I talking? No matter.

I sit still and stare at my phone, willing it to ring. Who else can I call? I don't have anyone else.

My brother's name pops into my head. Tim? No, I'm still not certain it wasn't him who did this. Or am I? I slap my temples a few times to try to dislodge the obsessive thinking that goes round and round in my head.

Doug snuffles around my ankles. He's still wearing his harness with the lead attached and dragging behind him. I forgot to take it off earlier. I unclip it and pull it off over his head. He does a full-body shake that ends right at the tip of his tail. He seems completely unaffected by the traumatic experience on his dog walk earlier.

I check my phone. No calls, no messages. It's 5 p.m., Doug's dinner time. I've been crouched here, a tornado charging about in my head, for two hours. Jamal's coming round at 7 p.m. That's not far away. Two hours hiding in a corner. If whoever slashed my car seats was going to do something, they would've done it by now, surely.

I pat Doug. He's almost dry. Knowing I need to get up to feed him energises me into standing. My muscles ache, and I feel light-headed, but I make my way into the kitchen and sort Doug's food.

That little act makes me feel stronger. I'm meant to be making Jamal a moussaka. It's one of his favourites. I found a recipe and bought all the ingredients the other day. I force myself into action. I pull the recipe up on my phone and begin to methodically go through it. I get out everything I need and prep the vegetables. It's a fussy recipe that involves quite a few steps, but the action of following instructions soothes me. Step by step, I don't need to think about anything else apart from slicing the aubergines, browning the lamb mince, and making the tomato sauce.

By the time I've assembled the ingredients and have the dish ready to go in the oven, I'm feeling better. It's 6.30 p.m., and Jamal will be here soon. He's always very punctual. I realise I'm still wearing my soggy clothes from earlier, now smelling a bit damp and musty. I head upstairs for a quick shower and to put on a fresh outfit. It revives me, and my thoughts become clearer.

I know what I need to do – I need to take some photos of the back seat and the knife for my diary. Write everything that happened down in my Singapore notebook. Stay alert and safe and build a case for the police. Try to catch whoever is doing this red-handed.

I head back downstairs and sit at the dining table. It's ten to seven. Should I put the moussaka in to cook or wait until Jamal arrives? It needs to cook for fifty minutes. I debate this for a while, and then at five to seven, I put it in the oven and put a timer on my phone.

I check WhatsApp. It shows that Jamal was online twenty minutes ago. He hasn't messaged me since his customary morning message to wish me a good day earlier. Ashley hasn't been on the app since 10.30 a.m., so she must definitely still be with Kevin. Neither of them has called me back.

It surprises me that Jamal hasn't called because he's been on WhatsApp, so he's been on his phone. Did he not get my voicemail? He would've seen I'd called, though. Perhaps he's waiting to talk to me in person. He'll be here any minute. At least I'll know when the doorbell goes who it is.

I decide to go all out. It's been a terrible day, but I can make it a good evening with my sexy man. I lay the table with my aunt's fancy tableware and china and light some candles. I get one of the artificial roses from my aunt's large display in the kitchen window and put it in a tall glass vase I find in a cupboard and put that in the centre of the table.

The clock in the kitchen says it's ten past seven. This is the first time he's ever been late. He must've been held up. I look at WhatsApp, and it says he's online. I wait to see that he's 'typing', but after a few minutes, I realise he's not going to message me. Then he's no longer online.

Weird. I message him:

Hey babe, are you running late? Let me know cos I can hold off on dinner, no probs xx

I put my phone on the table and decide to prepare the salad and get the garlic bread ready. When I've done that, I stand in the middle of the kitchen, the delicious smells of the moussaka cooking circulating, and twiddle my fingers. He still hasn't replied.

On WhatsApp I see he's read the message but hasn't responded.

My alarm goes off, and I jump. It's now almost 8 p.m. I turn off the oven but leave the dish in to stay warm.

This is so unlike him. A lump of dread lands in my belly. Is he ghosting me? Why? No, there must be an issue. Perhaps he's been in a car accident, or his mum has taken ill.

He clearly has his phone with him because he's looked at my message. But maybe it's not him looking at his phone. Visions of movie kidnapping scenes infiltrate my mind – of Jamal tied to a chair in an abandoned warehouse.

I need to stop jumping to wild conclusions, so I call him. He doesn't answer. It goes through to voicemail, but I don't leave one this time. I call him another few times. He can just answer and tell me he's fine. That's all I want to know.

On the fifth time, he answers.

"Jess," he says sternly.

"Jamal, is everything all right? You were meant to be here at seven. I'm really worried."

He doesn't reply, but I can hear his breathing.

"Jamal?" I nudge.

He tsks sharply, and I'm not sure if it's at me or at something else. "It's over. That voicemail... it went on for seven minutes. It was crazy. You sounded mental. You are not quite all there in the head. Blake, you have told me about. But this... this Tony? Is he another ex-husband? How many do you have?"

"No, Toni is a woman—"

But for the first time ever, he's not listening to what I say, and he interrupts me. "All this chat of people after you? Of people trying to kill you? Am I going to end up someone who's after you too? No, it's not right. You need to get yourself sorted."

I can't quite comprehend what I'm hearing. My sweet man is telling me I'm 'mental', telling me it's over? "Someone slashed my car seats at Brean Down with a knife! I'm not making that up! It freaked me out; it would've freaked anyone out," I say hysterically, desperate for him to believe me.

"You have way too many issues. I can't deal with the theatrics. It was probably kids or something like that."

"That's what the police said – but it was a warning, I know it!"

He tuts. "Goodbye. Don't contact me again." He hangs up.

Ice shoots through my heart, and I clutch my chest, dropping the phone on the floor. He can't mean that. We were getting on so well. He was such a gentleman, so kind and caring. I thought he could be the one. I had such a good feeling about him, no warning signs, no hunch he wasn't fully into me in return.

I need to explain. He doesn't know about my history, my

previous breakdown. My mental health is more robust now after that. It just had a jitter today, that's all.

I call him back, but he's turned his phone off, and there isn't even the option to leave a voicemail, just to call back later. I tap out a message, but he's already blocked me on WhatsApp, and it doesn't send.

I crumple to the floor in the kitchen and sob. The front door rattling startles me, and I freeze mid-wail.

15

The key turns in the top lock and then the deadlock, and the door handle goes.

It's Ashley. It has to be Ashley. She's the only one with keys apart from me.

The chain catches as the door opens.

"Oh!" Ashley exclaims. "Jess, are you in there? You've put the chain on, hon!"

I stumble up from my knees and to the front door.

"Coming," I mumble.

I undo the chain and open the door to Ashley, moving back into the hallway.

"Thanks." She bustles in, closes the door, locks it and puts the chain across. "Wow, something smells delicious."

Then she sees my face. Her eyes widen with questions.

I wipe away the tears. "Jamal just dumped me. I cooked us moussaka."

"What? But I thought you two were solid? I'm so sorry, hon." She grabs me into a big embrace, and I rest there in her arms for a while.

I pull away and stare at my feet. I don't have the energy to even hold my head up. "I honestly thought we were going somewhere. I really liked him."

"What happened?"

"I'm unlovable, that's what happened. I'm not worthy of love. I'm a freak."

Ashley gives my shoulders a gentle shake. "What? Absolutely not. Don't think like that."

The sobs spill forth once again, and Ashley leads me through to the dining area and sits me down on a dining chair. I put my arms on the table and then rest my head in them.

I mumble, "Something awful happened earlier today at Brean Down, and I told him, and he thinks I'm crazy."

"What awful thing?"

I look up from the nest I've made for my head. "I called you, but you didn't answer."

"Oh, gosh, sorry. I've not looked at my phone all day. I've been with Kevin." She puts her bag on the table, pulls off her coat and then finds her phone in the bottom of her bag. She looks at the display and must see all my missed calls. "Shit, sorry. What happened at Brean Down?" She looks around. "Was it Doug? Where's Doug?"

"Doug is fine." I sit up and tell her about the slashed car seats, the knife in my car, the couple helping and the police's indifference.

"You called the police, and they didn't do anything?" She's incensed and shakes her head. "I can't believe that. And then Jamal thinks you're crazy because someone messed up your car?"

The mention of Jamal's name sends me off again. My emotions are rolling through me like great rumbling tanks: fear from earlier, grief at the loss of an amazing relationship, anger at being targeted by whoever it is. They churn together, and I can't get a fix on anything. I feel dizzy.

Ashley comes over and puts her arm around my shoulder, crouching next to me. "You're a wonderful, amazing person. You will find a decent guy. You will get through this."

"I am not a wonderful person. There's something not right with me."

"Oh, Jess. That's not true and you know it. Listen, have you eaten dinner? Shall I dish up that moussaka? It's a shame to let it go to waste, and Jamal didn't deserve it anyway."

I know what she's trying to do. She's trying to cheer me up and take my mind off things, but each time she says his name, it's like my heart is being wrenched out and stomped on.

"You carry on. I'm not hungry."

"Sure?"

"Yeah."

She heads into the kitchen and takes the dish out the oven and sorts herself a plate of food. "I'm guessing all the drama at Brean Down is why you parked in the disabled spot over the road? Do you want me to move the car? Otherwise, you'll get a parking ticket when they come round and check tomorrow morning."

A parking ticket is the least of my worries. But she's right, the car needs to be moved. It was inconsiderate of me. But I can't face going outside this house right now to do it. "Yes, please. If you don't mind. The keys are in my bag. I'll get them for you in a bit."

She brings the plate back to the table and digs in. "I'll do it after I finish this. Jeez, I'm starving. Haven't eaten anything since breakfast. Kevin and I just talked for hours, and suddenly it was way past lunchtime."

Watching Ashley eat and talk about her day brings a sense of normality to the evening, and I feel myself calming slightly. I need to stop thinking about my worries and think about my friend for a moment. I wipe away my tears. "How'd it go with Kevin?"

"We might give it another go, but I'm just not sure. I love him so much, and he's promised to change his ways, but I've asked him for some time to think about it. We kinda just talked around in circles. I need to just sleep on it, I think."

"That's a good idea. There's no rush, is there?"

"No. If it's meant to be, it's meant to be."

"I know it hadn't been long, but I really thought Jamal and I were meant to be."

She shakes her head in disbelief. "He *was* such a lovely guy. I really didn't expect him to be such a prick to you."

"He *is* a lovely guy. It's me. I'm the problem."

"Jess, I know you're hurting, and this is going to feel raw for a while, but that's not healthy thinking."

"I know it's not." I rub my eyes. "I'm going to go to bed. I'm shattered. If Doug needs to go out later, please can you make sure you lock the back door? And double lock the front door and put the chain across when you've moved the car?"

"Of course, no problem at all. I'll move the car straight after dinner."

"Thanks, mate." I give her a small smile and then head up to my bedroom, leaving the car keys on the side table in the hallway.

I change into my pyjamas and get into bed, lying dead still. I listen to all the sounds inside and outside the house, attempting to pinpoint where each one is coming from and coming up with a plausible, sensible explanation for every sound so my mind doesn't immediately think it's someone out to get me. It's obsessive behaviour, I know, but I find it calming.

I hear Ashley eating, the scrape of cutlery on her plate, and then hear her pottering in the kitchen – the fridge and dishwasher opening and closing, drawers and cupboards being used. Her footsteps pad through to the hallway, and I hear the keys being lifted off the side table. The front door opens and then closes. A few moments pass before she comes back in the house. The deadlock goes, and the chain is put across. Moments later, the telly comes on in the lounge. It's very faint, a background hum in my room, really, but I feel reassured that she's not far away. That life is carrying on as normal.

I'm too wired to sleep, but I don't want to think about today. I need to protect myself, so I listen hard to the sound of the telly for a long while. There's canned audience laughter, and I hear Ashley laugh out loud or snort a couple of times. It's probably a sitcom or reality TV show. Ashley loves those. She doesn't have it on loud, being considerate of me, but it's enough of a sound for me to focus on.

As I'm drifting off to sleep, the doorbell goes. My heart pounds in my chest. It's them again. The prankster who slashed my car seats. It has to be the same person.

I hear Ashley open the front door. Oh no, she should've just left it. What if they overpower her and force their way in the house and up the stairs to get me? I scan around the room for something to use as a weapon. I used to have my old hockey stick at my house in Oxford under the bed, but I don't have anything like that here. Stupid for not arming myself. Stupid.

There's murmuring at the door. A man's voice. I get out of bed and creep to the bedroom door. How could I escape if there's someone in the house?

The door closes, and footsteps pound up the stairs and straight to my bedroom door. Oh shit, they've overpowered Ashley and are coming for me. I grab my aunt's vase from the top of the wardrobe. That'll have to do. I stand poised to strike.

There's a soft tapping on the door. "Jess?"

It's my friend. Thank God. I lower the vase.

She continues, "Kevin's here. He wants to talk some more.

I've left him on the doorstep, but can he come in? Otherwise, I'll go back to the apartment."

The thought of being left alone in this big house on my own tonight fills me with horror. And if Ashley goes back to the apartment, will she ever return here? That's her home, after all. "Of course he can come in," I blurt. "No problem at all."

"Thanks, hon. Are you okay?"

"Yep, just reading," I lie.

"Cool, thanks again."

Ashley pads back downstairs, and the front door opens.

Immediately, Kevin says, "I've been such a fool. Forgive me, Ashley. I love you so much. I'll do anything for you..." His voice breaks and becomes weepy as he manages, "Anything."

Ashley shushes him. The front door closes and then the lounge door. I can't hear them over the telly noise.

There's a scratching and whimpering outside my door. I replace the vase and let Doug in. He jumps up on my bed. I get under the covers. His heavy weight leaning against my leg reassures me.

Hours later, my phone goes and wakes me up. I usually put it on silent, but I must've forgotten tonight. I read the message from Ashley:

Can Kevin stay over?

It's past midnight. I tap out a reply.

Sure. All going well?

Yep, really, really well :-)

Cool. I'm going to work from home tomorrow, so don't wait for me in the morning.

Ashley replies with a thumbs-up emoji.

I hear them creep up the stairs and into the back bedroom, but I don't hear anything else. I'm pleased that she's repairing things with Kevin. That she seems happy. But also feel desperately sad. Will she move back in with him? Will I not see her so much anymore? She's my only friend in Weston. I can't lose her now I've only just found her. And I can't lose her now that I've just been cruelly dumped and I'm single again. Hopefully, they'll need some more time to work things through.

Stop, Jess, stop. I berate myself for being so selfish, for wishing for Ashley's relationship to fail because I like having someone else in the house with me and want her to stay. On top of everything else, I'm a bad friend.

I cry myself to sleep, my negative self-talk dialled up to the max.

16

I come awake blearily with the noise of Ashley and Kevin getting ready in the bathroom next to the back bedroom. I stay in bed, listening to them pottering around and heading out the front door. I don't hear any conversation, and I'm thankful that they're keeping their voices down, knowing I'm still in bed.

After a while, I sit up. The movement nudges Doug awake, and he stretches elaborately and then paws at me. I made the right decision not going into The Hive. I'm not in the right frame of mind to be around lots of people today. And what if I bumped into Jamal there? The thought of it is overwhelming. I'm not even sure if I can face doing any work, but I have clients waiting on things and deadlines to meet. The pressure of clients' expectations makes me want to go back to sleep, to withdraw, to hide from all responsibilities.

But Doug paws at me again and then jumps from the bed and scratches at the door. He's eager for breakfast and a walk. And I need to let him out for a wee. That can't wait. Unless I want to be clearing up a little puddle on the carpet in a few minutes' time. Which I definitely don't.

"Come on, boy," I say and get out of bed. I wrap my dressing gown around me and pop on my slippers as I head downstairs.

I let Doug out the back and watch as he sniffs and lifts a leg, then trots in happily, giving me a look that says *breakfast now, if you please.* He waits by his bowl. I sort his breakfast and then make myself a coffee. My appetite is non-existent, and although I know I should be hungry because I skipped dinner last night, I'm really not.

Doug wolfs down his food as I sip my coffee slowly. When he's done, he goes and finds his tennis ball and drops it at my feet. A sure sign he wants a walk.

"In a bit, Doug. Just let me finish my drink and wait for your food to go down."

He whimpers. Then a whiff of dog fart permeates through the smell of my coffee.

"Ew, Doug," I say as I bat the smell away. "Okay, I get it. You need to go out. You could've done a number two in the garden."

He cocks his head at me and then picks up his ball and drops it again at my feet.

"I get the message." I head upstairs to get changed and brush my teeth. I pull on a beanie to cover my bed hair, having no energy to brush it or wash it right now.

I put his lead on and open the front door. The cool air rushes me, and I stand there for a moment. Terror grips me, and I can't take a step any further. Is the person who slashed my car seats out here, ready to slash me?

The mail carrier gives me a wave as she pushes her red trolley past my house. "None for you today," she says cheerily as she walks up the path to the house next door with a wedge of letters.

I force a smile and a friendly nod. It's not so bad out here. There are good people around. It's half nine, and the street is bustling with cars and people coming and going. Nothing is going to happen in broad daylight.

Doug tugs at the lead, pulling me toward the front gate. It's the encouragement I need.

I close the front door, and we head out. Doug turns towards the little park a few streets away, but I don't want to go there – too many places for someone to hide, too many big trees casting long shadows. So we walk a loop around the busier streets. Buses come and go, and I pass numerous pedestrians and cyclists all going about their day.

Every few steps, I scan all around me and check behind. I can't shake the feeling I'm being followed. But I don't see anyone. Doug does his business, and I pause to pick it up, allowing a group of laughing college kids to pass me.

I drop the poo bag in a bin, and we head home. I pass the mint-green Honda and am thankful Ashley moved it for me. It's on the other side of the road, and I pass it quickly, not wanting to catch a glimpse of the destroyed seats or the knife. Would Ashley have moved the knife? I've no idea, and I don't feel like checking. But I'm certain she wouldn't have touched anything. I need to take a photo for my diary, but I can't face it. Another time. My heart races as I pass the car, and I speed up my pace, dragging Doug past quickly.

As I let myself in the front door, I take a deep breath. It was fine, all fine. I take off my coat and decide to set up my laptop on the dining table to work.

Doug settles himself in his bed under the table and snores softly. I could just go back to bed. That's always been my coping mechanism when I'm stressed – to retreat to bed and sleep all day and night. Sleep until the awfulness has passed. But I have work I need to do. I'm self-employed and don't have a team to pick up my slack. I have to keep functioning and forget the heartbreak and stalker and continue living. I know work will take my mind off things.

I log in to my laptop and write out my to-do list for the week, something I do every Monday morning, then go through emails and reply to a few before getting my head into a proposal for some new LinkedIn advertising for a long-standing client.

It distracts me, and before long, I'm suitably in the flow, quickly typing up my ideas for a new ad campaign.

But a noise from upstairs stills my fingers. *Did I just hear something? Or was I imagining it?*

I look up to the ceiling, as if that will give me a clue. I shake my head. Stupid. I'm alone in the house. Doug is by my feet, fast asleep.

My fingers poise to type again when a loud creak sounds above my head. The old floorboards in the house protest as someone walks over them.

There's somebody upstairs. An intruder in the house. They must've got in when I was on the dog walk.

My gut rolls over, goosebumps erupt all up my arms, and my heart rate shoots through the roof. This isn't the first time this has happened, but then I was asleep. Footsteps creak across the landing and towards the stairs.

As the intruder descends, my mind transports me to that terrible night three years ago in Oxford.

I'D BEEN DREAMING about lounging on a sunny beach. It's crazy how I remember that so vividly. Fast asleep. I thought I was safe, secure, cocooned in my home of almost twenty years. But a creak on the floorboard in my bedroom woke me. It was the floorboard I'd been meaning to get fixed for years. It was a comforting sound... when it was me who was stepping on it.

Something in my sleeping brain heard it and knew it was wrong, all wrong, and sounded the alarm.

At first, I could sense there was another person in the room. Perhaps I could hear the light breathing, or the shape of the air was different, or the smell was slightly off. Perhaps I could feel the sinister energy like an electric current zapping my skin. My eyes pinged open, but they took a while to adjust to the darkness. I stayed completely still, attempting to continue to breathe as before, to pretend I was still asleep.

In the gloom from the streetlights creeping through the heavy curtains, I could see a figure standing at the end of my bed, watching me sleep. How long had they been there? How did they get in? What did they plan to do?

Whatever it was and whatever they had planned, I was not waiting to find out.

I shot up in bed and grabbed the hockey stick that I knew was propped up next to the bedframe. The figure raised an arm – was that a knife at the end of it? I couldn't see. The intruder came towards me...

I SHAKE off the memory before it paralyses me and focus on the present. Think, Jess, think. A weapon. I need a weapon. I edge the chair out as slowly and quietly as possible and creep into the kitchen. I grab a large kitchen knife out of the block on the counter.

I hold it in front of me. My hand shakes, and the blade wobbles.

Had I left the back door unlocked when I let Doug out for a wee this morning? I rack my brains but can't remember. Did I allow another intruder into my house? Foolish woman. I grab the knife tighter as the intruder comes down the stairs and pads through to the open-plan kitchen-diner.

I brace myself, knife in hand, as a tall, broad-shouldered man steps into the room.

17

"Who the fuck are you?" I scream at the man and jab my knife at him.

He immediately holds up his hands in surrender and jumps back, startled.

"Kevin! I'm Kevin," he squeals. "Ashley's boyfriend. Don't hurt me!"

I frown but don't lower the knife.

He rambles, "I stayed over last night. I slept in late because I'm not working today. Ashley said she'd let you know. She must've forgotten. I just came down for some coffee. I'm sorry. Please, please lower the knife."

I take him in. He's absolutely terrified of me. His body is in a stance that looks like he might at any moment make a run for it. His face is ashen, and his eyes are bulging. He's still holding up his hands, and I notice they're shaking.

He's clearly quite a bit older than Ashley and not what I was expecting at all. His hairline is receding back from his forehead and so thin on top the scalp is visible. His hair is longer on top than the sides, but it isn't gelled and sticks straight up in a frizzy, wispy halo. It's a dreary light-brown mousy shade with grey at the temples and around the ears. He has a beard, but it's not a trendy beard, more fluffy and patchy, and is a few different colours – gingery on the upper lip and along the top of his cheeks, grey on his chin and then a dark brown on the sides. It's a different colour and much thicker than the hair on his head. His eyebrows are almost non-existent, a shade much lighter than his hair, which makes his face seem almost upside-down.

He has a long, rectangular face with a normal, unremarkable nose and no errant nose hairs. But his big, fleshy ears and long-hanging lobes with prominent creases definitely age him. His grey-blue eyes are dull, small and deep-set with a few pronounced wrinkles lining his forehead.

He wears a neatly ironed pale-blue shirt tucked into brown trousers with a perfect crease ironed down the front. I realise he's groomed in a tidy kind of way and well presented. His clothes, although they look old and slightly worn, are clean and fit well. He's tall, about six feet, with a trim but solid figure. It's clear he takes care of himself and his appearance. He reminds me of a slightly stuffy science teacher I used to have at school.

His feet are bare. And that's when I know he's not here to harm me. What intruder would have bare feet?

I lower the knife.

"Oh, thank goodness," he says, relieved. "I really am terribly sorry for startling you."

He lowers his hands carefully to his sides and very slowly gives me a smile as if trying to calm a skittish horse. He has thin lips, and his top lip almost disappears when he smiles. It reveals yellowing, wonky teeth, which are a surprise because he's so put together otherwise. But his smile is warm and trustworthy, forming pleasant crinkles around his eyes. It lights up his entire face.

His presence is actually strangely comforting. He comes across as a sensible, harmless, slightly nerdy chap.

"I'm sorry, Kevin. I thought you'd left with Ashley this morning." I put the knife in the block. "She didn't message me to say you were here."

He rolls his eyes dotingly. "She must've forgotten. And caused such a to-do. I reminded her last night, but she has a brain like a sieve sometimes. I really am terribly sorry."

His voice is quiet, and I can barely hear him. His entire demeanour is meek and mild, and I have an urge to want to protect him. Maybe that's what Ashley sees in him? Some women like men to look after, don't they? Otherwise, from first impressions, they don't seem well-suited in the slightest.

"Would you like a coffee?" I ask.

He looks at his watch. It's small with a leather strap. "Ahh, it's a bit late for me now."

"Late?" I look up at the clock on the kitchen wall. "It's just gone eleven."

"Precisely. I couldn't possibly drink caffeine *after* 11 a.m. Keeps me up all night if I do. And sleep is very important for good health." He smiles at me again. "But I'll take a glass of water if it's not too much trouble."

"Of course."

He hovers while I get a glass of water for him and switch the kettle on.

I hand him the glass and gesture to a dining chair. "Please, take a seat."

"Thank you, very kind."

He pulls out a chair and sits. He takes a coaster from the stack in the centre of the table and places his glass on it. Then he fiddles with the stack so all the corners are neatly aligned. His nails are clean and filed with neat white crescents. They put my own tatty nails to shame.

"So, Kevin, what do you do?" I ask as I make my coffee and sit down opposite him, moving my laptop out of the way.

He folds his hands in his lap and sits upright with impeccably straight posture. "I work in IT. I'm remote for a government organisation in Salisbury. I can't really say more than that about it."

"Oh, right."

He takes a sip of his water. "Ah, that's better. Was feeling a tad dehydrated. Eight glasses a day is the optimum. This is number one for me."

"Er, yes, it's very important to keep hydrated."

"It certainly is. I'm always reminding Ashley to meet her recommended water intake."

There's a pause as I ponder what to reply. The conversation is definitely not flowing. Which is odd, as I get on so well with this man's girlfriend. But I did just brandish a knife at him, so I guess we didn't get off on the best of terms. "So, you've got a day off?"

"Yes."

When he doesn't elaborate, I shift in my seat.

He takes it as a cue to carry on talking. I have to lean forward slightly to hear what he's saying.

"I knew it would be a late night with Ashley. She doesn't have a particularly stringent night-time routine, although I remind her how important that is. Anyway, I simply can't function unless I have eight hours of sleep per night. We didn't retire until eight minutes past two, so I took today off, knowing full well I'd need to sleep until ten. My employer is very understanding. There aren't many who can do what I can do, so they are flexible with me."

"Well, that's good." I stifle a yawn. The adrenaline rush of thinking Kevin was an intruder is fading, and now the awkward conversation is taking its toll on my energy levels.

Kevin picks up one of his hairy feet and rests it on the

opposite thigh. He then begins to massage his toes and the arch methodically while continuing to look at me. I'm not entirely sure why, but it turns my stomach, and I fight back a gag. I have a thing about other people's feet. I find them repulsive.

He continues to rub as he says, "I really am terribly sorry about earlier. Certainly not an ideal first meeting."

"Forget about it. I'm a little jumpy at the moment."

The doorbell blares, and I jump.

"My, you are jumpy," Kevin observes.

I'm frozen to the spot. Moving to go to the front door feels all too much right now. I don't know who it might be on the other side.

"Can you go?" I ask.

Kevin blinks twice at me. "A strange request, but one which I shall honour."

He stands, performs a slight bow towards me, and then strides towards the front door.

I hear it open and close, and then Kevin reappears holding a white box about the size of a shoebox.

He hands it to me. "Someone left this for you. They'd gone by the time I opened the door. It has your name on it."

'Jess' is scrawled in marker pen across the top of the box. When I don't take the box from him, he puts it on the dining table in front of me.

He sits back down in his seat. "Well, are you going to open it? I love to receive packages. Don't you?"

No, I don't. And especially not when I'm not expecting a package and there's no branding on it to indicate it's something innocent from a shop I know. I don't even want to touch it. I debate whether to ask Kevin to open it. But we've only just met, and that would be even weirder than my asking him to go to the door of my own house. I'm not sure what Ashley has told him about the things that have been happening to me, but I'm guessing not much... because why would she?

I look at the box. It could be something from Jamal, an apology. Or perhaps my aunt and uncle have sent me a treat from the local bakery.

Good or bad, I need to see. I need to just get it over with.

I compose myself and open the box. The smell hits me first. Fish.

"Urgh." Kevin grimaces. "Fresh fish should never smell. Did you know that?"

I shift the greaseproof paper to the side, and the stench intensifies. It's a rotting fish, gutted and bloody with its head removed. The head is loose in the box, and there's a folded piece of paper tucked in its mouth. I pull it out, retch, and shove the box away from me.

I open the note. It reads:

Slippery, festering little fucker, just like you.

Anxiety clutches at my chest and squeezes.

I bolt out of my seat and try to run, to where I'm not sure, just away. Away from the reeking monstrosity that is in that box. I get as far as the kitchen area before I collapse. I can't breathe. Waves of panic hit me, and my skin feels clammy with sweat. Bile surges up my throat, and I think I'm going to vomit. My heart is beating a strange irregular pattern that alarms me.

Kevin is next to me, saying something I can't hear. The entire room is spinning, and his voice is carried around in the whirlwind.

He crouches next to me, and I see his mouth moving. I focus in on his thin lips and yellow teeth.

"Breathe," he's repeating. "Breathe."

I try to do what he's telling me and concentrate on

inhaling and exhaling. Then he touches my shoulder with his hand. His hand that has just massaged his feet. Yuck.

I shake him off and crawl to the corner of the room and prop myself against the fridge, my legs straight out in front of me. I feel like I'm drunk and have just gone through the washing machine's spin cycle. I try to focus on relaxing images like my counsellor back in Oxford told me to do. A pristine white beach, a snow-capped mountain, a trickling stream in a sunny forest.

Kevin stands and pulls his phone out of his trouser pocket. "I'm going to call Ashley," he tells me. I hear him speaking into the phone.

He kneels in front of me. "Ashley is on her way back from the co-working place. She won't be long. Can I get you anything?"

"Water," I stutter.

He sorts me a glass of water. I take a few sips.

It takes me a while, but I get a handle on my breathing as Kevin watches me with concern. Ten minutes later, Ashley flies through the front door, out of breath from running, and into the kitchen.

She puts her arms around me but talks to Kevin through pants. "What... the hell... happened?"

"There was a box left on the doorstep, and I'm deducing from Jess' reaction that it didn't have particularly nice contents."

"What was in it?"

"I haven't looked. That's an invasion of privacy."

"Oh, for heaven's sake," Ashley says.

"It smells decidedly like rotting fish. And I believe there was a note. It's still on the table should you care to look."

Ashley turns to me. "I'm just going to take a look, and then we'll put it outside, okay? Get it out of the house."

I nod weakly at her.

She walks the few steps to the dining table and covers her mouth with her hand. She looks in the box and audibly gags. She peers at the note and frowns. She steps away and comes back over to me.

"Kevin, will you put the lid down and put that whole thing outside by the bins? Don't leave it on the ground. We don't want Doug to eat it. And then open some windows and get the room spray and give this place a spritz. It stinks."

"Certainly, my dear." Kevin does Ashley's bidding without a second thought.

After he passes us on the way to the back garden, holding the box out in front of him with a grimace, Ashley says, "Do you feel up to moving into the lounge? You'll be more comfortable there."

I allow her to slide me up and onto my feet, and we head into the lounge. She settles me on the sofa with a blanket wrapped around me.

"What was that?" Ashley asks me gently.

"A panic attack – similar to what happened at the museum. But worse. Full on."

"Right." She heads into the hallway to get her bag and comes back with her phone and Kevin.

Kevin takes a seat on the sofa, crosses his legs, and interlocks his fingers.

Ashley sits next to me and looks on her phone for a while. "She had a panic attack," she tells Kevin.

He gets out his phone and starts to scroll. After a while, he says, "No wonder she's feeling a bit discombobulated."

They begin to discuss panic attacks, what to do after, how I might be feeling, and I let the conversation play out without me. It's nice that they care about me. Care about getting me right again. But I feel utterly drained, and their voices are like drums booming in my ears.

Someone out there believes I'm a slippery, festering little

fucker. Wants to scare me. Tim? But he came across as such a reformed character when he visited. Blake? He's still bitter about the divorce and failed pregnancies and the police warning and still hates me for how it all ended. Or maybe Toni still wants to get back at me, the home invasion not enough in her vengeful head to punish me for the affair with Marcus.

I tremble. It turns into a full-body shake, almost like a convulsion.

Ashley notices. "Shit, Jess, what's happening?"

"I think I need to go to bed," I mumble and try to get up. Ashley and Kevin both spring to my aid and help me up.

"Do you need to eat something?" Kevin asks. "It says that replenishing the body after a panic attack is a good idea."

"I'm not hungry. But maybe later." The smell of fish still lingers in my nostrils and congeals in my gut.

Ashley leads me up the stairs to my bedroom, leaving Kevin wringing his hands at the bottom of the stairs.

"There you go," Ashley says soothingly as I get into bed in all my clothes.

I feel vulnerable going to sleep while someone is out there. I need to be vigilant, awake, alert, but my head is a fuzz, full of cotton wool.

I cling to her sleeve before she can turn away. "Ashley, could you and Kevin stay in the house today? Overnight? I really don't want to be on my own."

"Of course, hon, we're right here. We're not going anywhere. You rest up and don't worry about a thing. Shout down if you want anything, a cup of tea or piece of toast, anything, okay? And I'll bring it right up."

When I'm alone, I know this isn't good, as if a loose thread on a seam has been tugged and the stitches of my mind have unravelled scarily fast to leave a gaping hole.

18

The next morning, a soft tapping at my bedroom door stirs me from a deep slumber.

"Jess, are you awake?" I hear Ashley say from the other side. "Can I come in?"

"Yeah," I reply groggily. I went to bed yesterday after the panic attack and haven't left it since.

The door is pushed opened gently, and Ashley sticks her head around, sees I'm up, and then comes in. I prop myself up in bed.

She puts a steaming mug on my bedside cabinet. "I've brought you a cup of tea."

"Thanks." I pick it up and blow on the hot liquid before taking a sip. It's just what I fancied.

"How are you doing this morning?"

How am I doing? I take a moment to ponder this. I feel anxious, angry, frustrated and powerless all at once, like I'm on a late train and know that I'm going to miss my connection but can't do anything about it. "Not great," I reply.

"Do you feel up to coming to The Hive today?"

I barely have enough energy to pick up the mug; the

thought of getting out of bed is too much for me to comprehend. It feels overwhelming. "No, I think I'll have a duvet day. I can't face moving from here."

Ashley smiles sympathetically. "I think you've taken a bit of a knocking, and you just need to rest."

I notice then that Ashley is dressed and has make-up on. My nerves turn into a jangling mass. "Will you and Kevin be leaving?" I ask her wide-eyed, my breath already coming in shorter, shallower bursts. I can't be left alone in this house. The idea terrifies me. Vulnerable in my bedroom, in my bed.

"Please don't leave me on my own," I beg.

She reaches out a hand and places it gently on the duvet on top of my foot. "Well, I was going to head to The Hive, and Kevin was going to go back to the flat... but we can stay right here with you. No problem. We can both work remotely. Kevin works in IT. He'll just need to pop back to the flat to get his laptop and a few things, but then he'll be right back, and I'll be just downstairs."

"Thank you. Thank you so much."

There's another tap on the door. "Can Kevin come in?" Ashley asks.

I nod. Ashley stands and beckons him in.

"I've brought you some breakfast," Kevin says, almost proudly, and gives the tray to Ashley, who puts it on my lap.

It's a perfectly presented full English with bacon, scrambled eggs, tomato, sausages, mushrooms, hash browns and buttered toast. And a little pot of baked beans on the side. There's bottles of ketchup and brown sauce and a glass of orange juice too.

"Wow," I say, and my stomach grumbles appreciatively. "This looks delicious."

Ashley smiles and kisses Kevin on the cheek. "That looks so good," she says to him.

Kevin beams at the praise and then turns to me. "We were

worried that you hadn't eaten properly. I don't think I saw you eat anything yesterday. And you need to eat to keep your strength up."

"Thank you so much," I say and take a bite of toast.

Ashley takes Kevin's hand. "The Tesco food shop was delivered yesterday, I'm not sure if you heard? So there's plenty of food in the house. We opened the door to the delivery person before they could ring the bell because Kevin saw them coming up the pavement."

"Oh, that's good. No, I didn't hear."

Ashley's tone is gentle as she says, "Listen, you don't need to worry about anything, okay? We'll look after you until you feel better."

I nod with relief, my mouth full of the best scrambled eggs I think I've ever eaten.

She leans in to Kevin. "Did you make me any?"

He looks at her with such love, the magnitude of it almost pushes me out of the room. "Of course, my dear, and I added chilli flakes to your scrambled eggs just how you like it." He kisses the tip of her nose, and she melts into him.

Kevin continues, "Come on then, let's leave Jess to her breakfast in bed."

He steers Ashley from the room, and she says to me as she's leaving, "Kevin's a great cook." She looks out the door at him, "Gets really into it, don't you, babe?" Then she turns back to me. "He'll make sure we eat well."

From outside the door, Kevin says, "Yes, I certainly will. I have already devised the menu for lunch and dinner today."

Ashley gives me a thumbs-up and a look that says *aren't we lucky* as she leaves the room and pulls my bedroom door closed. I hear them pad down the stairs, talking quietly.

I wolf down the breakfast. I'm starving, not having eaten lunch or dinner the day before. There are chives in the scrambled eggs, parsley with the mushrooms, and the tomatoes look drizzled with olive oil and have a hint of something I can't quite place. I'd be hard-pressed to think of a better breakfast I'd eaten out at a restaurant or hotel.

I finish the lot, put the tray on the floor and get back into bed. I'm not sure if it's the big meal or being mentally exhausted or both, but the movement makes me dizzy. I lie back down and close my eyes against the topsy-turvy feeling. I fall asleep almost immediately.

THE SHRILL SHRIEK of the doorbell wakes me. It burrows deep into my ears like a worm digging deeper, deeper.

"I'll go," I hear a man's voice shout downstairs. Kevin, I remember.

"Okay," a woman's voice replies. Ashley. My friends.

I force my feet onto the floor and stay half in the bed, half out for a count of two before heaving my top half up. I wobble on my feet and have to take a moment to steady myself. I shuffle to the bedroom door and open it.

"I see you!" I hear Kevin's voice drift upstairs from out the front. "You won't get away with this!"

I concentrate on putting one foot in front of the other and get to the top of the staircase. I hold the banister for support.

"Kevin?" Ashley says as I see her run to the front door as Kevin walks back in and closes the door behind him.

"I almost caught the prankster. I saw them running off around the corner and gave chase but to no avail." He sounds frustrated and slightly out of breath. I notice he's barefoot again.

"Oh, well done for trying, handsome. Hopefully, you might have scared them away. Who the hell would keep ringing the doorbell? It's ridiculous," Ashley replies.

"Well, they might think twice, now they know there's a man in the house who almost caught them." He sees me stood at the top of the stairs and indicates my presence to Ashley. "Ah, Jess, how are you doing? Are you ready for some lunch?" He looks at his watch. "It's ten to one. I do like to have lunch at 1 p.m. sharp, keeps me on track throughout the day, and I don't like to break with my routine. It won't take me a moment to prepare."

Even though I ate a big breakfast and haven't done anything physical, I do feel inexplicably hungry. But along with the hunger I feel out of sorts, as if I'm floating in some kind of sensory-deprivation tank. I almost feel claustrophobic in my own body, with sounds, sights, smells all blurring together and being held at an arm's length from my brain. My tongue feels thick and heavy in my mouth, and my voice is stuck somewhere behind it. I manage a nod.

Ashley hurries up the stairs and helps me down as Kevin heads to the kitchen, pottering about.

She settles me at the dining table and then jogs back upstairs to retrieve my breakfast tray and my dressing gown. She puts the tray on the kitchen counter and then puts the dressing gown around my shoulders.

"Don't want you getting cold," she says and squeezes my shoulders tenderly before taking a seat.

"Here we are," Kevin says as he brings in two plates. He puts one in front of me. "Mediterranean chickpea salad with feta. Very healthy after your breakfast."

It looks absolutely delicious, fresh and green with the cheese cut in perfect cubes. "Thank you."

He puts another plate in front of Ashley. "And here's yours, my dear, with some jalapeños. I know how you love your spice."

Ashley's eyes light up at her lunch. "The spicier, the better. Even salad."

Kevin picks up a third plate from the kitchen counter. "And here's mine, sans the feta." He sits and then looks at me.

"I'm a vegan," he explains. He picks up his knife and fork and announces, "*Bon appetit.*"

I take a mouthful. "It's really good."

Ashley finishes her first mouthful, then leans across the table and kisses Kevin. "Perfect amount of heat."

She sits back and continues to eat. I glance around the room and see two laptops on the side. Kevin must've gone back to get his this morning when I was asleep. There's a large suitcase and a duffel bag against the wall.

Kevin notices me looking and says, "I picked up a few bits and pieces when I collected my laptop. But I haven't taken them up to the bedroom or unpacked or anything. I wanted to check with you if you wanted me to stay a little longer? I am more than happy to head home this evening after making dinner if that is more agreeable to you."

Ashley gives Kevin a loving look and then turns to me. It feels good to have a man in the house. To have them both in the house. If Kevin leaves, then it won't be long before Ashley heads off too. Maybe she'll even go with him tonight. Although they are like chalk and cheese, they seem to fit together well. They won't want to be apart now they've just got back together.

Could I manage on my own? No. I know the answer is no. Aunt Alice came to stay with me when I was like this before. I couldn't cope with doing anything. And I feel like I'm going that way again. The targeting has knocked my confidence to the point that I don't want to leave the house, to leave my bedroom. Sitting here at the dining table in my own home is making me feel anxious.

They're both looking at me keenly, and I realise there's been a long pause, and I still haven't replied. It's as if all my functions are running out of energy: sluggish and grinding to a halt.

"No, please stay." My voice comes out in a wibble.

Kevin dips his head at me in a cordial gesture. "Ah, good. I hoped you'd say that. I'd really like to catch this prankster who is bothering you. I almost had them today. And when I set myself a goal, I always meet it."

"He's not lying," Ashley adds with a fond glance at Kevin. And I believe them both.

I'd like him to try to catch this... prankster too. Or at least scare them off. And then perhaps this will all be over and I'll get back to normal.

The couple continue to chatter and attempt to include me in the conversation, but it's too much for me to cope with. I concentrate all my energy on eating my lunch. Ashley finishes her meal and then puts her feet up on Kevin's lap. He quickly finishes his salad and then massages her feet through her socks. She relaxes, slouching down into her seat, and gazes lovingly at him. It's clear she likes to be doted on, and he likes to do the doting.

They seem blissfully happy, and I feel like a third wheel. Guilt settles over me. They should be together in their own home, not looking after me.

"Thank you so much for being here with me," I croak.

"Of course," Ashley says. "What are friends for?"

"You'll be fit as a fiddle in no time," Kevin adds.

I put down my knife and fork. My plate is empty, and I'm disappointed that there's not more food to eat.

"Do you want to go and sit in the lounge? Put some telly on?" Ashley asks.

I nod. The dining chair suddenly feels too hard to sit on. I stand and almost topple over. "I'm feeling a bit out of it," I say.

Ashley guides me into the lounge, and I settle on the sofa. She turns the telly on and then gives me the remote. "We'll just be working on the dining table. Call if you need anything."

"Here you are." Kevin comes in and puts a glass of orange squash on the coffee table in front of me. "To stay hydrated."

"You and your hydration," Ashley teases as they head out of the room and pull the door ajar.

There's some daytime show on about house renovations, and it washes over me as I roll in and out of consciousness, picking up words like 'foundation' and 'architect' before everything sounds like gobbledygook.

Then a noise splits me in half like a chunk of wood on a chopping block, and I claw at my ears to try to make it go away. It's a baby crying. Wailing, shrieking in that pitch that only babies can manage.

I stare at the telly but can't make out the picture. The crying intensifies, so loud that I think my head will explode with it.

"Stop!" I yell, trying to cover my ears with the scatter cushions. I writhe and bang my head on the back of the sofa. "Stop, stop, stop!"

But the baby keeps wailing.

Kevin is before me. "Jess?"

I stare at him, his face the only clear thing in the room, which fades in and out, my aunt's quirky décor swimming together. "Can you hear it? Make it stop, make it stop!"

"Hear what, Jess?"

"The baby! The baby is screaming."

"I don't hear any baby," Kevin says, alarmed.

"Where's Ashley?" I demand.

"She's just taken Doug out for a short walk around the block. She'll be back any second."

"Ashley!" I yell. I know, deep down, that Kevin isn't lying to me, but all I can think about is how I need her right now. Right here.

"Let me phone her," Kevin says. He stands and pulls his

phone out of his trouser pocket. As he's calling Ashley, I notice his bare feet.

I stare at them. They enlarge and shrink. Pulse with the baby's wailing. The hairs on his big toe move like a can of worms. I screw my palms into my eye sockets to block out the image.

A few moments later, Ashley stands in front of me. She still has her coat on and holds Doug in her arms. The fine baby hairs around her hairline and in her side parting stick straight up, dislodged by the wind outside, I assume. "Jess, what's happening?"

I stare at her. "Can you hear the baby crying?"

Ashley looks around the room and then at Kevin, who shrugs. "No, Jess, I can't hear any baby. Are you sure that's what you can hear? And not something on the telly?"

I blink at her. The screeching lessens until it's gone, and the inane, harmless background prattle from the renovation show fills the room once again.

"What day is it?" I ask. I can't remember, and I need to know.

"Tuesday," Ashley replies.

This knowledge soothes me, and I slump against the side of the sofa, utterly spent. My eyelids droop.

"Let's get you back to bed," Ashley says in a motherly way that I find comforting.

19

I thrash and writhe in my bed. Nightmares about screaming dead babies pulsate behind my eyes. The screeching baby pounds between my ears so loudly that I feel it throughout my body like a vibration.

I had seven miscarriages. Is it my children trying to tell me something? Trying to communicate? But they're not happy. A baby doesn't cry like that unless there's something very wrong.

Shush, I say in my dream, shush.

There's a cot in an empty room, and I walk towards it. That's where the wailing is coming from, I'm certain. But when I get there, the cot doesn't contain any babies. It contains the rotting fish, its head separated from its body. The fish eyes swivel to look at me.

I wake with a start, panting. My hands grip the duvet cover so tightly it takes me a while to loosen them. I'm in my pink bedroom. It was just a dream.

Except it wasn't just a dream.

The baby wailing still thrums through my body. It's so

loud. I switch on my bedside lamp and squint as the light illuminates the room.

All the furniture seems to vibrate with the noise too. My wardrobe recoils from the racket like a frightened child. My bed trembles. Even the light flickers.

I need to find the baby. It wasn't in my dream. There's a baby in this house.

I roll out of bed, and the floor caves in. I grab at the radiator on the wall to stop me from falling through the black hole that has opened up. My bed teeters and is sucked into the void. I edge around the gaping chasm in the floor, finding my way onto the landing.

Listen. The noise is not coming from downstairs. I turn towards the staircase that leads up to my aunt and uncle's room in the attic.

There. It's coming from up there.

I lurch forward, bouncing off the walls, and reach out to the banister. I've never been up there. I've not needed to. That's their bedroom and bathroom. They told me they had locked it.

But the baby's crying is definitely coming from up there. I step closer to the bottom of the staircase and look up. It's dark. I need light. I press the light switch on the wall, and suddenly the stairs are too bright to look at. The floral pattern on the carpet moves, and flowers and stalks twist around one another.

The baby is up there. That is definitely where the noise is coming from. I have to go up the stairs. But they look menacing, like an angry garden with vines that will grab you and wrap around your limbs to suck you down.

I take a deep breath and look up. Something catches my eye on the ceiling above the staircase.

Looking closer, I see. It's a baby. It's crawling along the ceiling. Upside down. Wailing.

I ignore the threat of the vines to run up the stairs and try to reach it. To help, to get it down. But it's too far away. I try grabbing at it, standing on tiptoes. Again and again, I reach out. But it's no use.

The crying booms in my head. The poor baby, stuck up there. It can't get down. And I can't help it.

A guttural scream gushes up from the depths of my being and erupts. It scares me. I didn't even know I could make such a noise. My legs give way, and I slide down the stairs to land at a heap at the bottom. I'm still screaming. Now it's started, I can't stop it. I grab at my hair, at my pyjamas.

Lights snap on in the main hallway, and Ashley and Kevin come running out of their bedroom at the end of the corridor. The wailing stops. The light must've scared the baby.

"Jess!" Ashley shouts. She reaches me and crouches next to me.

Kevin stands over us.

My screaming stops so I can shout, "Up there! On the ceiling! The baby. Can you see it? Help it! Get it down."

They both look up for a long time.

Quietly, so as not to startle me, Ashley says, "There's nothing there, honey."

She holds my hands away from me. They clutch at the air as if they have a mind of their own.

"Didn't you hear it?" I ask in a raspy voice, hoarse from the screaming.

Ashley shakes her head. "No. We didn't hear anything apart from you."

I begin to weep. Tears glug out of me like a tipped-over carton of juice.

Ashley gives me a hug, and we stay there for a long time before she says, "Shall we get you back to bed?"

"No," I blurt. I can't face the nightmares again. "I want to stay awake."

"Sure," she says.

"It's 5 a.m." Kevin says in his practical manner. "I could make us an early breakfast. If you feel up to eating?"

My head drops forward, and all I can do is cry. I hear them whispering to each other over my head. I hear the word 'hallucination'.

Hands grip my arms and heave me up. But I feel detached from my body, as if I'm being left behind while my body is taken away.

The next thing I know, I'm on the sofa in the lounge, as if my brain has caught up to where my body is located.

"I think I might be having a mental health breakdown," I say.

Ashley and Kevin exchange glances. They look worried.

"Let me get you a cup of tea," Kevin says and heads out of the room.

"It happened before, when Blake was abusive. But not this bad. I thought I'd got over it with the therapy and my two years away..." I trail off.

"Shush," Ashley soothes. "You've had a really stressful time of it recently. Moving here, all the shit that's happened, splitting with Jamal. You're mentally exhausted. No wonder your mind is playing tricks on you."

Kevin returns and hands me the tea. I take a sip. It's weak and sweet.

"It's decaf, and I added some extra sugar," Kevin explains. "I think you need it. I think you've had a bit of a shock, and it will help stabilise your blood sugar level after all that adrenaline coursing through your body. But the caffeine is counterproductive, hence the decaf."

"It'll do you good," Ashley says reassuringly.

I drink the tea as they watch me. Kevin rubs Ashley's shoulders and kisses the back of her head. The drink tastes a bit weird, but I never have sugar in my tea or decaf. Ashley tucks a seahorse blanket around me.

Her head bulges and shrinks in front of me, and I close my eyes. Behind them, snow falls. I'm somewhere dark, but the snow shines as if lit by car headlights on a long, dark road.

I rest my head on the sofa's armrest and tuck up my feet. The movement makes me feel nauseous, and I swallow repeatedly.

"Are you going to be sick?" Kevin asks.

But I don't reply. I'm going somewhere else. Far away from the lounge. Floating like a snowflake, drifting in the wind.

20

A shley shakes me. "Tim is here."

"Tim?" I groan. It takes me a moment to piece together who that is. "My brother?"

"He says you called him," she says.

"Let me through," Tim's voice demands in the hallway.

"Just wait there one moment, please," Kevin replies.

"This is nonsense. She called me to come over. She didn't sound well. I demand to see her right now. Who the hell are you, anyway?"

I called him? I look down at my hands. My mobile is in one of them. I'm dressed, no longer in my pyjamas. I don't remember getting dressed. I don't remember calling him.

"How did I get dressed?" I ask Ashley in a whisper.

She screws up her forehead as if I've asked her a trick question. "Er... you had a shower and got changed earlier."

I touch my hair. It's damp. I must've washed it, but I have no recollection.

"Jess," Tim shouts from the front door. "Jess!"

"I really think you ought to wait—" Kevin is cut off, and suddenly Tim appears in the lounge.

Once again, he's impeccably dressed in low-key but obviously expensive clothes with the collar of his smart navy-blue peacoat turned up against the cold. Kevin arrives hot on his heels.

"Look," Tim says, holding up his phone. "I received a call from Jess forty minutes ago. And here I am."

He hands the phone to Kevin, who scrutinises it. He looks up at Ashley and nods. As Kevin gives it back, it rings.

Tim looks at the display and then rejects the call. "Damn work. Not important right now," he says almost to himself. He switches his phone to silent on the side and pockets it.

Drowsily, I tap in the pin code to unlock my phone. It takes me a while, my fingers not doing what I want them to do, but I eventually find my phone records. I did call him. And now he's here.

"It's okay," I say to Ashley. It comes out in a slur.

I attempt to move, and she helps to prop me up on the sofa. My entire body feels so heavy, I can barely keep my head up. It feels like a bowling ball crushing my neck into my shoulders.

"I'd like to talk to my sister," Tim says and then pointedly looks at Kevin and Ashley. "Alone."

Ashley glowers at him for a long while until Tim shifts his feet. She turns back to me. "Listen, Jess, we're just in the next room. We'll get back to work and leave you to it. But if at any time you need us, just holler." She leans in to kiss me on the cheek and whispers in my ear, "I don't trust him. Be careful. He could be the one targeting you."

She pulls away and gives me a knowing look and then leaves with Kevin. Tim watches them go and sits on the sofa opposite.

I struggle to keep my eyelids open and my gaze focused on him.

"Forgive me for saying this, sis, but you're in a right state."

It takes me a while to reply, to unpick the jumbled thoughts in my head. "What do you care? Hmm? You're the one who's done this to me. It was you, wasn't it? To mess with my head, it's all been you. The rotting fish, the slashed seats, the doorbell... all of it." The words come out at a snail's pace, an effort to form each one.

Tim listens patiently, waits to see if I have any more to say. When I don't open my mouth again, he says, "Jess, I don't know what you're talking about."

"Someone has been targeting me since I came to Weston."

"Well, that someone sure as hell isn't me. I've been waiting for you to get in touch with me and going about my business. I was thrilled when you called me, but now I'm really worried about you. I want to catch this someone and get them to stop. Look at what they're doing to you."

I try to raise my hand to point at him, but I don't have the energy. Instead, I lift my index finger. "You! You did this to me... before."

He hangs his head and then rubs his face. "I'm utterly ashamed of my behaviour back then. I was a drug addict, desperate, stupid. I fully admit to stalking you and making your life hell. And I will always regret that. But I'm not that person anymore. I've moved on. You have to believe me. It's been more than ten years."

"What happened to us?" I say, almost as much to myself as to him. "We were so happy as kids."

"We weren't happy as kids, Jess. Maybe when we were really little, but we had a shitty childhood. Always moving around with Dad's job and starting new schools every few years."

"They did their best for us..." An image of my parents appears in my mind – of them hugging and laughing together in the garden when they thought no one was looking. "They loved each other, and they loved us."

"In their own way," Tim says.

Grief hits me like humid desert heat, and I can't break free from the heavy, smothering emotion. I weep.

"Oh, Jess," Tim says. "I could've been a better brother to you, I know. But after Mum's illness..."

I look down my deep well of grief and see Mum in hospital, her bald head due to the chemotherapy. It sets me off even more. I blub.

Tim looks forlorn. His eyes glisten, and the corners of his mouth turn down. He takes a short breath to steady himself. "Listen, I've never been back to their graves in Stafford. It's something I've been meaning to do. Do you want to go now? I can drive us. My car's right outside."

"How long would that take?"

Tim shrugs. "Couple of hours?"

I open my mouth to say no, but something tugs at me. I do want to see their graves, I do want to think about them, and I do want to do it with my brother. It'll be cathartic. I feel like I need to get all this grief out of my body; otherwise I might burst with it. It'll be like popping a blister – painful but necessary.

"Let's go," I say.

He nods, stands and heads out to the hallway, calling for Ashley and Kevin.

I drag myself up off the sofa and follow him.

"Are you sure you're up to this, Jess?" Ashley asks. She pulls a tissue out of the box on the hallway console table and hands it to me.

I blow my nose, wipe my tears and smile weakly at her. "I haven't been to their graves for years. I want to pay my respects."

"Well, if you're sure." She hands me my coat and handbag. I slip my phone in the front pocket and hitch on my coat.

Kevin comes bustling out of the kitchen. "I made you

some lunch – beetroot and halloumi salad with pomegranate and dill. I've packed it in a tub. You need to keep your strength up." He hands the tub of salad and a knife and fork to Tim. "She's not eaten breakfast this morning, didn't fancy it."

"She can eat it in the car," Tim says and nods his thanks at Kevin.

"Oh, wait." Kevin hurries back to the kitchen.

As we hear the kettle boiling and some clanging, Ashley studies Tim. It's clear she hasn't made her mind up about him yet.

"I'll be fine," I say to reassure her.

She nods but doesn't take her eyes off Tim.

He fidgets under her intense scrutiny. "Let me take your mobile number, just in case."

"Good idea," Ashley replies. She waits for him to take out his phone and then tells him her number, watching carefully as he types it in.

Kevin returns with a flask. "And here's some more sweet tea. To keep your spirits up." He hands it to me with a warm smile. "Take care of yourself. We'll see you soon." Then he glances at Tim and steps out of the way.

Tim guides me through the front door and to his fancy car parked up the road. It's a two-seater BMW and awkward to get into – especially as my hand-eye coordination appears to be completely shot. He opens the door for me and gathers his Apple laptop, a tablet, a notebook and some papers off the passenger seat. He slips them all into a stylish leather satchel and puts it on the back seat. He makes sure I'm comfortable before closing the passenger door and getting in himself.

"Right, Stafford." He presses a few buttons on the car's in-built screen, and the GPS navigation comes up. "Can't remember the name of the church, but I'm sure I'll remember the way once we get into the town. We lived there for... how long was it?"

"Three years. One of the longest places."

"That's right."

He sets off, and I fumble to open the tub of salad. "Do you mind if I eat this now? I'm actually really hungry."

"You go right ahead. It sounded delicious."

"Yes, Kevin's a great cook. Have you eaten lunch?"

"Yes, I had something earlier before I came over. You enjoy."

The satnav gives directions to get out of Weston and towards the M5 motorway. I eat greedily, my appetite swinging from not hungry this morning to absolutely ravenous now.

Tim drives sensibly in his flashy car, sticking to the speed limit and letting cars out in front of him. We don't talk much, me too busy eating and Tim too busy listening to the directions.

When I'm done with the salad, I take a few swigs of the tea and guess Kevin's given me decaf again, not wanting to load me up on caffeine in the afternoon. It's a sweet gesture.

Tim's phone rings. "Sorry, work call, do you mind if I quickly answer?"

"No worries."

He answers the call through his car's console and says hello.

A male voice replies through the speaker in the car. They begin to talk about a three-bed semi-detached property on the outskirts of Leeds that's just come on the market.

The rumbling of the car on the motorway rocks me into a trance. I rest my head against the windowpane and zone out, watching the cars whir past.

·   ·   ·

"JESS, WAKE UP. WE'RE HERE," Tim says softly and taps gently on my arm.

My eyes ping open, and I see the church in front of us.

Tim continues, "Plenty of parking today, guess not so busy on a Wednesday. We made great time. It's just gone four. And I stopped and picked up some flowers." He leans through the front seats and picks up two bouquets from the back. He hands one to me.

"I slept the whole way?"

"Yep. And all through my cursing and beeping at an idiot driver who cut me up." He chuckles.

"Ha." This is how I remember Tim – always the joker, always ready to make people laugh. But the joviality fades as we both contemplate the graveyard through the car windows.

Tim puts a hand on the door handle. "Are you ready for this?"

I nod and get out of the car. We walk around the back of the church and through the graves to the two gravestones that sit closely together near the back.

My breath hitches as I see the names inscribed on them: *Lily Salmon* and *Colin Salmon*.

But it's Tim who breaks first. "Mum was only thirty-eight when she died. And Dad was forty-one. That's my age now. So young." Tears stream down his cheeks as he gently places his bouquet on Dad's grave.

He sniffles as I place my flowers on Mum's grave.

"They did love each other," he says through his tears. "For all their ups and downs. Mum knew what she was signing up for, but Dad definitely wore the trousers. She was meek and submissive."

Dad's job as a pub landlord for a national chain meant they moved around a lot. That was what he excelled at – taking poor performing pubs and turning them around. And then moving to the next place. Mum followed him without question. Then, when we came along, we went all over too. I look at her grave. "But she was strong in her own way."

"She was. She was the best mum. Always tried to get us settled quickly in each new place and at each new school. But it was hard."

"Then the bowel cancer took a hold…" I trail off and hug myself. Silent tears etch a line down my face. I'd only been fourteen, Tim sixteen.

He shakes his head. "Just when we needed her."

"Dad did his best to bring us up."

"No, he didn't. You're being kind. He wasn't really interested. He did a terrible job of coping with his grief and an absolutely shit job at helping us cope with ours." Tim chokes back a huge sob. "Do you know he used to beat me?"

"What?" I stare at him, but he doesn't look at me, his attention on the graves in front of us as he cries.

He puts his hands in his coat pockets and takes a moment before replying, "You turned inwards and studied hard, got left alone by the bullies for the most part. You kept your head down."

This is true, but I'd never thought Tim had taken that much notice. I used to stay out of the way, hide in my bedroom, read books, keep quiet. We had to get ourselves up in the morning and sort breakfast, lunch and dinner because Dad worked late shifts at the pub and was never up before 11 a.m. Then he'd go down to the pub and be there until gone midnight most days. We barely saw him. "I liked the structure and rules of school because it was a complete contrast to the chaos at home."

"Exactly. But I went the other way. Rebelled, got in with a bad crowd, didn't do well academically. Dad spiralled out of control, drinking heavily and never fully accepting that Mum was gone. Late at night, when you were safely tucked up in bed, I used to wind him up and goad him when he was drunk, and he'd beat me. It was a strange release for both of us. But our relationship completely broke down, and we hated each other towards the end."

I look away from Dad's grave and at the well-tended hedge behind. When I look closer, I see a thorny bramble poking through and realise that nothing is ever what it seems. "I didn't know he beat you. I'm so sorry. I thought he used to be angry with you because you were in trouble with the police for joyriding and shoplifting and vandalism and all of that."

"I don't know what came first. It was a vicious cycle. I see that now."

"And then two years later he..." But I can't bring myself to say it.

"He committed suicide," Tim says bluntly.

It stings, but it's the truth. "He was still heartbroken over Mum."

"He was a coward." Tim's sobs escalate, and I put my arm around him. It's the first time I've touched him since we were children.

Tim continues, "He left us. We weren't important enough for him to live for. It felt like a big fuck you."

Something cracks and falls away inside me, and I know it's true. I'd blocked that thought, plastered over it, determined not to hate Dad for leaving us.

Tim leans into me. "We needed him. I needed him. I needed a father. But I was eighteen, and I turned to drugs. I thought I was a man and could fend for myself. Those were terrible years."

"You could've come with me to live with Alice and Edwin."

He shakes his head. "Not after the inheritance bullshit. I hated you then. Hated everyone."

I take a short, sharp inhale at the mention of that drama

and tense all over, bracing myself for an altercation.

But Tim's voice softens. "Listen, I said it before – I'm over that now. I get it. Dad hated me. And you thought I'd spend it all on drugs and likely kill myself."

Dad had left all his and Mum's money to me in his will – about one hundred thousand pounds. I could've given half to Tim, but Dad hadn't wanted any to go to him, and I could understand why. But I was torn between honouring Dad's wishes and doing right by my brother. "I wanted to give you half, but you were off the rails. That's why I said to get clean and go to rehab and then I would. I'm sorry."

"God, don't be. I've made my money now. I've come good. It's taken me years, but I understand why he did what he did. Why you did what you did. I would've blown it all on heroin and probably killed myself. So I'm pleased I didn't get anything." He hugs me. "You kept me alive, Jess. Thank you."

On the way home, I ask Tim if he has a girlfriend.

"Nope, I'm working on that. I wasn't really in the right frame of mind before. There's been women come and go but nothing serious. But now I'm clean and doing well for myself, I'm going to get on the dating scene. I want a family of my own. A couple of kids. You?"

I debate whether to tell him about Jamal but decide not to pick at that wound. "Nope. Not in any rush after the divorce from Blake."

"What happened with him?"

That's another sore spot I don't want to reopen. "It didn't work out." I lift up my hair and flip it to the other side.

He glances at me with a smirk. "You know, I totally forgot about your weird, pointy elf ears."

"Ha. Well, I hadn't forgotten about your wonky nostrils. In fact, I think they've gotten wonkier over the years."

We continue to reminisce and laugh about fun times from our childhood. But I start to feel sleepy again. And hungry. So the conversation trails off, and we drive in amicable silence.

As we near my house, Tim says, "Ashley and Kevin, how well do you know them?"

"Why?"

"I get a funny vibe from them, that's all."

"I met Ashley at the co-working place I go to, and we hit it off. Kevin is her boyfriend, and I know he's a bit weird, but he's a nice guy. They've been nothing but amazing to me. I've been all over the place. Still feel all over the place."

"I know it's none of my business, but you're my sister, and I'm worried about you. So I'm just going to say it, do you think you should see someone? A doctor or therapist?"

He's right. My GP and counsellor in Oxford were both brilliant with my breakdown before.

"Yes. I should. I've not signed up with a GP surgery in Weston yet." The thought of organising that overwhelms me, and suddenly, I just want to get home to bed. I yawn.

He pulls up outside the house. "I'm back up to Leeds tomorrow to look at that property, but I'll be back on Friday. I'll pop by and check in on you if that's all right with you?"

"Sounds good."

"And message or call me if you need anything, okay? I'm here for you."

"Thanks. And thanks for today. I needed to do that."

"Yeah, me too."

I touch his elbow and turn to him. "I'm sorry I wasn't there for you more. Didn't stop Dad from—"

"All water under the bridge, sis. There's nothing you could've done."

We smile at each other as I get out of the car and head to the front door. I let myself in, turn and wave. He waves back and then drives off.

21

That night, even after feeling drowsy all day, I lie in bed wide awake. I feel alert and energised, but also agitated and panicky. I'm desperate to talk to someone, anyone. I momentarily debate waking up Ashley for a chat, before dismissing that idea as inconsiderate and rude. It's 1.48 a.m. They'll both be fast asleep.

Kevin made us chicken fajitas for dinner – normal for me, extra spicy for Ashley and vegan for him – with some of the best guacamole I think I've ever eaten, and I had all the time in the world to talk then but didn't. I felt lethargic. The four-hour round trip to Stafford, the crying, the revelation about my dad and brother's relationship getting violent and the grief stirred up after so long submerged all combined to scupper my conversational skills.

But now, like my appetite, I've swung the other way. My heart races, and I'm burning up. I glug back the water from the glass by the side of my table to moisten my dry mouth. But it doesn't make a difference. I toss and turn and debate whether to get out of bed and go for a wander around the house. But I decide that's a bad idea and will probably just freak me out unless I turn on every light.

Maybe I should go and find Doug and talk to him. He's not sleeping on my bed tonight. He likes to rotate sleeping locations.

At least it's silent in the house. No screaming babies tonight.

But I speak too soon. The doorbell buzzes, and I jump as if someone's fired a gun. That's it, I'm going to catch the bastard. I leap out of bed and dash onto the landing.

Kevin and Ashley are also up. Kevin's already halfway down the stairs.

Ashley grabs me and stops me from going any further. "Kevin will handle it. Stay here, babe."

I'm fidgety, can't stand still and switch from one foot to the next.

Kevin opens the door and runs out, shouting down the road, "Whoever you are, piss off!"

Words tumble out of me in quick succession. "Do you think he'll catch him? Do you think that'll work? Who do you think it is?"

Ashley blearily looks at me, half asleep.

I continue, "I mean, I think I know who it might be, but it could be anyone, you know? Oh, Ashley, you and Kevin have been such good friends to me. I really appreciate everything you're doing for me. Do you want to go downstairs and have a cup of tea and a chat?"

"Umm, not right now. I'm knackered and think I'm going to head back to bed."

"Right, yeah, of course. It's late. I just feel really chatty right now."

She rubs my arm sympathetically. "Your moods are all over the place, and I think your sleep cycle is out of whack because you slept a lot the past few days. We'll have a catch-up in the morning. Sound good?"

"Yep, perfect. Great. Thanks. In the morning. Yep," I ramble, desperate to keep her talking, to keep talking myself. What is wrong with me? It's the middle of the night.

Kevin comes back up the stairs. He purses his lips in frustration. "Didn't catch them this time. But next time. I've got my ear out. Just need to be quicker."

"Well done, my love. Nearly got 'em," Ashley encourages. "Let's all get back to bed. Hopefully, that'll be it for tonight."

She leads Kevin back to the bedroom and shuts the door. I hover in the landing, feeling flooded with energy. I jog on the spot to burn some of it off. Doug comes trotting up the stairs and sits watching me.

"Come on." I usher him into my bedroom and close the door. He jumps on my bed, and I pace the few steps in my room from wall to door, wall to door, inanely chattering to the dog.

An hour or so later, when I'm all talked out, I get into bed. But I still can't sleep. I'm wired. I feel like I used to when I went clubbing all night long in my early twenties. Although those days, I had alcohol in my system that helped me drop off to sleep. I never took illegal drugs, although I was offered. My mind brings up those days, and I reminisce fondly over happy memories. But as if someone reaches inside my head and flicks a switch, suddenly I'm desperately sad.

I drop off crying silent tears about my friend's cousin's mate's boyfriend who took an ecstasy tablet and died at nineteen.

The doorbell rings and jolts me awake. But this time, my limbs don't spring up from bed. They feel sucked down like I've fallen in thick mud. I hear Kevin run down the stairs and to the front door. I hear him shouting, but I can't make it out.

A few minutes later, I hear him pad up the stairs, breathing heavily.

"Any joy?" Ashley's voice asks.

But there's no reply from Kevin, and I guess he's gestured in the negative, as there's silence after that.

I look at my phone. It's 4.42 a.m. I stare at the ceiling until I drop off again.

ASHLEY'S PRODDING me wakes me up. "I've brought you a cup of tea and some cereal. How you doing? Still up for a chat?"

I eye her from under the bedsheets. I'm most definitely *not* up for a chat now. My head pounds with an impending migraine, and I just want to hide from the world.

She puts the cereal and tea on the side. I grunt my thanks. My appetite pendulum has swung towards 'stomach as tight as a coiled spring', and the thought of chewing, swallowing or even putting a morsel in my mouth is repulsive.

"Listen, hon, Kevin brought up a good point this morning. He asked if you've let your clients know you're off sick? I mean, it's Thursday, and you've not touched your laptop all week. I know it's none of our business how you run your business, but we're worried about you. I don't want you to lose clients because you need a bit of time off. You want them all to still be there when you're fit and healthy again and return to work."

She's absolutely right. I've barely thought about work since Monday morning. The thought of stacks of unread emails piling up in my inbox, missed deadlines and unhappy clients is too much for me to bear.

I groan.

Ashley continues, "Shall I bring up your laptop? It's downstairs. You could do it now and get it out of the way."

"I just... I just can't bring myself to do it," I say. And that's when I know depression has firmly seized me in its grip. It's what happened before. All I could manage was to exist. Daily activities, work, even dressing myself became too much effort.

Ashley notes my distress. "I can help. Tell me what to do, and I can send the emails. It won't take a moment."

Aunt Alice helped me before. And now it's Ashley. I feel blessed to have such a wonderful aunt and friend in my life. I'm so lucky to have people who care when I'm like this. When I'm so useless. The thought makes me teary.

Ashley pats my knee and heads out of the room. She returns with my laptop. She powers it on and hands it to me. But I can't even face touching the damn thing.

She sits on the floor cross-legged and rests the laptop on her knees.

"What's your password for your laptop?"

"Lily123. Capital L."

She efficiently types it in.

"And your email?"

"Same."

She types, then looks at me. "Who should I email?"

My brain throbs with the effort of thinking.

"Let's just do it one at a time," Ashley encourages. "There's no rush."

I force the cogs in my brain to turn. "Barbara Fleeks."

Ashley clicks a few times. "Okay, what do you want to say?" She looks up at me, but when I don't respond immediately, she continues, "Shall I say that you're unfortunately not well and haven't been in work this week and will be off sick for the rest of the week? I'll apologise profusely, etcetera, etcetera."

"Perfect," I reply, relieved that I don't need to think about words. A sentence. A paragraph. Anything.

Ashley types swiftly. Pauses to read what she's written.

Adjusts a few things. "Sent. I'll just copy and paste that for your other clients. Easy. Now, who's next?"

I reel off the names of my eight clients, and Ashley pings them all an email.

Ashley closes the laptop lid. "There, all done."

I swell with gratitude for my friend. "Thank you so, so much."

"Absolutely no problem at all. I'd better get on with my work now." She stands. "I'll pop your laptop back in the bag downstairs out of the way. And you don't need to think about work until next week."

I 'hmm' weakly at her.

She indicates the cereal. "Try to have a few mouthfuls before it gets soggy. Kevin'll get upset with me if I don't encourage you to eat. He's a real feeder, that one. Which is perfect because I'm a big eater." She laughs. "We'll just be downstairs. You do whatever, head down or stay here all day. Take it easy."

"Thanks, mate."

"Come on, Doug." She nudges the dozing dog. "Time for breakfast, and Uncle Kevin's going to take you for a walk this morning." When Doug makes no sign of moving, she scoops him up. "Seems we're all a bit tired this morning after that bloody doorbell going off at all hours." She nuzzles his head and carries him out of the room.

The bloody doorbell. Who the hell keeps ringing it? Although such an inane, innocuous thing, it's driving me mad.

22

I don't think it's my brother anymore. He's a reformed character. He's moved on. But someone clearly hasn't. I lie and stew for hours, and when I can't take it anymore, I get out of bed. I take a sip of the cold tea and grimace.

"Ashley?" I call as I head downstairs.

She meets me in the hallway from the kitchen. "Yeah? What's up?"

"I need to work out who's targeting me, and then I can get my life back on track."

"*Okay*," she replies, dragging out the 'a' sound. "Let me just go and save my work, and I'll be right with you." She gestures towards the lounge, and I head there. There's some murmuring from the kitchen.

Kevin shouts, "Do you want a hot drink, Jess? I'm making Ashley one."

"No, thank you," I shout back, my stomach still screwed up tight like a crumpled ball of paper.

A few moments later, Ashley heads back in with a mug of black coffee. "So," she says after a sip, "who do you think it is?

You mentioned that wife of that guy you were seeing for a bit. Do you reckon it was her?"

I think back to the home invasion. Terrifying as it had been, it hadn't played out as Toni had expected. Her plan to scare me, to exert control over me, to warn me off her husband had been royally scuppered.

My mind latches onto the idea. "It has to be her," I reply. "She still wants her revenge. To get back at me for taking Marcus away from her."

"So she and Marcus split up?"

"As far as I know. That was what he told me in the last conversation we had three years ago."

Ashley takes another sip. "You think she's still bitter about it."

"I think so. She's somehow found out I'm back in the country and living here and is out to terrorise me."

"So what are you going to do about it? Send her a message on Facebook or something?"

My lethargic mood from earlier is replaced by a sizzling hot rage. It burns away the haze of the exhaustion. "No. I confront her face to face. This has gone on long enough. She'll just ignore a message or a phone call."

"Jess... I'm not sure that's a great idea," Ashley says tentatively.

But it's in my head now, and I'm fixated on it. "It's a great idea."

"How are you going to organise this meeting? She won't want to meet you," Ashley says.

The plan slots together in my head, forming so fast I have a job keeping up with it. "I'm not going to organise anything. I'm going to go to her house. I know where she lives."

"She might've moved," Ashley says. "It would be a wasted journey."

I can tell she's eager to steer me off this course. But I won't be deterred. "Then I'll go to where she works. She was an HR manager at a big insurance firm in Reading. Marcus always said she loved that job and would never leave. I'll find her."

"Maybe she won't be in?" Ashley tries again to dissuade me.

But I look at the clock. I'm surprised to see it's almost four. It'll take a couple of hours to get to Reading, and by then she'll be home from work.

"I'm going to have a shower and get changed. I'm going right now. This all needs to stop. I'm going to make it stop."

"You've already had a shower this morning, hon."

"What? No I haven't."

"It was just before I brought your breakfast because Kevin also wanted a shower, so he went in after you because when your shower is on, we don't get any hot coming through in our bathroom."

"Oh. I don't remember." But then I didn't remember calling Tim the other day, either. Perhaps this is a thing now, the not remembering.

She laughs. "And I was surprised to see you back in your PJs in bed when I came in."

"Right. Well, I'm just going to get changed, then."

I head up to my bedroom before Ashley can try to convince me otherwise. I get dressed and head back down, throwing on my dog-walking coat, grabbing my handbag and my phone charger for the car, as I'll need it for the satnav.

But the car keys aren't in the usual place on the hallway console by the front door.

"Ashley, have you seen the car keys?"

Ashley and Kevin come through from the kitchen. She holds up the car keys. "We really don't think you should do this, Jess."

Kevin adds, "I'm not sure you're fit to drive."

"Give me the keys," I demand. I know they've been

wonderful to me, and they're only looking out for me, but I have to do this. I have to stop Toni playing her mindfuck games once and for all.

But Ashley doesn't make any move to hand me the keys.

I explode, feeling like a child being denied the one thing they want. I scream, "You can't keep me prisoner in my own home!" I grab at the keys, and Ashley relinquishes her grip on them.

They both looked stunned. Ashley flicks her attention to Kevin, but he's gaping at me, his mouth in a perfect O.

Ashley lunges towards me, and I hug the keys into my chest, expecting her to grab them off me.

But she yanks her coat off a hook. "I'm coming with you, then. If you're so determined to do this, then I'll drive."

"Ashley," Kevin says in a tone that indicates he's not on board with that idea. Not on board at all.

She dismisses his concern with a hand wave. "I'll message you when we're on our way home. Don't worry. It's better that I'm with her."

Kevin wrings his hands, clearly fretting. "But Jess hasn't eaten anything today. She turned down lunch."

"I turned down lunch?"

Ashley nods. "Yeah, I came up at one-ish, but you said you weren't hungry."

I frown. I have zero recollection of that. But I shake it off. That's not important right now.

We head out the front door, and Kevin closes it behind us. Ashley gestures for the car keys, and I hand them to her. I realise I have no idea where the car is parked. But Ashley heads straight towards it, and I remember she moved it a while ago from the disabled spot.

We get in the mint-green Honda, and Ashley starts the engine. She pulls away from the kerb and starts heading out of town. I haven't been in this car since... I'm filled with horror. The knife, the slashed seats. I slowly look over my shoulder.

There's no stuffing spilling from gashes. There's no knife. The seats look perfectly normal. I'm stunned. I wind down the window because I think I might vomit. Is that another thing I made up?

No, it can't be. Toni did it. I'm on my way to confront her right now about it.

"Ashley," I begin but then stop myself. If I ask Ashley about the seats, will she think I'm crazy? That I imagined it? She'd turn the car round. No, the rotting fish definitely happened. Kevin was with me. The doorbell ringing. The note nailed to the door – Ashley saw that.

She doesn't notice I don't finish what I was saying. She's an anxious driver, not paying me much attention, constantly looking in her mirrors.

"Do you have an address?" she asks. "I've got no idea how to get to Reading from here. I'm guessing the M4 towards London? It's in that direction, isn't it?"

I plug Reading into the satnav, and it starts to direct us. It'll take one hour fifty-two minutes, apparently. Ashley visibly calms and settles into the drive. She's the complete opposite to Tim. Her driving is jerky and heavy on the brakes. She weaves in and out of traffic on the motorway impatiently. The Honda groans with every gear change.

I have the address on an email I sent myself. After Toni rumbled us in that hotel, I had to see for myself. I followed Marcus home one night from where he worked and, I'm not proud to say, watched them for a while through the windows. The wife. The kids. The dog. The family home. He'd well and truly lied to me.

But when I'd spoken to him days later, he told me they'd split up. That he'd left the home, the kids, the family, the dog. I'd been overwhelmed with guilt.

On the outskirts of Reading, Ashley pulls over, and I put the address in the satnav app. Fifteen minutes later, she parks up outside the house.

"Are you sure you want to do this? We could just turn around and head home," she says hopefully.

I take in the sweet family home and notice the two cars in the driveway. Toni must have someone visiting. It doesn't deter me. "It's now or never," I say and get out of the car.

I stomp towards the house, Ashley following a few steps behind, and ring the doorbell more than once. To give Toni a taste of her own medicine. Then I thump on the door.

"Coming," I hear a female voice calling from inside.

The door opens. Toni stands before me. She's clearly just got in from work. She wears a brown cropped blazer over a brown frilly shirt with black trousers and sensible, smart black court shoes. Her bobbed afro hair is parted in the middle, and subtle make-up accentuates her great skin. A slick of lip gloss draws attention to her lips, and she looks very professional. Not like the last time I saw her. Then, she was the crazed wife of a cheating husband, wearing a balaclava and hooded top, breaking into the other woman's home to frighten them.

The pleasant expression falls away as she recognises me. Her eyes harden into pinpricks, her nostrils flare, and her mouth puckers into a hard line. She takes a slow, appraising look at me up and down. I don't look professional. I must look dishevelled with baggy joggers, a tatty sweatshirt and a grubby coat I use to take Doug for walks. I don't remember looking in a mirror for days and know my face is devoid of make-up, and my long hair is knotted. I can't actually recall the last time I brushed it.

"What the hell are *you* doing *here*?" She articulates each word slowly, as if I'm stupid.

It riles me up. "I know it's you, still trying to get back at me. Well, it has to stop. Right now."

"What are you blathering about?"

I yell, "You're tormenting me! Did you hire someone? Or have you been coming to Weston-super-Mare? I wouldn't put it past you. You're sick in the head, full of revenge. You'd enjoy torturing me yourself, wouldn't you?"

"Hire someone?" Her bravado breaks, and she visibly deflates in the face of my fury, instead looking ever so slightly scared of me.

I lean forward and point at her. "To attack me in the street! To ring my doorbell, leave rotting fish on my doorstep, write messages on my car, tip over my bins... and all the rest!"

"You're demented. I've not done any of those things," she insists, her voice rising a notch.

"Bullshit," I holler, practically spitting in her face.

"You're scaring me!"

"What's all this about?" A man's voice comes from behind Toni.

And then he appears at her side, edging her behind him in a protective manner.

Marcus.

My heart skips a beat. I take him in, his bald head, wide nose, thick lips, neatly trimmed goatee, and beautiful brown eyes. His double chin is still prominent, but it always suited him, matching his chunky, solid figure. He's wearing a crisp white polo T-shirt with the collar turned up just like he always used to. I glance down at his feet, and as expected, he wears a pristine white pair of trainers.

"What are you doing here?" I ask, stunned.

Marcus glares at me. "I live here. What are you doing here?"

"You got back together?"

Toni's head pops up over Marcus' shoulder. "We never split up."

My eyes bore a hole into Marcus.

He licks his lips. "You were a minor blip, Jess. Toni is the woman for me, has always been the woman for me and always will be."

This news propels me backwards, and I take a step away from them.

A child's voice comes from somewhere deep in the house. "Mummy! Daddy!"

Toni turns and says sweetly, "We'll be right back, munchkins. You stay right there."

"I meant nothing to you?" I ask Marcus quietly.

We were together for three months. I thought he was my ticket out of the Blake hell I'd been in. He was so romantic and loving. I thought he'd be my next serious relationship. Until I discovered he had a wife and kids. No, scratch that, until his wife discovered us. We could've gone on for years if she hadn't found out. I trusted Marcus implicitly when he told me he was divorced and single.

He shakes his head. "No. You meant nothing to me."

I splinter into pieces and clench every muscle in my body to keep myself together.

It must show on my face because Toni extends a hand to me in a pitying gesture. "Oh, Jess, we're blissfully happy. You were the wake-up call we both needed to repair our relationship."

As if to prove the point, Marcus turns and kisses Toni tenderly.

The piece of me that contains my heart falls out like a lump of coal on the ground.

She continues in a voice she might reserve for children, "I'm sorry for that night at your house. I shouldn't have done that. I should've apologised before. But it took me a long time to heal after the beating you gave me. You could've killed me. But I totally understand you needed to protect yourself. Thank you for not going to the police."

I blink at her. My mind is blank.

She continues, "We're sorry you're having a tough time. But it's nothing to do with us. I have my man." She hugs Marcus and rests her head on his shoulder. "You've been out of the picture for years."

Marcus kisses his wife again, and it makes me queasy. They look like lovestruck teens.

He puts his hand on the door. "Listen, Jess, we're going to close the door now and go back to our children and our dinner."

I don't move or reply, so he slowly shuts it in my face. When it's an inch from closing, he looks pointedly at me and then at Ashley, who I know stands behind me, and says, "Perhaps you need to get some professional help? It's been years. This can't be healthy."

Then the door is shut.

Ashley takes my arm and guides me back to the car. I'm in a trance, staring into the space in front of me but not seeing anything. Ashley gets me seated in the passenger side, then gets in the car. She drives a little way down the road and then pulls over.

"I think we should head home," she says gently. "Are you up for the drive? Shall we get some food? A Maccy Ds?"

"I thought Marcus might be the one. I thought Jamal might be the one."

"You'll find someone who isn't a bastard. Not all men are awful."

"Blake was awful."

Ashley rubs my knee. "I'm going to drive us home. It's clearly not Toni."

The thought of going home unsuccessful sends a sensation like pins and needles but ten times worse all up my spine.

I ball my hands into tight fists. "It has to be Blake."

Ashley sighs. "Jess, I don't think..." But she sees the look on my face and doesn't finish her sentence.

23

"Blake still lives in Oxford. That's only an hour's drive from here."

"We're not going to Oxford," Ashley replies. "I think you've had enough for one day."

"Yes. We are. I'm not going home until I stop whoever is doing this to me."

Ashley shakes her head.

I continue, "Fine. I'll get out and walk to the train station and get a train there. You can't stop me." I open the car door and put one foot out.

"Jess!" Ashley leans across the car and grabs my arm. "Okay, okay. I'll drive you. You're in no fit state to be walking for miles to the train station and getting on trains. I can't leave you on your own. Get in the car."

I get in.

Ashley lets out her breath, a relieved expression on her face. "Where are we going, then?"

"I have his new address from finalising a few things about the divorce." I bring up my emails on my phone and search for my solicitor's emails. I find the address and plug it into my satnav app.

Ashley taps out a quick message on her phone – I assume to Kevin to let him know our next destination – and starts the car, following the directions to Oxford. It will take an hour, and for the first ten minutes or so we travel in silence. Ashley fidgets: chewing her lips, tapping her fingernails on the steering wheel, shifting in her seat every time we come to a stop, and tucking and untucking her growing-out fringe from behind her ear.

Finally, she speaks. "What did Toni mean when she said you almost killed her?"

"I... er..." I reply, unable to form into words what had happened. But the memory starts up unbidden, and I play it through again.

THE FIGURE STOOD over my bed, arm raised with what looked like a knife.

I stood and swung the hockey stick. It connected, and there was a yelp.

I hit again and again. A red mist descended like I'd never experienced before, and I couldn't stop. The figure dropped to the ground. I pounded and kicked.

"Stop!" a female voice yelled. "Please stop!"

A woman? I was hitting a woman? It jarred me, and I paused. Panting, I switched on the lamp on the bedside cabinet.

"Toni?" I blurted.

She pulled down her balaclava so I could see her face. She bled heavily from her nose and had cuts on her hands and face. Her eyes were already purpling with bruises. I think I might've killed her if she hadn't yelled.

I slumped on my bed and flung the blood-slick hockey stick away. "What are you doing here?"

"I... I wanted to scare you. To warn you to keep away from my husband. But... but..." Her voice came out thick through her bloody nose. She touched it tentatively and flinched from the pain. "I think it's broken."

"I thought you were here to murder me."

Toni heaved herself up to sitting. "You're insane."

"No, you're insane. You broke into my house!"

"And you almost killed me!"

We were both silent then, catching our breath, thinking things through.

Finally, she said, "You'll be in the same amount of trouble with the police, if not more, than me."

I knew she was right. UK law said you could use reasonable force when defending your home from intruders, but I'd almost beaten her to a bloody pulp. Would that be considered reasonable, or had I taken it too far?

"What do we do now?" I asked.

"I'm willing to let it go if you are?" Toni said through gritted teeth. It was clear this wasn't the outcome she had expected.

"Deal."

She snarled at me. She picked herself up, leaving a smear of blood on my wall, and limped out of the bedroom. I heard her hobbling down the stairs. But I didn't follow. I was too shocked to move, the adrenaline of earlier crashing and leaving me spent and close to tears.

"How did you get in?" I shouted after her.

"Your back door was open, you stupid bitch."

I TAKE A BREATH. "Toni broke into my house and threatened me. I fought back."

"Right," Ashley replies. The word is shot through with what sounds like uncertainty. But I must be imagining it because I know she's on my side.

She continues to fidget for the rest of the journey. But I sit as still as a rock. My insides are in turmoil at the thought of seeing Blake again, and my entire attention is on dealing with that. I have nothing left for movement of any kind.

By process of elimination, it has to be him. The last time I saw him properly was when he moved out of the house after I got an occupation order – an injunction that banned him from entering the home and surrounding area due to domestic abuse – and a second non-molestation order. He hated me so completely. He refused to acknowledge that he'd raped me, couldn't believe that a husband could be accused of doing that to his wife. He insisted it was consensual although my bruises told a different story.

Then he hung around outside the house for a while, just to spook me, until the police gave him a warning, telling him that if he broke his injunction again, he'd be arrested. The idea of confronting him now brings bile to my mouth. But I can't let him plague me forever. If I don't stand up to him, he'll take control. Just like in our marriage, just like in our fertility struggles. I've fought back against him before – soon after my seventh miscarriage. I can do it again.

"We're here," Ashley announces and parks the car. She points to the house opposite. It's in darkness with not one light on, not even an outside light. "Looks like nobody is home."

It's a modest semi-detached home in a nice part of Oxford. I got nothing from Blake in the divorce, and he got nothing from me. He'd made me sign a prenuptial agreement, which meant the house – which I'd purchased before I met him with the help of the inheritance, a student mortgage and my aunt and uncle as guarantors, which we'd lived in for years and which had tripled in value – belonged solely to me. He earned a good wedge from his sales job at a big pharmaceuticals firm and didn't want me getting my hands on any of that. I know with his salary he would've had no problem getting a mortgage, even though he'd never had one before.

Ashley shifts in her seat. "What do you want to do? I feel a bit creepy sitting here."

I know Ashley isn't likely to bring me back here tomorrow or another day. And she was right earlier – I'm not sure I've got it in me to manage a train journey.

"We wait," I say.

She gets her phone out and opens the Scrabble app, which I introduced her to, while I stare at the house. About twenty minutes pass when headlights flash behind us. An estate car comes up the road and pulls into the driveway of Blake's house.

I nudge Ashley, and she looks up, putting her phone away. She scoots down in her seat in an attempt to hide. But I watch on brazenly.

Blake gets out of the car, oblivious to our presence across the road. He still has a good head of ginger hair for forty-one, with a side parting and swept over to one side with gel. A security light pings on from above the garage, activated by his movement, and highlights him in a spotlight. He still looks trim and healthy, his cheeks a ruddy pink. But he now wears glasses. He always had beautiful blue eyes and perfectly straight white teeth. He was always proud of his teeth, paying a lot of money for them and insisting I get mine done too. But I resisted. I hate the dentist, and I always thought my oddly spaced teeth were just fine, thank you.

He still has his ginger beard. He rubs it and then walks around the side of the car. He opens the passenger door and helps out a woman. As she stands, I see she's heavily pregnant. A lump lands squarely in my throat. She's obviously younger than him. And also taller. I was taller than him too. But his charm would've won her over, like it did me. Who cares about height when you're in love?

He smiles widely at her, and she beams back. She stands to one side as he opens the back door and brings out a baby car seat and carrier. He leans in to grab a bag and then turns, and I see the beautiful sleeping baby in the carrier.

They walk together to the house, and she lets them in. The door closes, and a few moments later, various lights go on in the windows, and curtains are drawn.

"Looks like he's moved on," Ashley whispers, still crouching down in the car. "With a baby and another on the way."

"He looks so happy," I mutter, still staring at the house.

I feel completely flattened. Heartbroken even. "Both Marcus and Blake have moved on and are happy, and I'm what? I'm miserable."

"It'll pass," Ashley encourages. "You'll be happy again in no time."

I shake my head. My depression is so deep that I simply don't believe her. "I'll never be happy again."

"You will," Ashley insists, always the optimist.

"But someone is still out there targeting me."

Ashley folds her arms, at a loss for words.

I continue forcefully, as if my friend has the answers, "Who? Who, Ashley?"

"I don't—"

But her words are cut short by a banging on my window. Ashley gasps.

Blake is right there on the other side of the pane of glass. His pale skin is fiery, all the muscles in his face tensed. He's furious.

He gestures for me to open the window. When I don't, he thumps the glass again. "Open the damn window, Jess."

I open it a crack.

"What the actual fuck?" he yells through the gap.

Ashley starts the engine. It's clear she's planning a quick getaway if this beast attacks.

He continues to shout, "I just saw you from my bedroom window, spying on us from your car. I knew you wouldn't be able to stay away, would be back to ruin my life all over again. Wouldn't be able to let me move on with my new family. I just knew it! Once a lunatic, always a lunatic. You're stalking me again now? Well, you can fuck off and leave me alone. Do you hear me? Fuck. Right. Off."

"I never stalked you in the first place," I shout back.

He taps the side of his head. "You're nuts. Have you forgotten everything that happened? Those last five years of our marriage were a living hell. You became a monster."

"You became the monster!"

"Well, I see nothing has changed these past few years. You're still full of lies. You're still deluded."

He leans down so he can see Ashley. "You there, don't believe anything this woman tells you. Anything. She conveniently forgets things. She'll manipulate and use you. That's what she does. You must be her only friend. She drove all the rest away with her attention-seeking behaviour. But you're here, aren't you, so you're witnessing it first-hand."

I shift forward so that his attention is on me again.

But he stares straight past me at Ashley. "Oh, and beware – she has a temper. She's violent."

I slap the dashboard to get his attention. "None of that is true, Blake, and you know it."

He sneers at me. "What I know is this. If I see you anywhere near here again – or if you come anywhere near my wife or children – I won't be responsible for my actions. Do you understand? I will protect them no matter what from you and your poison. Fuck off before I call the police. Right now, you crazy bitch."

He steps back and slaps his palm on the roof of the car and then kicks the door.

Ashley screeches away from the kerb and speeds off. She drives like a maniac until she finds a garage to pull into.

She's breathing heavily, her hands clasped around the steering wheel, and stares straight ahead. That bastard has frightened her. I'm used to his venom, but this was her first taste of his evilness.

"It's okay, Ashley. I told you he was a monster," I say in a reassuring voice.

Her head swivels to look at me. "*He's* the monster?" she blurts.

I take in her face. She's looking at me in a way she never has before. With doubt. It's the same way some of my old friends had looked at me after Blake had filled their heads with lies. He'd pushed them all away, eventually.

"Don't believe anything that comes out of that bastard's mouth. He distorts reality. He's always gaslighted me. Always. All of that was rubbish. I never stalked him before. I've never lied about anything. You have to believe me, Ashley."

Ashley takes a few deep breaths and then nods at me. "I'm going to fill up, and then we're heading back to Weston. How much will a full tank be, do you reckon?"

"Here, take my card and do contactless. It's not fair for you to pay to put petrol in my car." I get my debit card out of my wallet.

She takes the card and gets out of the car before I can say any more about Blake, and I watch as she pumps petrol into the tank and then heads to the shop. She comes back with two bags of Haribo sweets. She hands my card back, opens both the bags and gets her phone out of her pocket.

"Just going to let Kevin know we're on our way home," she

explains as she taps out a message. She puts her phone in the storage compartment between the seats and then grabs the gear stick.

I put my hand on her wrist. "Ashley, you believe me, don't you? Blake is a liar."

She looks at me. "I believe you. Of course I do."

But I see the uncertainty dancing around the edges of her lips, across her brow, in her eyes.

She starts the car.

24

It's gone 10 p.m. by the time we get in. We both head to the lounge and slump on the sofa. Kevin jumps up and flings his book aside to head to the kitchen. I hear his bare feet slapping on the kitchen lino and wonder briefly if he ever puts socks on.

For something to do, because it's clear Ashley isn't in the mood to talk, I pick up the book and read the title: *Seven Brief Lessons on Physics* by Carlo Rovelli. Never heard of it, and probably not something I'd ever pick up. It's well-thumbed. Perhaps he's read it more than once. Or maybe it's second-hand. Either way, it's almost the perfect book for him to be reading. It'd be odd if it were a Western or a space opera.

A few moments later, he hands a mug to me and then one to Ashley. "Hot chocolate. To settle your nerves."

"Thanks," I say and take a sip.

He kisses Ashley on the top of her head and sits next to her. She snuggles into him.

"How did it go?" he asks in his quiet voice.

Ashley glances at me but stays mute.

"Not great," I reply.

"Oh?" he asks.

"Neither of them is targeting me."

"Ah."

I drink some more of my hot chocolate, appreciating the smooth, creamy flavour. I feel highly strung, but the hot drink smoothes all the hard edges like a balm and makes me feel drowsy.

We sit in silence, decompressing. Ashley and I are knackered. But Kevin is restless, clearly eager for conversation after being left alone for most of the day.

"Have you eaten anything?" he asks Ashley.

"Not really," she replies.

"'Not really' doesn't sound like a particularly nutritious dinner, I must say."

"Oh, don't start, darling. I'm really not in the mood right now."

"I just asked what you had for dinner, that's all. I care about your health—"

"Sweets," she replies just to shut him up.

"Just sweets?" he asks, but she doesn't respond.

When he realises she's not going to volunteer any more information, he looks back to me.

"So who do you think it might be?" he asks brightly as if he's asking me how my day was.

I burst into tears. I don't even get the tingle warning, it just happens. The waterworks turn on, and I bawl uncontrollably.

I don't know who it is. I don't have any clue whatsoever. Marcus and Blake have moved on and are happy. Toni has her man. Jamal dumped me. Someone hates me. Everything blitzes together and sprays everywhere like fruit and milk in a smoothie blender when you've forgotten to put the lid on.

"Jesus, Kevin," Ashley reprimands.

She puts her mug down and comes to me. She takes the now-empty mug from my hands and helps me up.

"What did I say?" Kevin asks.

"We're going to bed. It's been a long day," she replies.

I WAKE from a deep sleep hours later, needing to wee. I'm in my pyjamas, but I don't recall putting them on. Maybe Ashley helped me? Doesn't matter. I put my dressing gown on and tiptoe to the bathroom, relieve myself and then creep back to the bedroom, avoiding the creaks in the floorboards.

But outside my door, I pause. Although my head is foggy, I don't want to go back to bed. I have the urge to move.

I wander aimlessly around the house in the darkness. I head downstairs and notice Doug is asleep in his bed under the dining table. I want to fuss him but also don't want to wake him up. He looks peaceful. Almost dead. I stand and watch his little chest moving up and down in the moonlight that comes through the window.

When my body starts to ache and my eyes hurt, I realise I've been there for some time. I yawn, and my stomach grumbles. I didn't eat any dinner, and Ashley ate most of the sweets in the car. I open the fridge and cupboards, but nothing really appeals. I grab a chocolate bar and put it in my dressing gown pocket, not really fancying it, but maybe I'll change my mind in a few minutes. I decide to head back to my bedroom.

I plod up the stairs, watching where I place my feet in the dim light, and look up when I reach the landing.

But there's someone there, coming out of the bathroom next to the back bedroom. I stifle a scream, clapping a hand over my mouth. It's not Ashley or Kevin.

It's a boy.

He freezes, eyes wide, and gawps at me.

He's perhaps ten years old. My first baby, a boy, would've

been ten years old if he'd survived. Is this him? Has he come back to find me? I had so much love for him. So much. Perhaps he's ready to receive it now?

No. I know he's a figment of my imagination. Just like I hallucinated that baby on the ceiling. I blink a few times, but the boy remains as still as a statue in front of me.

Neither of us moves, and we stare at each other for a very long time. Maybe he's just as surprised to see me as I am him. Perhaps I've crossed into some other realm, another dimension, a parallel universe or whatever, where he survived. I want to say his name to reassure him that I'm his mummy, but Blake and I didn't give him one. We hadn't decided on one by the time he died.

Not entirely sure what I'm going to say, I open my mouth, but the boy, my son, brings a finger to his mouth in the gesture for silence. I nod. Then he points to my bedroom, and I understand he wants us to go there.

I head to my room, and he follows. I take a few steps inside and slowly turn back to him. I want to turn on the main light to get a good look at him, but I don't want to scare him off. I'm curious about my son and want to get to know him. I wonder what my life would be like now if he'd survived. I always wanted to be a mother. Perhaps this is my chance, in my own head, in my dream world, in my insanity, to form a bond and make a connection.

"Hello," I say quietly, not wanting to startle him.

"Hi," he replies in a whisper, slowly closing the door behind him. I switch on my side lamp. He takes a step back into the shadows, looks at his feet and wrings his hands.

The sound of his voice fills me with joy. I'm finally hearing my son's voice. It's perfect. But he's clearly shy, or perhaps just wary of me. I need to carefully coax him out of his shell. I can manage that. I'm his mummy, after all. "How are you this evening?"

"Okay," he replies, still not looking at me. He chews his lip.

I remember the Snickers in my pocket. "Do you want some chocolate?"

I pull out the chocolate bar and hold it out to him. He stares at it uncertainly and makes no move to take it from me.

"I know, let's share it," I suggest, and he nods. I break it in half and give him a chunk. He takes it from me. I know I'm imagining this entire thing, like a child pouring tea for their dolls, but I go with it.

"Thank you," he says politely, then nibbles at it. I eat too. Moments after he swallows the last bite, his face relaxes, and a small smile replaces the anxious frown.

I want to bombard him with a million questions, to find out everything about him. But I know I need to play it cool. I don't want my eagerness to drive him back to the other universe he came from too fast. I want to spend some time with him now he's here.

"Is chocolate your favourite food?" I ask.

He shakes his head. "No. Spaghetti bolognaise with lots of cheese on top. I like to suck up the spaghetti strand by strand." He makes a slurping noise and chuckles, then looks away from me and blushes as if he's said something very embarrassing.

"I love sucking up spaghetti too," I say with a reassuring smile.

His face lights up. "Once I ate too much too quickly and made myself sick!"

"Oh dear!"

He chuckles. "But I still love it."

I nod. He goes quiet and chews his lip again. I want to keep him talking. I ask, "So, if you could be any animal, what would you be?"

"A pigeon," he says without hesitation.

I raise my eyebrows. Not what I was expecting, but brilliantly quirky. "A pigeon? Why's that?"

"I watched this TV show about them, and they're fascinating. Did you know they can fly at nearly one hundred miles per hour? And they can do backflips in mid-air to get away from prey. They're intelligent too and can learn the alphabet and recognise humans. And they form flocks with their friends."

"Wow, I didn't know that. Pigeons sound pretty cool."

"And they make a sound like this..." He coos. "And do this..." He jerks his head back and forth and struts around.

I laugh, and he laughs too. The wonderful sound gives me the warm-and-fuzzies.

"Do you want to see a silly face?" he asks eagerly.

"Most definitely."

He turns his back to me and then spins around with his fingers pulling out the corners of his mouth, his tongue out and cross-eyed.

"Aargh!" I say and shield my eyes with my hands. "That's too silly. I can't handle the silliness of that face."

I drop my hands, and he beams at me. He points at the stack of books on my bedside cabinet. "Do you like to read?" he asks.

"I do, very much."

"Me too. I've read the *Harry Potter* books more times now than I can count."

"I've read them too. And watched the movies."

"When I grow up, I want to make potions."

"A scientist?"

He looks sad all of a sudden. "Mmmhmm." He fidgets. "I'd better go."

Although I'm disappointed, I nod.

He leans closer to me. "Don't tell anyone about me. Promise?"

"I promise."

He grins at me. It's cheeky, fun, and it brightens his little face. "I'll be back another night."

"Sure," I reply.

"Well, that's if you want to see me again?" he asks, suddenly unsure, his face falling.

"Absolutely."

The grin returns, and he drifts away into the hallway. I close my bedroom door and sit on the edge of my bed. My elation at meeting my child fades, and I hold my head in my hands. I've truly gone mad, talking to my imaginary grown-up son. About pigeons, no less. There's no way I'm going to tell anyone about seeing him. They already think I'm on the brink of a monumental breakdown. Hallucinating about babies crying and boys walking the house at night is not a sign of a healthy mind.

I need help. Tim was right.

25

I doze on the sofa, watching some early-afternoon weekday crap on the telly. I got up earlier, ate breakfast in bed – chia pudding with blueberries, raspberries and strawberries prepared by Kevin – fell asleep for a few hours and then woke up dressed and showered and on the sofa with no memory of getting there. But blanks in my memory are normal now. I ate lunch – Kevin's chicken noodle soup – and then nodded off again.

The doorbell goes. But it doesn't really register. I'm probably imagining it like I imagined the boy last night.

But I hear footsteps pad to the door and hear Kevin's voice. I'm relieved that some of my senses are still functioning: I did, in fact, hear the doorbell. I feel like a zombie, lying on the sofa, spaced out, hollow inside.

"Come in," I can just about hear Kevin saying. "This way."

He steps into the room, followed by Tim, another man I don't know who carries a chunky briefcase, and Ashley.

All four of them look at me, and if I could move my body, if I actually cared, I would squirm at the concentrated attention. But I sprawl there unmoving.

"Jess, this is Dr Clegg," Tim says gently. All of them stand motionless, as if any move might startle me and set me off flapping into the sky.

The doctor gives a brief nod. He's middle-aged, greying, portly and has a chubby face. His manner is warm and friendly. He wears a long black coat, which he takes off and looks around for somewhere to put it. Kevin takes it from him with a small bow like a butler. Underneath, the doctor wears a smart tweed jacket, white shirt and navy trousers.

"Dr Clegg?" I ask, confused. Where has this doctor suddenly come from?

Ashley sees my confusion and takes a step forward to kneel in front of me. "You called Tim and asked him to organise a doctor for you," she explains.

"I did?"

"We spoke earlier, Jess. You asked me for help. Don't you remember?" Tim says.

I shake my head. My mobile is on the coffee table, but I don't bother looking at my call history. I know what it will tell me. Next to it is my closed laptop, but I don't remember using it. My memory is shot to pieces.

Tim glances at the doctor, then continues, "I told you I would get it all sorted. Dr Clegg is a private doctor. I'm paying for it all, so you don't need to worry about that. He was good enough to come out at short notice and make a home visit. I explained the situation to him, and we didn't think you were up to going to his GP clinic."

"Sure," I mumble, not having the energy to do much else.

The doctor clears his throat. "Jess, I'd like to talk to you alone if that's okay?" He has a northern accent, not a Somerset accent like the locals.

"Sure," I say again.

He smiles at the others, and they get the hint. They file from the room. He watches them out and then closes the lounge door. He picks up a footstool and brings it close to me on the sofa. He sits and looks at me kindly.

"So, Jess, what's been happening with you? Your brother is quite worried, but I'd like to hear it from you."

I prop myself up on my elbows so I can look at him better. "What day is it?"

"Friday."

"Ah."

"Do you find you're losing track of time? How else are you feeling? Talk me through it."

His kindness opens a gate, and the words bundle through. "I'm just finding everyday life hard. I can't seem to function properly. I can't work or do anything or think properly. My mood is all over the place, from lethargic to angry to wired to uncontrollable crying. I feel so overwhelmed with everything."

"I understand. And how is your appetite? Have you noticed any changes?"

"Yes, it swings from being ravenous to not wanting to even drink water."

"Right. And your sleep?"

"It's all over the place too. I might sleep for hours all day and be awake at night. Today, I've got extreme fatigue. I can't remember things happening, like calling my brother earlier. It's as if I'm doing things, but my mind is actually asleep."

He nods. "And has there been anything else?"

"Yes. I... I think I'm having hallucinations. I keep seeing and hearing things that aren't really there. But at the time, it feels like they are really there." I sigh and have an urge to cry. My face crumples, but I do my best to hold the emotion back.

"I see. I think you're having what is called a nervous breakdown or a mental breakdown. It's essentially a mental health crisis. It's a period of extreme mental or emotional stress brought on by trauma or grief or a particularly stressful time. It can be very frightening."

"This isn't the first time."

"Oh? I'm afraid I haven't had a chance to request your notes from your last GP, so I'm not aware of your history."

"That's fine. It was a few years ago now after coming out of an abusive marriage. But this time is worse."

"Hmm. But you recovered. So you'll know the good news is that it's temporary. But everyone is different in terms of recovery. It could last anywhere from days to weeks to months. How long were you unwell before?"

"A month."

"This time could be different. It could be shorter. Or much, much longer."

I groan. "I hate feeling like this."

"I know, it's not pleasant, but you have people around you who care for you. And I'm going to prescribe you some anti-depressants and a sleep aid to help when you can't sleep at night. Did you have either of those before?"

"No, my GP in Oxford was very keen on talking therapy in the first instance. So I had psychotherapy treatment, and that seemed to do the trick."

"Mmmhmm. But I believe, and as you've indicated, the severity of this breakdown is more significant, so I'd like to start you on medication in the first instance."

He opens his briefcase and searches for something within. While he's looking, he says, "If the medication doesn't help, then we may need to consider a short stay in a residential treatment facility."

A hospital stay is the absolute last thing I want to happen. "No. No, I don't want that."

"I don't think it will come to that. You have a good network around you, by the looks of things, to take care of you, to make sure you eat and take your tablets, especially if your mental fatigue is leading to forgetfulness."

"My aunt cared for me before."

"Ah, and could she care for you again, perhaps?"

"No. She's away on a cruise. My friends and brother are here."

"While you are in the midst of it, you might want to consider organising lasting power of attorney."

He starts to tell me what power of attorney is, but it's too much information for my brain to handle, and my forehead throbs.

I wave my hand at him to stop. "I'm sorry, please could you get Tim and explain this to him? It's not going in."

Dr Clegg smiles warmly at me. "Certainly."

He stands and goes to the door, calling for Tim. Tim enters the room moments later, a concerned look on his face.

The doctor sits once again, writes out something on a pad, and signs it. "Mr Salmon, your sister is suffering a mental breakdown. I have prescribed her antidepressants." He hands the note to me, but I indicate for him to give it to Tim. He gives it to Tim, and Tim glances down at it.

Dr Clegg continues, "And I was just mentioning lasting power of attorney. It is a legal document that gives another the permission to make decisions on someone's behalf when they lack the mental capacity."

Tim frowns. "I don't know what that is."

The doctor shuts his briefcase and stands. "Your sister can appoint you to help manage her affairs, just while she is unwell. It can last for as long or short as you need it."

"No way, Jess'll be fine soon. We don't need that."

Dr Clegg smiles. He turns to me. "I would also suggest resting but also making sure you eat a healthy diet, getting outside in nature if you can manage it, and perhaps a short walk. Exercise is a natural mood booster."

I stare at him. I can't even face moving off this sofa, let alone doing some kind of exercise.

He continues, "I will schedule another visit with you soon. But in the meantime, please start your course of antidepressants as soon as you can."

He strides from the room, and Tim sees him out the front door before heading back into the lounge. He clasps the prescription note in his hand.

"Oh, sis, I had no idea you were suffering this badly. I'm so sorry you're feeling this way."

His sympathy sets me off crying. He comes forward and hugs me awkwardly while I'm still lying on the sofa.

He breaks away and sits on the stool that the doctor had used and puts his hand on my forearm. "What can I do to help? Do you want me to go and pick this up?" He holds up the prescription note.

"Yes." I sniffle. "I think I should get started on those right away."

He checks his nice watch. "I'll go to the pharmacy right now."

"Thank you."

He stands and leaves the room with purpose. I hear him call down the hallway. "Ashley? Kevin? I'm just popping to the pharmacy. I won't be a moment. Jess is in the lounge."

The front door opens and closes, and a moment later, Kevin and Ashley come in. Kevin hands me a cup of tea.

"Thought you might need this," he says.

"You're so kind. Both of you have been so good to me."

Ashley blows me a kiss. "It's not a problem, honestly." She puts her arm around Kevin's waist. He presses his nose into her blonde hair and inhales, his face full of bliss. She continues, "You drink your tea and chill out. We just need to get on with work in the next room. Kevin's got a call in a bit, and I just need to finish off a few things before the weekend."

I shift my position to sit upright and take a sip of the tea. "Of course."

They leave the room and close the door. I drink the tea and immediately feel sleepy. Tim will be back shortly, and I need to stay awake. But it's no use. I'm exhausted from the conversation with Dr Clegg.

"JESS? JESS, I'M BACK."

I come to as Tim shakes me gently.

He holds a small package in his hands and continues, "Sorry I've been ages. What a drama. The first pharmacy I went to didn't have these in stock. So I walked to another. Same thing. So I had to walk back here and get the car to go into town, and then there was a long wait, and then they didn't have it anyway. So I went to a fourth place, and they had it. But then I got stuck behind a learner driver and couldn't find any parking nearby." He rolls his eyes. "But I'm back now. Here." He hands me the package, then takes a seat on the sofa next to Ashley.

I open it and see a handful of boxes in there. Tim moves to one side, and Kevin comes over with a glass of water for me. He puts it on the coffee table in front of me and then hovers.

I fumble with the boxes and just tip the lot out on the sofa. Kevin watches intently.

"Would you like some assistance?" he says eagerly.

Ashley chuckles fondly. "Oh, let him help, Jess. He loves stuff like this. He's so anal. If it says you have to take the pills twelve hours apart, he will set a timer so you take them at precisely the right time."

"I like to be precise," he replies. "Precision makes the world go around."

Ashley smirks at him. "If you say so, darling."

I scoop up the boxes and hand them to Kevin. I don't have it in me to read all the small print.

His eyes brighten as he takes them. Then he shifts the stool to one side, sits and opens the first box. He pulls out all the contents and places them neatly on the table. He picks up the first leaflet and begins to read.

Ashley raises a glass of wine at me. "That'll keep him busy for a while. Thanks, babe." She notices me looking at the wine and explains, "I got all my work finished early, hurrah. So cheers to the weekend!"

I long to be well to celebrate a Friday night with her again. I rub my face, then sigh deeply. Tim chews the side of his mouth. He looks like he wants to talk to me, but he eyes Ashley and Kevin.

"Right," Kevin announces. "These are the antidepressants. You need to take two per day for a duration of six months. They'll probably start to work after one to two weeks." He looks at his watch. "It's four o'clock now. So I would suggest taking one with dinner in a few hours' time, as it recommends taking with food to avoid the potential side effect of nausea. And then take the next one with breakfast. I think that's manageable, don't you?"

It's exactly what I need, someone to manage this for me. Alice had done it all before. "Yes, thank you, Kevin."

"Shall I keep these in the kitchen for you? Or do you want them in your room?"

"Keep them with you."

He picks up the medication and indicates the box he's left on the coffee table. "And these ones are sleeping tablets. I'd suggest you keep them on your bedside cabinet. You can take them when you need to."

He stands. "Right, I'll put these in a safe place and then finish off my report before making dinner. Veggie stew sound good to you, Jess? With cheese and potato dumplings for the non-vegans, of course." He does a little chuckle. "Nice and hearty."

"Delicious, thank you."

"Will you be staying for dinner, Tim?" Kevin asks formally.

Tim considers Kevin for a moment. "Ah, not sure just yet. Can I have a word with Jess privately?"

Ashley finishes her glass of wine. "I need to pop to the shop anyway to pick up another bottle. I'll take Doug out to stretch his legs."

She and Kevin exit.

Tim watches them leave and then turns to me. "I'm really worried about you."

"I know. I just can't think straight. I have no idea what day it is half the time. But this isn't the first time this has happened. I was in a right state when Blake and I divorced. The same is happening again. But this time it's worse."

"I'm sorry to hear that. I didn't know."

I shrug. "You weren't around."

His face falls. "Look, I'm around now, and I want to help you. I wasn't sure about Kevin and Ashley at first, but they seem like good people. But I think I'm going to make arrangements to move in here to help them look after you. I mean, they do so much for you, but you're my sister. We're family. I want to be here for you. What do you think about that? Is there room for me?"

"That's really kind of you. But honestly, you don't need to do that."

"I want to. Even if it's just for a couple of days. We've only just reconnected. I can't abandon you now."

But before I can answer, my mobile rings.

26

W e both stare at my phone. I can't remember the last time it rang.

"Do you want me to get it?" Tim asks after a while.

"No, I can manage. It might be Alice and Edwin." I pick up my phone and see it's a mobile number that I don't have saved in my contacts.

I answer with a tentative, "Hello?"

The male voice on the other end sounds familiar but polished and professional. "Hello, Ms Donovan?"

"Speaking," I reply, expecting some kind of sales pitch or junk call.

"Hi, it's Kiran Ramesh from Scott and Sons Estate Agents. I'm just following up to get the ball rolling on the property you put an offer on this morning via email."

"I'm sorry... property? What property?"

"Yes, number forty-three Willacre Drive in Worle. You offered double the asking price, cash. Which, of course, was accepted immediately. You must really want it, and I can understand why. The house is definitely a doer-upper but has so much potential. Would you be able to share your solicitors' details?"

My frazzled mind throbs, attempting to decipher his words. I have no idea what he's talking about. Open-mouthed, I glance at Tim.

He mouths, "Who is it?"

Kiran says, "Ms Donovan? Are you still there?"

"I... er... can I call you back?"

"Certainly," he says cheerily. "I'm here until six and in tomorrow all day."

I hang up and shake my head.

"What was that all about?" Tim asks.

"It was an estate agent. Apparently, I put an offer in on a house this morning. Double the asking price."

"What?" Tim blurts.

"I don't remember doing it, Tim," I say, alarmed.

I grab my laptop off the coffee table to power it up. When I lift up the lid, I realise it's already on. The first thing I see is a browser open with a house listed on an estate agent's website. I look closer – it's 43 Willacre Drive in Worle. I click through the photos of the house.

It's an absolute dump with rotting walls, holes in the floor, and an overgrown garden. What was I thinking?

I look at the asking price and nearly choke when I realise I must've offered half a million pounds for this place.

There's a tab with my email inbox already open. I click into it and navigate to the Sent Items folder. There at the top is the email to the estate agents, sent at 10.18 a.m.

I reopen the house listing page and hand my laptop to Tim.

He scans the page and then clicks through the photos. "Jesus, Jess, this is a hellhole. I wouldn't touch this place with a barge pole and would strongly advise my clients not to, either. But if it's somewhere you've got your heart set on—"

"No! I definitely don't want to buy it." My voice rises a pitch or two. What else have I done that I don't remember? What else could I do?

"Okay, don't panic. Call the estate agent back and withdraw your offer."

Panic pitter-patters around my lungs, and my breath comes in short, shallow bursts. "I can't..." I manage.

"Stay calm. Don't worry about a thing. I'll do it." He holds out his hand, and I give him my phone. It's already unlocked, and he taps the screen a few times and holds it to his ear. I hear the faint sound of the dial tone, and a man answers.

Tim stands and paces around the room. "Hello, I'm calling on behalf of Jess Salmon."

I catch his eye and shake my head.

"Jess Andrews," he says my married name, and I shake my head again.

"Donovan," I whisper.

"Jess Donovan," he says finally. "I believe she made an offer on a property. Who am I speaking with?"

The voice on the other end talks, and I hear a low murmur, but I don't hear the exact words.

Tim listens patiently and nods. "Kiran, thank you for following up, but Jess would like to withdraw that offer. She's had a change of heart and doesn't feel it's the right place for her anymore."

There's some more chatter from Kiran, and then Tim hands me the phone. "Kiran would just like to hear it from you."

"Hi, Kiran?"

"Yes," he replies moodily.

"This is Jess Donovan. I'd like to withdraw the offer."

"Understood. Well, we're here if you change your mind or if you see anything else on our books that takes your interest. Just call me direct or call the main switchboard."

"Thanks." I hand the phone back to Tim.

Tim lifts it to his ear, then lowers it and places it on the coffee table. "He's rung off."

"I can't believe I did that," I whisper. "What a mess that could've been. I feel like I'm going insane."

"No harm done."

"This time. What happens if I do something crazy like that again?"

Tim just looks at me. He chews at his lip. I can tell he can't think of anything to say that might alleviate my worries. Then he says, "Your medication should kick in soon."

I nod. Soon. But not soon enough – a couple of weeks. What could happen in that time? I try to buy another dump? I give all my money away to charity? I spend it all on lottery tickets? I have around one million pounds from the Oxford house sale sat waiting in a couple of savings accounts and safe investments for when I'm ready to buy somewhere. I can't trust myself with it. I can't trust myself to handle my own affairs, full stop.

Maybe the doctor was right. I need someone else to manage these things while I'm unwell. I've proven myself unfit. I'm worse than I was before, when Aunt Alice came to look after me. I didn't have blackouts then or hallucinations. Those are new symptoms and are more worrying. I grab my phone and search for 'power of attorney'.

I read the government website:

A lasting power of attorney (LPA) is a legal document that lets you (the 'donor') appoint one or more people (known as 'attorneys') to help you make decisions or to make decisions on your behalf. This gives you more control over what happens to you if you have an accident or an illness and cannot make your own decisions (you 'lack mental capacity').

I scan down the page. There are two types of LPA: Health and Welfare, and Property and Financial Affairs. I can choose to make one type or both. Health and Welfare will give my attorney the power to make decisions on things like my daily routine like washing, dressing and eating, medical care, and life-sustaining treatment.

The second one gives me pause. A property and financial affairs LPA gives an attorney the power to make decisions about money and property. Things like managing a bank account, paying bills, selling a home. It can be used as soon as it's registered as long as I give my permission.

I look up at Tim. He's patiently waiting for me and tugs at his beard nervously. Could I really sign myself over to him? Or to Ashley and Kevin? Would any of them want to do it? Want the responsibility? There's no way I'm going to get Alice and Edwin to call short their holiday to come back and care for me. It's their once-in-a-lifetime trip. I can't ruin that. It would have to be Tim, as a family member.

I sigh heavily. It's a massive thing, to sign everything over to someone else, but I'm clearly not capable of taking care of myself or my affairs right now. So what other choice do I have? And really, they wouldn't need to do all that much, just keep me fed and taking my medications and keep me away from my bank accounts so I don't do anything stupid while I'm out of it. Maybe by changing the passwords and not letting me know, or something like that, so I couldn't log in. It would only be for a while, and then when I'm better, we'd put everything straight again.

Perhaps Tim's moving in is a good idea. And then I can see how I go and approach the power of attorney with him after a few days.

"Tim, I'd really like you to move in. I think I need your help. You're right, you're family. Ashley and Kevin are incredible friends, but I've already put so much on them. Hopefully, it won't be for too long."

"That's absolutely fine. And I can stay for as long as you need me."

I nod. He stands and comes over with his arms out. I heave myself off the sofa and hug him back.

"Thank you," I mumble into his shoulder. He's much taller than me. Always has been, ever since we were children.

He steps back and smiles. "I've got a few bits to sort out tomorrow, but I can probably move in on Sunday, if that works with you?"

"Sounds good. Sunday it is."

"Should I go and let Ashley and Kevin know?"

"No, I'll do it." I head from the room and towards the kitchen with my brother following.

Kevin is cleaning the kitchen fervently, his face inches away from the sink as he scrubs, while Ashley lounges to one side, drinking another glass of wine and painting her nails on the kitchen counter. Doug sits at her feet. I bend down and pick him up. He feels chilly, and I guess they've only just got back from their walk to the shop.

"Guys, you've been so good to me, but I've asked if Tim wouldn't mind moving in to help me. I'm really struggling and need all the help I can get."

Kevin stops what he's doing and looks up. A weird look ripples around the three of them. Kevin looks at Ashley; Ashley glares at Tim; Tim flicks his eyes between the two of them. I'm too exhausted to decipher what it means. If, in fact, it means anything. It's likely just my mind playing tricks on me again.

Ashley steps closer to me, her hands in the air and fingers splayed so as not to smudge her drying polish, and nudges me to one side with an elbow and a pointed look. "Are you sure?" she whispers and glances back over her shoulder at Tim.

"I'm sure," I say, thankful once again that I have such a protective friend.

She smiles, then turns to Tim. "Great news," she says.

Kevin blinks twice at her and then turns back to his cleaning, attacking the taps with zeal.

Tim frowns at her and looks confused. I realise that he might've thought that they would move out. But I don't want them to go anywhere. They've been so good to me. Ashley has been such a great friend, and Kevin, although a bit nerdy, has really looked out for me.

"You guys can stay for as long as you like," I say to Ashley. "It's a big house. There's plenty of space."

Kevin's tense demeanour seems to soften.

She comes over and gives me a hug. "We're worried about you, so we'll stay a bit longer, just to make sure you're getting better." She turns to Tim. "The more the merrier, hey?"

His face transforms as he beams at Ashley. "Absolutely," he says.

27

Coming awake, I notice it's pitch-black outside. I reach for my phone and check the screen. It's Saturday and almost midnight. I've slept all day. I took my first antidepressant at dinner last night, then another when Ashley woke me up with breakfast, and I don't remember anything else of the day. It's like a complete blackout. A void.

Did Ashley or Kevin bring me dinner and another pill to take? I'm certain they would've, Kevin being a stickler about the instructions. But I have no memory of it.

I feel utterly exhausted. Groggy. I know depression causes fatigue, and I remember sleeping a lot before, but I've pretty much been out for the count for twenty-four hours. Perhaps it's the medication that's screwing up my body clock and making me drowsy. A side effect.

The house is still. Ashley and Kevin must be in bed. I switch on the bedside lamp and scrunch up my eyes, opening them crack by crack until they're used to the brightness. Doug is curled up in his spot on the end of my bed tonight. I watch his little body rise and fall. He's not snoring for once and looks like a scruffy little teddy bear.

A soft tapping on the door startles me from my stupor, and my heart thuds like a herd of elephants stampeding.

Calm down, Jess. It must be Ashley or Kevin still awake. They've no doubt noticed my light glowing from under the door. "Come in," I say as I put my glasses on.

The door opens slowly, silently, and a boy's head pokes around.

It's the boy from the other night. My son.

Oh God, I'm having another hallucination. Or perhaps I'm still asleep. But this all feels so real. I suppose that's what happens in your mind. You dream about waking up, but you're actually still dreaming.

I've completely lost the plot. I know that now. I'm so lucky to have people here to care for me. I could just shout, and Ashley or Kevin or both would come running. And soon, Tim will be here. I'm so fortunate he's here too, that we've put our differences from the past behind us. Maybe when I'm well again, it's time I give him his share of the inheritance.

I'd used all the money to buy the house in Oxford. But I definitely have fifty thousand pounds I could give him now. I doubt he'd take it from me. He's done so well for himself anyway. It's clear he understands why I didn't give it to him before.

The boy creeps in and sits on the end of my bed. My thoughts return to the present from my Tim tangent. It's odd. I can feel the weight of my son, feel him pressing against my foot, see the duvet crumple where he's sat. But it's just my imagination. He's an apparition of my first dead baby grown up.

"Hi," he whispers.

I should force myself to wake up, to accept he's not really here. But I'm eager to find out more about him after our first meeting, after discovering he loves pigeons and slurping spaghetti and wants to be a potions-making scientist. He seems so real. And well, what the hell? I doubt my brain will do anything I want it to right now, anyway. "Hi," I reply.

Doug stirs and then opens an eye. He stretches out his legs, and we both watch him. Then he stands, stretches some more, and pads over to the boy, looking for fuss. The boy picks him up and puts him on his lap, stroking his fur. Doug licks his hand, and the boy laughs.

This is so bizarre. Am I imagining that the dog can also see my vision? Or am I imagining Doug, and he's actually asleep downstairs on the window seat? Who knows?

"We often meet in the middle of the night for a cuddle, don't we, Doug?" the boy says and continues to pat the dog. Doug laps it up, then woofs in happiness.

"Shh," the boy says urgently, "you'll wake up Mummy and Daddy. And we don't want that, do we? Not when I'm with my new friend." He looks up at me and beams.

Wake Mummy and Daddy...

Something's not right here. Something doesn't add up. My brain aches with thinking. I scrutinise the boy. He's skinny, short, with pale skin and a small mole next to the bridge of his nose on the right side. He's wearing a blue-and-white striped dressing gown and pale-blue button-down pyjamas and Spider-Man socks. His light-brown hair is neatly trimmed, clearly using clippers, but not too short. And he has green eyes.

He notices me looking at his socks and pulls out a small Spider-Man figure from his dressing gown pocket.

"I love Spider-Man," he says.

"I love superheroes too," I reply.

He hands me the figure. I hesitate.

He gestures again for me to hold it. "Go on, you can have a look."

I take it from him. It's solid. It's real.

And that's when it hits me. He's solid. He's real. With eyes like Ashley's and a haircut just like Kevin's.

Oh God.

He takes Spider-Man back and slots the figure back into his pocket. From the other pocket he pulls out a small pot. "Look, I brought us some slime to play with."

"Cool," I say. He scoops the purple putty out of the pot and splits it in two, handing me a blob. We both squidge and pull apart and roll it into balls.

After a while of playing, I ask as casually as possible, "So, um, are Ashley and Kevin your parents?"

"Uh-huh. But you can't tell them that you've seen me? Promise? I'm not allowed out of the bedroom. They don't know I sneak out at night. But I just get *sooooo* bored in there. And it's so hard being quiet all the time."

Ashley and Kevin have a son! I remain calm and focus on playing with the slime. I don't want to scare him away. He demonstrates how to fold the putty to make a bubble, and I ask, "How long have you been in that room?"

He pops his bubble and grins. "I moved in when Daddy did. Mummy was already here. I am allowed out sometimes, when you're out or asleep. And when Daddy pretends to Mummy that he's taking me to hospital."

"Pretends?"

"Can we be friends? I've never had a proper friend." He looks forlornly at his hands, and his bottom lip quivers.

"Yes, I'm your friend." I reach out and hold up my palm.

"Yippee." He high-fives me. He puts his slime back in the pot and takes my blob and pushes it on top, placing the pot back in his pocket. "I've brought *Harry Potter* for us to read." He produces a tatty copy of the first book from up the sleeve of his dressing gown. "Do you want to read it out loud? We could take turns. You can go first."

"Sounds great. I'd love to." I take the book from him and open to the first page. "Before we start, though, what did you mean by 'pretends'?"

His face perks up, and he leans towards me conspiratorially. "Can you keep a secret? That's what friends do, isn't it?"

"Yes, I can keep a secret."

"Well, Daddy makes me lie to Mummy. We've been doing it for four years now, since I was six. But I don't really want to do it anymore. I love Mummy, and it makes me feel bad."

"Lying about what, exactly?"

"That I've got"—he pronounces each word carefully and precisely, as if he's rehearsed them many times—"chronic recurrent multifocal osteomyelitis." He lets out a breath, clearly relieved he's said it correctly. "Or CRMO. It's this condition that means I can't go outside due to my weak immune system and risk of fractures. Daddy picked it because someone with it looks normal but has bone pain, which is easy for me to fake. It's managed with medication I swallow and can go away permanently. That's what Mummy's hoping for, anyway. But Daddy won't let me tell her the truth. When I'm with her, I have to pretend to limp and be in pain. She thinks I rarely go outside because I might catch something."

"Whoa," I say. "That's a big secret."

"Yep."

"Why is Kevin – your daddy – making you lie?"

"Because Daddy loves Mummy *sooooo* much, but I don't think Mummy loves him anymore."

"Why don't you tell your mummy?"

His voice rises a pitch or two. "Because then she'll leave us! Daddy says she only stays with us because I'm ill. And I can't be left with just Daddy. I just can't. He's never really loved me like Mummy loves me. He's only nice to me when Mummy's there."

His face screws up, and I think he might cry.

"It's okay," I soothe.

"Mummy thinks I'm taking lots of medicines, but I'm not really. Sometimes, he gives me pills to sleep because I'm so bored on my own, and she thinks it's because I'm unwell."

"Pills to make you sleep?"

"Oh yes, Daddy has a whole cupboard full of all sorts."

The penny dropping clatters in my head.

"What's your name? If we're going to be best friends, I need to know your name. I'm Jess."

"I know your name, silly. You're pretty much all Mummy and Daddy talk about." He chuckles softly, and I swallow back my growing unease. "I'm Noah."

"Noah, can you show me this cupboard?"

"No way!"

"Please?"

He squirms and twists, debating this request. "All right. But you can't tell them. And we can't get caught. And after we see it, we'll read some *Harry Potter*, deal?"

"Deal."

He picks up the book and stuffs it back up his sleeve.

28

We tiptoe from my room. Noah leads the way, holding my hand tightly. He takes two steps, stops, listens, and then turns to me with his finger to his lips. I nod back.

We repeat this until we're right outside the back bedroom – Ashley and Kevin's bedroom. And Noah's. Noah has been living in that room the entire time Kevin has been here. That's been a week. I still can't believe it.

But he's real. His firm grip on my hand tells me that.

The door is ajar, clearly left open by Noah as he snuck out earlier. He drops my hand and leans in close to me.

"They're heavy sleepers, but don't make any noise. Just in case," he whispers in my ear.

He gestures for me to stay put as he creeps forward and sticks his head around the door to peer into the bedroom. He takes a few steps further into the bedroom.

I can hear a heavy snore and a gentle snore. They are almost in unison, so it's like one continuous snore. I wonder how Noah can sleep with that racket. But that's probably why he wanders at night, to get away from the cacophony made by his parents.

I can also hear my own breathing. It's shallow and harsh. Noisy. I take a few deliberate, silent breaths, focusing on calming my racing pulse.

Eventually, Noah deems it safe and beckons me in.

I creep forward. The room smells musty, of too many bodies and night-time breath. It reminds me of the unpleasant aroma of some of the hostel multi-bunk dorm rooms that I stayed in when I was away. It's not a particularly large room. It's lit faintly by a small nightlight plugged into a socket near the door. I glance at the double bed and see two sleeping lumps under the covers. Ashley and Kevin, I know, but I can't quite see any distinguishing features. Then I notice a small sleeping bag in the corner on top of what looks like a single blow-up mattress. Noah's bed.

I haven't been in this room since Ashley had her miscarriage. And before that, I'd only been in once. Aunt Alice showed it to me when I had first arrived. It's known as the back bedroom but could also be the blue room, with blue bedsheets, painted walls and Aztec-patterned curtains in various shades of the hue. There are two big wooden wardrobes, a chest of drawers painted a light blue, and a dark-wood cupboard.

Noah points to the cupboard next to the bed. It's a little bit taller than me and thankfully on this side of the room, close to the door and the dim nightlight.

I reach for the handle. But Noah grabs my arms and frantically shakes his head.

Oh shit.

I glance at the sleeping figures, but they don't move. The snoring continues, perfectly in time. Noah jabs his finger at the other door handle.

"That side squeaks," he says in a barely audible voice.

I give him a thumbs-up to show I understand and put my hand on the other side. I pull the door open slowly and gently. There are shelves of men's clothes neatly folded – I'm not sure if they belong to Kevin or my uncle.

But on a shelf directly eye level, there are rows and rows of orange and brown pill bottles, medication boxes, plastic baggies of powdery substances, and glass dropper bottles containing clear liquid.

It's all perfectly lined up, with the labels facing out. And I know this is Kevin's hoard. I pick up one orange bottle and read *GHB* on the label. Another bottle reads *Lysergic Acid Diethylamide*. Then a blister packet of bright blue tablets that reads *Eszopiclone*. One box reads *Megestrol*.

My heart topples out of my chest as if given a massive shove and lands somewhere near my feet. Is Kevin drugging me? Why? How?

And does Ashley know? She can't know; she's such a great friend. He must be lying to her about me like he's lying about Noah. Oh fuck. Perhaps he's jealous of our relationship, like he's clearly jealous of Ashley's love for her son. He wants her all for himself. Drugging me gets me out of the picture. He puts it in the food, that has to be it. That's why he makes three versions of every meal – not because Ashley likes spice and because he's vegan but to make sure she's not eating any of the drugs.

Then I notice what looks like a baby's foot on the shelf, but I can't see the rest because it's hidden behind the squeaky door. A doll?

But before this can sink in, Noah grabs my arm and yanks it down. I drop to the floor into a foetal position, curling up as small as I can muster, as Kevin's voice grumbles, "Noah?"

I lie like a log on the carpet next to the bed. What will Kevin do if he finds me? What is he capable of? He comes across as meek and mild, but he's a tall, strong man – he's not skinny. I couldn't overpower him. I need to tell Ashley when he's not around. He's clearly dangerous.

"It's only me, Daddy," Noah whispers. "Just went to the loo."

Kevin tuts. "You know you should be doing it in your bottle unless I give you the all-clear to leave the room."

"Sorry, Daddy. But it felt like a really big one, and I didn't think the bottle would hold it all."

Kevin huffs impatiently, and the bed creaks.

Oh shit, is he getting up? He'll swing his legs down, and his feet will land right on me. I attempt to shuffle under the bed, but the rustling gives me away. I freeze. Noah coughs to cover the noise.

Then Ashley murmurs, "No harm done, Kevin. You go back to sleep now, Noah, baby."

"Yes, Mummy. Love you."

"Love you too, my little Spider-Man," she says automatically, still half asleep.

Noah gets into his sleeping bag, and I hear it rustle a few times and then go still. Kevin and Ashley shift positions on the bed.

My muscles are so tense I feel as if I might crack apart. But I wait. The breathing gets heavier, heavier, until the heavy snoring starts up again. Then the gentler snore begins, and after a while, they fall into unison again.

There's no movement from Noah. Should I crawl out? Or wait for him?

The indecision is killing me. My mouth is dry, and I'm starting to feel dizzy. But then Noah is there. He moved so silently that I didn't even notice. He helps me up and ushers me out, closing the cupboard door as I pass, and then the bedroom door behind us.

We linger in the hallway outside my bedroom. He looks at me with glee, clearly exhilarated by our close call. He looks very alive in that moment. I can almost feel the energy coming off him.

Why didn't Ashley tell me about him? Having a child is a pretty big deal and not something you keep hidden from a friend. Is it to do with his illness? Or something to do with Kevin?

Noah looks at me eagerly.

"You were very brave," I say.

"As brave as Spider-Man?"

"Braver."

He grins.

I hold up a closed hand, and he fist-bumps me. "Noah, does your mummy know about what's in the cupboard?"

"Uh-huh, she thinks it's my medication and your medication."

Terror seeps into every part of my being. Ashley knows about the drugs. She must be in on it. I stand up straight again. He points towards the back bedroom and whispers, "We'll read tomorrow night. I'd better get back." He waves and then skips back there, closing the door behind him.

I pause in the hallway until I'm certain I can't hear anything.

Back in my room, I grab my phone and google 'GHB'. It's an illegal drug, also known as the date-rape drug, because it causes sedative and anaesthetic effects. Is that what they gave me at breakfast that made me sleep all day? Is that why I can't remember things?

I search for 'lysergic' and discover it's LSD – acid – an illegal drug that causes hallucinations. Then I look up 'eszo' because I can't remember the weird spelling. But those four letters are enough to tell me that it's a drug that is prescribed to help with insomnia. Sleeping pills. Then I remember the last name and type it in. Megestrol is an appetite stimulant used to treat anorexia.

That hallucination was because they gave me LSD. And that baby's foot in the cupboard was a doll. They must've put a baby doll on the ceiling and played wailing from a hidden speaker. And they've been giving me drugs to make me hungry so I eat their tainted food.

Oh my God.

What were they planning to do? Keep me incapacitated so that they could live in this house rent-free? I pay for all the food and bills. They could be here for the next nine months until my aunt and uncle return. Why the hell didn't they tell me about Noah? I would've felt weird having the whole family in the house, that's why. Better to keep him a secret.

So that's what they are – scroungers looking for a free ride.

Ashley isn't really my friend. It was all an act just to get in the house. And Kevin is lying to Ashley about Noah? They are one seriously screwed-up family, and I'm in the middle of it. Was I a mark from the beginning? Or was it just an awful coincidence that I told Ashley I lived in a big house on my own when I first met her?

And then it dawns on me. They must be the ones who were targeting me, pretending to stalk me and leaving that rotting fish. It has to be them. It was all done to make me vulnerable so I'd invite them into my house and want them here because I was scared to be on my own.

I need to get out of here. No. I need to get *them* out of here. Out of my home. Out of my aunt and uncle's house.

29

I dial Tim's mobile. I know the police won't believe me. They'll think I have completely lost the plot. And Dr Clegg would confirm it. But he only thinks I'm having a mental health breakdown because Ashley and Kevin have been drugging me.

Tim doesn't answer. It's 4 a.m., so I'm not surprised.

His voicemail clicks on, and I leave a message:

"Tim, it's me, Jess. You have to come over as soon as you get this. It's Ashley and Kevin. They aren't who we think they are. They're out to get me, to live in this house. They're not my friends. They've been drugging me, making me have hallucinations, all sorts. I've seen the cupboard – Kevin has a cupboard full of drugs in their bedroom. And – get this – there's a boy living in that room. Their son! Tim, you need to come and save me. We need to get them out of the house. But don't let on that you know when you see them, okay? We need to work out a way to make them leave. They're danger-ous. I just know it."

I hang up and stare at the phone. I know I'll have to wait until the morning for him to reply. I pace my room, but my head starts to pound, and my entire body feels heavy, as if I can't support it anymore. I lie down. I know this must be a side effect of the drugs they've been giving me.

I rub my temples and close my eyes, and before I know it, sleep swallows me.

"Morning," Ashley says brightly. She comes into my room and opens the curtains. "It's a beautiful spring day out there. How are you feeling?"

I prop myself up in bed. I need to play this right. I can't alert them to the fact that I know their secret, that I've sussed out their game, that I know they're con artists, grifters. That I now know that everything that comes from their mouths is false. That might make them do something stupid.

"Morning," I reply. "Feeling really groggy."

Kevin follows her in with a tray of food. "It's Sunday, so you know what that means – full English, of course. And there's your medication to take once you've eaten. Always better on a full stomach."

He places the tray on my lap. It looks delicious, and my stomach grumbles. But I'm guessing that's because they've been giving me appetite stimulants to counteract the side effects of so many drugs, one of which must be loss of appetite.

"Thanks, Kevin. It looks amazing, but I'm really not hungry."

I look at the tea. But don't dare drink that, either.

"You need to eat, Jess, to keep your strength up," Ashley says, and she moves closer to Kevin, linking her arm through his.

They stand over my bed, and for the first time since they've been in my house, I'm terrified of them. Who are these people?

"Just try a mouthful," Kevin encourages.

"But I'm really not—"

"One mouthful," Ashley insists. Her voice has an edge that I've never noticed before. She stares at me. It's not kindly or friendly.

"Just eat a little, and we'll leave you be," Kevin says. "We can't let you starve. And you'll feel better taking your antidepressant after eating."

They watch me closely, and it's clear they won't leave until I've eaten. I need them out of my room, away from me. This close, they're unpredictable and could easily sink their claws deeper in me. I smile tightly at them. I pick up a forkful of mushrooms and force it into my mouth. I chew and mmm as if I'm appreciating the food and then make a show of swallowing.

"Delicious," I say.

"Just a little more," Ashley urges. "Do you want me to help you? We're really worried about you. The least we can do is make sure you don't waste away."

Will they force-feed me if I don't eat? That seems to be what Ashley is implying by her offering to 'help' me. I quickly shovel in a few more mouthfuls.

"And now your medication," Kevin says and points to the little pill that he's put in a shot glass.

I pop it in my mouth and take a sip of tea.

Ashley squeezes my shoulder. "Well done, mate. You'll be right as rain in no time."

Kevin takes the tray off my lap.

Ashley continues, "Do you want to come downstairs? Watch some crap weekend telly with me?"

I shake my head, then edge down in the bed and turn my back to them.

"Let's let her sleep," Kevin says.

They leave the room, and I hear the door close. I listen as

they both traipse down the stairs. As soon as I can't hear them anymore, I jump up from the bed and pull the old-style sash window down. The bottom doesn't move, only the top pane. I pull over the pink velvet bedside chair and knock off my pile of clothes that have accumulated on top of it. I stand on the seat.

I lean out the window, the bottom pane as high as my waist, and spit the pill out from under my tongue. I've no idea what it is. It's unlikely to be the antidepressants the doctor prescribed me. It could be absolutely anything from Kevin's little stash in the cupboard. Then I stick my fingers down my throat and vomit.

It splatters on the flat roof. This roof can only be seen from my window. It's the extension off the kitchen with the utility area and back door.

After I've purged, I feel more lucid. I can't trust anything they give me to eat or drink. I know this now. But I do still feel weird. I don't know what cocktail of drugs they've been feeding me, but perhaps this spaced-out feeling is a side effect. Or maybe it's a withdrawal kicking in now some of the drugs are wearing off. Either way, I almost fall off the chair, my head spinning. I land on the floor with a thump. Although my mind feels clearer, my body is struggling.

Maybe some of the tainted breakfast managed to get into my system? I head to the bathroom and stick my head under the cold tap, drinking greedily. Water from the tap is clean. They can't tamper with that.

After I glug a few mouthfuls, I wash my face and replace my glasses. I feel marginally better.

The doorbell goes. *Tim! Oh, please, let it be my brother.*

30

I haul myself out of the bathroom and to the top of the stairs. I watch as Kevin goes to the door. I hear Tim's voice.

Relief sweeps through me like a fire in a field. But I have to play this right. I mess up my hair and stumble down the stairs in my pyjamas and dressing gown. "Timmm."

"Jess, are you okay?" Tim shouts up the stairs.

"Jess!" Kevin launches himself up the stairs to catch me as I trip, and helps me down. "I gather you wanted to watch the television after all," he jokes and attempts a little laugh.

Ashley comes running from the kitchen and takes my other arm. Together, they help me into the lounge. I drag my feet as if I can't pick up my legs and let them place me on the sofa and tuck a blanket around me.

"I haven't seen you in *weeeeeeks*, bro," I garble.

"I was here on Friday. It's Sunday," he replies, his face full of concern. He glances at Ashley.

She catches his eye and looks at her feet. She looks sad, worried. But I know it's all an act. Kevin hugs her to him.

"She's not doing so well today," Kevin says to Tim, his voice tinged with sadness and worry too. Faker.

They're both faking it. I need to get Tim on his own.

Kevin continues, "Jess wasn't really hungry this morning. Only ate half her breakfast. Which isn't like her, because she's always got a good appetite."

Yeah, because you're giving me a drug that makes me hungry! I feel like bellowing, but I don't. I have to keep my cool, maintain the advantage.

"Can I talk to my big bro? I need to tell him what happened to that CD I stole and said I didn't when we were kids." I turn the corners of my mouth down in an exaggerated upset face.

Tim gestures to them that he's got this, and they retreat without question, closing the door behind them.

He sits on the stool that the doctor sat on, close to me. Articulating every word carefully, as if I'm blind drunk, he says, "Jess, I've got my bags in the car. I'm going to move in. Do you remember us talking about that?"

I swing my legs out so I'm sitting bolt upright and angle myself toward him. "Tim, did you get my voicemail?"

He reels back at the sudden change in my manner. "Er, no, what voicemail?"

"Doesn't matter. Don't make a sound, okay? Or say anything just yet, but Ashley and Kevin are drugging me."

"What?" Disbelief rings loud and clear in his tone.

"I've seen their cupboard full of illegal drugs. I vomited up their food this morning, and I feel better. I'll never eat or drink anything they give me again – and you shouldn't either. I don't know what their game is, but they're up to something. They're dangerous."

"Jess..." Tim says my name in a way that sounds immediately like he doesn't believe me.

"Listen to me, I'm not crazy. I'm being manipulated. They have a son who has been hidden in their room for the last week. I've seen him."

"This all sounds a bit far-fetched. Have you taken your antidepressant this morning?"

"No, I spat it out. I didn't know if that's what it was, anyway. And I don't need to take it." I grab his arm. "Tim, they're lunatics. You need to help me."

Tim sighs deeply and takes my hand, gently undoing the vice-like grip I have on his bicep, and holds it in his. He still thinks I'm having a mental health breakdown. It's obvious. I know I must appear like a babbling fool concocting improbable fantasies – perhaps some of the drugs are still in my system? – but I have to convince him.

I continue, "I'll show you. And then you can tell the police and get this sorted."

"The police?"

"Yes. They'll think I've lost the plot because of the doctor's diagnosis, but they'll believe you. You're a rational, credible witness."

"Oh, sis, I'm so worried about you. I think you're really unwell."

"I'm not, though! I'm *perfectly healthy*!"

"I know this might be hard to comprehend right now, but I think you're having a paranoid delusion. I was looking up lots of stuff last night about your condition. And maybe it's worse than we thought. Perhaps I should get the doctor back."

I let out a frustrated '*aaaarrrggghhhh*'. "Tim, they're drugging me."

"Ashley and Kevin have been great friends to you. They've really looked after you. There's no boy in the house. Why would they have a child here and not say anything? That makes absolutely no sense. You're having irrational thoughts that are simply not true."

"I'm telling the truth," I insist. There's only one way to prove it to Tim.

I stand abruptly and strike out for the door. Tim follows. "I'll show you. You can see the cupboard and the boy for yourself. As proof."

"Sure," Tim says in a defeated voice. He appears resigned, as if playing along with my fantasy. But I know it's true. And soon, he will too.

Kevin and Ashley are still in the kitchen as we head up the stairs. I move quickly. I can't risk them stopping us. I grab Tim's wrist. "Hurry up! Before they catch us."

We take the stairs two at a time.

"Get your phone out," I tell Tim at the top. "Take photos, in case they try to cover things up later."

Tim does as instructed and gets his phone out of his back pocket.

I slam open the back bedroom door, hoping to catch Noah unawares. I don't want to frighten the boy, but Tim needs to see him before he can hide. Then I immediately pull open both the doors to the cupboard, the hinge on the left one squeaking as Noah said it would.

"See, look!" I move out of the way and point in the cupboard.

Tim stares in at it. "I see jumpers."

"What?"

I stick my head into the cupboard. The shelf eye level with me, last night full of rows of medication, is full of neatly folded clothes. I pull them out onto the floor, stick my arms in and sweep from side to side and reach right to the back.

"No, no! Where are all the drugs? The bottles and boxes and bags..."

I spin around and point at the floor. "The boy!" I yell but then choke on my words.

There's no blow-up mattress. There's no sleeping bag. And there's no Noah.

31

"They must've moved everything!" I protest. "He was right there, I swear it."

I grab the front of Tim's jumper and yank, attempting to pull him closer to the spot where Noah was last night. But Tim doesn't move. He rests his hands lightly on the tops of my arms as if to steady me.

I continue, "We have to search the room... the house... We need to get them out... We..." But I know deep down that there's no point.

The despairing, troubled look on Tim's face says it all. He's close to tears. He slowly shakes his head at me. And I know. I let go of his jumper and put my hand to my mouth. It was another hallucination. A paranoid delusion. I'm stunned by the realisation. I wobble, and Tim's hold on my arms keeps me from tumbling into an abyss.

That's it. Game's up. I've finally lost it.

I made it all up. The boy, the drugs. My mind has shattered, and the fragments are scattered here, there and everywhere. I'm not sure I'll ever piece it together again.

Tim gently guides me out of the room and into the hallway, soothingly saying things like "There, there" and "Easy does it."

I gape. I'm speechless. It was all so real last night. I was so certain about it all.

A few steps are all I can manage before I fall in a heap on the hallway floor. I cling onto Tim's hand, looking up at him as if he's saving me from drowning.

"I need help," I wail at him. "You need to help me!"

"Anything. What can I do?"

What can he do? The doctor prescribed me medication. He said this breakdown could go on for months and that if it got worse, I'd need to go into a facility. Oh, fuck, no, I don't want that. What was it the doctor had said...? I read about it on a website... *help when someone lacks mental capacity and can't make decisions for themselves...*

The solution materialises so suddenly I start. My brain fixes on it, and it's all I can think about. "Will you sort power of attorney? Please, Tim, please."

"Er..." He shifts his feet uncomfortably.

"I know it's a lot to ask, but I read up about it. It shouldn't take too long to get it certified once it's sent off, and we need witnesses and a solicitor to sign the document."

He considers me for a long, sad moment. "I think that might be best. We'll have to get Aunt Alice and Uncle Edwin back from their cruise."

"No! I can't ruin their holiday, I just can't. I'd never live with the guilt of cutting short their once-in-a-lifetime trip. You can be my attorney. I can't trust myself anymore. I can't wait for them to get back. Please, Tim."

He chews his lips. "All right, Jess."

"Can you get a solicitor here tomorrow with the papers? Get them to come to the house? Ashley and Kevin can be witnesses."

He nods. "I'll sort it all out. Don't worry."

I rest my forehead on his hand. "Thank you, thank you."

"Let's get you back to bed, hmm? And then I can move my stuff in. Ashley says there's a bedroom at the front that I could probably take. Would that be okay?"

"Yeah, of course. Ashley knows best."

Overwhelm presses heavily down on me, and I hang my head, staring at the carpet. I just want to shrivel up into nothingness.

"Come on, I'll help you up," Tim says and puts a firm hand under my armpit.

As he heaves, I notice something by my knee. It's the belt of a dressing gown. I ponder it for a moment. It's not my dressing gown. Mine is white. I follow it with my eyes. It's poking out from under the door to the airing cupboard. It's striped blue and white.

A distinctive blue-and-white dressing gown... *It's Noah's!* He's worn it both times I've seen him. The airing cupboard door isn't quite closed properly. *He has to be hiding in there!* I shove off Tim's hand and yank open the airing cupboard.

Hidden under the boiler is Noah. He's all bunched up, pressed into the towels and bedsheets.

I turn to Tim. "See! He's real. That's the boy! They made him hide, and they've moved all the drugs. They must've known I'd found them." I see the phone in Tim's hand. "I'm calling the police."

I grab the phone, but Tim won't let go. He snatches it away from me and holds it high in the air.

Noah crawls out of his hiding place and looks up. His face falls as he sees my brother, and he cowers, tears springing to his eyes.

He whimpers, "I'm so sorry, Tim. I didn't mean to do it. I didn't mean to let her see me."

32

"**D**o you know him?" I ask Noah.

He glances up at Tim and then at me. He wipes his nose with the sleeve of his dressing gown. "Uh-huh. He knows Mummy and Daddy."

I glare at Tim.

My brother's eyes are scrunched, lips pursed, a deep furrow between his brows. He pinches the bridge of his nose. I stand slowly. His expression calms, and his face changes before my eyes into one of friendly concern once again.

He smiles at Noah, and then his gaze falls sadly on me. "Of course I know Noah, Jess. You do too. He's been here all along. You've met him numerous times, had dinner together. You told Ashley and Kevin they could move him in. Don't you remember? Oh, sis, you're very confused about everything."

I stare at Tim. My instincts tell me to trust him. But my instincts aren't always right. In fact, they've often let me down. I'm too trusting. It's a lie. It must be. But then, I can't tell truth from fiction, and I have whole days that I can't remember. I'm torn with indecision.

Noah clears his throat timidly and says innocently, "Oh, no, we've never had dinner together. This is only the third time we've met."

Why would this boy lie? What's in it for him? I glance at Tim. All the muscles in his face harden, and a vein bulges in his neck. He gives Noah a look like he's about to tear him to shreds. And that's when I know Noah speaks the truth.

I gesture at Tim. "Nothing you say is true. You're in on this with them, aren't you?"

I launch myself at him, grabbing for his phone. I have to get the police here. But he's large and strong. He slaps me full force across the face and effortlessly flings me off him.

I slam against the wall, and all the air is knocked from my lungs. I'm stunned, subdued.

Noah wails.

"Shut the fuck up, Noah, before I rip your tongue out and feed it to the dog," Tim yells at him.

The threat only makes Noah cry harder.

Tim keeps his eyes on me but puts his chin over his shoulder to bellow down the stairs, "Ashley, Kevin, get here now and sort your fucking brat out!"

But they must've already heard the commotion and come running up the stairs seconds later. Ashley pushes past Tim and goes straight to her son. She crouches on the floor next to him.

"Are you hurt? Have you fractured anything?" She looks him over, touches all his limbs, examines his face and eyes.

"No, Mummy," he sobs, and she hugs him to her.

"Get him out of my sight," Tim hollers. He's livid. I see him for what he really is – a bulked-up, bald thug.

Ashley picks Noah off the carpet and hurries him into the back bedroom. He limps. I look between Tim and Kevin. They block the stairway. There's no way out that way. Ashley comes back and stands next to Kevin. She sneers at me. But Kevin looks disappointed.

"I knew a child would be a fucking liability," Tim shouts at them.

Ashley purses her lips petulantly, like a child getting told off by a teacher.

Tim continues, "But you wouldn't do the job without bringing your brat along. You told me you'd keep the little shit under control."

Kevin shifts his feet and can't look Tim in the face. But Ashley maintains eye contact, not cowed by Tim's threatening behaviour. Her nostrils flare, and defiant anger sizzles off her. It's clear now – she's the dangerous one in that relationship. She's the loose cannon.

Tim thumps his fist into his flat palm. The slapping sound makes Kevin jump. "It was all going to plan until your brat fucked it up. So we're going to need to restrain her and do this the hard way."

Ashley glances at me, her eyes cold, then dips her chin once in agreement. Kevin glances at Ashley and then stares at his feet.

Tim's the puppet master. He's the one calling the shots here. Why did I ever trust him? Why did I ever believe he was a reformed character? I'm such a fool.

He turns to me, and his bulk is now intimidating. "You're going to sign those power of attorney papers. My solicitor will be here Monday."

"No. I won't sign anything."

He cocks his head in a patronising manner. "Now, now, Jess. Don't be hasty. It would've been so much easier if you'd complied, but we have ways to force you."

"I would never have complied!" I shout at him, but I know it's not true. I was so close to signing everything away to him. I thought it had all been my idea.

"Oh, yes, you would have." His eyes fall on Doug, who is watching the scene unfold in the hallway. He picks him up with one hand and then places his other around the little dog's throat. He squeezes. The dog yips and squirms in distress.

"Let him go!" I shout desperately.

He tightens his grip, and Doug makes a high-pitched squeal that breaks my heart, but I understand. *Tim doesn't make empty threats.* My brother laughs. He drops the dog. Doug darts away, tail between his legs.

Tim wipes his hands together as if brushing dirt off his palms. "We would've kept you incapacitated until that document came through. Whether it took weeks or months, you would've been none the wiser, out for the count on GHB and sleeping pills like a zombie, believing you're in the midst of a mental health breakdown."

"And then what?"

"And then what?" he repeats, mocking my voice. "You really have zero imagination. Then I'd take my money out and give you an overdose. We'd tell the authorities that you committed suicide. A likely story after all your"—he taps the side of his head with a finger—"issues."

"That's what this is all about? You getting your fifty thousand pounds off me? You never got over the inheritance snub from Dad?"

"Oh, my dumb sister. I don't want fifty thousand pounds. I want *five hundred thousand* pounds. You're sat on more than a million from your Oxford house sale. And we"—he indicates himself and then Ashley and Kevin—"plan to split that fifty-fifty."

My mouth flies open. "How do you know that?"

He smirks. "That bastard ex-husband of yours told me everything. We never liked each other. He used to pay me to stay away from you, to keep your stress levels down while you were trying to get pregnant. It started the day after I jumped you in that car park. But when that payment stopped, I came looking for him. It was because you two were getting a divorce. And we discovered we had something in common – we both hated you. He blabbed all about your mental health issues, your miscarriages, your affair. He really is a vile man."

"You're a vile man! Why don't you just kill me?"

"Oh, no, we couldn't just *kill you* because then we would've needed you to change your will to leave the money to me. That would've been trickier because it always looks suspicious if a will is changed shortly before death. But a power of attorney is perfect. We just need to keep you alive until this document comes through. We'll have to force-feed you now. It's going to be ugly. But hey-ho, I'm willing to do anything for my pathetic little sister."

I have to get out of here. I run forward and kick Tim in the shin and flee past him, heading for the stairs.

But Kevin grabs me and holds tight before I can even put my foot on the top stair. I wriggle and scream and stomp on his bare feet. He winces but holds tight.

"Put her in the bedroom," Tim commands. "I'll get something to tie her down with."

Kevin shoves me towards my bedroom. I can't let them restrain me – that will be the end. I have to escape.

Ashley moves out of the way to let us past, and everything about her is hard, no longer the friendly, cheerful woman I used to know. She sneers at me, disgusted, like I'm dog poo on her shoe.

But there's something I know. There's something that might help me.

"Ashley," I spit her name to get her attention. "Noah isn't really ill. Kevin has been lying to you."

Kevin tenses and stops but keeps his grip on me. Tim makes a guttural sound like a deep growl. Ashley's eyes narrow.

"Noah," I shout at the top of my lungs, "tell her! Now's your chance! Tell your mummy everything!"

I hold my breath. Time seems to stand still. We all stare towards the back bedroom.

When the door doesn't open, Ashley glares at me. I don't recognise her. It's as if she had two completely different faces, and now I'm seeing the true one. She hisses at me, "Don't bring my son into this, bitch."

I shrink away from her, bracing myself against the violence she looks ready to commit.

"Mummy," a small voice says from a crack in the door. Ashley's attention snaps there. Then the door opens fully, and Noah shuffles into the hallway. He touches his toe to the other one, gazing at his feet. He wrings his hands and chews his lips. Then he waggles his head as if locked in an internal struggle. Honesty must win out, as his shoulders straighten, and he looks up at his mother. "It's true."

Ashley softens and kneels so she's eye level with him. She takes his hands in hers. "It's all right, my little Spider-Man. You can tell me anything. I love you no matter what."

Noah blinks and sniffs. "I don't really have a limp. My leg is fine, look." He jumps up and down.

Ashley gasps. "Be careful, baby." She attempts to hold him still.

But Noah doesn't stop, shrugging off her hands, doing star jumps and running on the spot. "I'm not poorly! I don't have any pain."

She watches him, her eyes travelling all over his body. "What... I don't understand..."

Noah pauses his dance. "Daddy and I have been tricking you, and I'm so sorry." He points at Kevin. "Daddy made me do it. He made me lie because he said you'd leave us otherwise and told me to keep quiet."

Ashley's face contorts from confusion to realisation to anger, and she twists to stand facing Kevin. "Explain."

There's so much venom in that one word that Kevin shudders, and I hear him gulp next to me.

When he doesn't answer, Ashley yells, "Prove to me that Noah is sick."

Kevin shakes his head. All the colour drains from his face.

"Prove it!" she repeats.

His mouth opens, and in the faintest of voices, he says, "He's got CRMO... his limp... the doctors confirmed it. I showed you the test results. I'll find that document..."

But Noah is on a roll, clearly relieved to be finally spilling his secret. "I've never even been to a hospital, Mummy. He made that on a computer at the library and printed it out there. We'd go to the park or the cinema when we told you we were going for my treatment."

"Noah," Kevin says desperately, "what have I told you about telling fibs?"

Noah raises his voice. "You're the biggest fibber of them all!"

Ashley flicks her gaze between them. And, just like I did, she chooses to believe the boy.

She thumps Kevin on the chest. "I can't believe it. You've

been lying to me for the past four years. You knew I'd never question it because I wouldn't ever go with you to the hospital because of my phobia. You fucking bastard."

"Ashley, my darling, I did it for you. I love you so much, and you threatened to leave me. You're my entire life…" Kevin blubbers, his voice cracking.

Tim shouts, "We don't have time for this shit right now." But Ashley and Kevin both ignore him.

Ashley lets out an almighty scream in Kevin's face. He closes his eyes against the force of it. She grabs Noah's hand. "I'm leaving you and taking Noah."

"You can't leave me. You can never leave me." Kevin's grip on me lessens as he reaches out to Ashley with one hand in a desperate bid to save their relationship.

But she swats it away. "Get out of my way!"

"No," Kevin replies. "We're meant to be together, forever. I gave up everything for you."

Ashley pummels and slaps at him hysterically with the one arm not holding Noah. Kevin doesn't react, just lets her hit him.

Tim steps between them like a nightclub bouncer breaking up a fight. "You two are screwed up. I knew Noah was ill, but not that Kevin was pretending, but you know what? *It doesn't fucking matter.*"

"Noah and I are leaving," Ashley says defiantly to Tim.

He jabs a finger in her face. "Neither of you is going anywhere. We've got a job to finish. Whether the boy is sick or not sick, who gives a shit? There's a million pounds up for grabs."

Ashley snarls at Tim, shoves past Kevin, and yanks Noah past his father. "Fuck the job, fuck the money! My poor baby. We're going."

She makes it to the top of the stairs before Tim shoulder barges her into a wall. She drops Noah's hand and fights back:

snarling, kicking, biting, hitting like a scrawny alley cat cornered and fighting for its life against a bigger foe.

Tim attempts to restrain her, but she thrashes and flails her arms. He quickly loses patience, and when her long fingernail draws blood across his cheek, he headbutts her.

The damage is instant. Ashley's nose explodes with a crack. Her eyes roll up into her head, and she slides unconscious down the wall onto the carpet.

"Mummy!" Noah steps towards Tim, his little fists pumping, but Tim pushes him away with zero effort, and the boy lands in a crumpled mess by my feet.

Kevin lets go of me and leaps on Tim's back. "How dare you touch my wife!"

ife? But I have no time to dwell on this as Kevin and Tim tussle. They're about the same height, but Tim has a weight advantage. They struggle and punch and grunt.

I see my chance.

I grab Noah up and drag him into my bedroom. Doug races in after us. I slam the door shut and tip the bedside cabinet over to block the way. I look around my room for a weapon. My eyes settle on the vase, but I know that won't stop him.

Tim thumps on the door. "I won't let you get away, Jess. You're not going anywhere."

Noah yelps. Tim attempts to open the door, but it catches on the bedside cabinet. The door rattles on its hinges, and I guess Tim is ramming it with his shoulder to force the obstacle out of the way.

"Stay there," I say to Noah.

I grab the chair that I'd used to stand on earlier and throw it against the window with all my strength. The window shatters just as I hear a crack from the door.

I punch out the glass, ignoring the pain in my hands as the shards slice my skin.

"Get out there, now," I say and usher Noah to me.

I help him climb through the window onto the flat roof. I pick up Doug and hand him to Noah. The door flies open wide enough to let Tim through as I climb out the window.

"Get back here," Tim yells, jumping over the toppled cabinet.

I clutch Noah to me, and we run to the far end of the flat roof. I look over the edge, but the garden below us is too far to jump.

Tim steps through the window. He looks deranged: his eyes bulging, his cheeks enflamed, his lips parted to show his teeth.

"Noah, you need to hang off the edge and then let go—" I start, but Tim grabs me.

I put Noah behind me and scream for help. Noah shouts too, "Help! Somebody, please help us!"

Tim puts his arms around me and slams a hand over my mouth to silence me. He attempts to wrestle me back towards the window, but I struggle and kick at his legs. I bite his fingers that cover my mouth.

"Fuck's sake," he hisses. "Get back in the house."

"No! Leave us alone," I wail before his hand clamps down on my mouth again. Doug barks, chasing around our feet. I twist and turn to break free of his grip, but he's stronger than me and drags me closer to the house.

Doug growls.

Tim pauses, looks down, and grunts. "Little shit."

The border terrier has his mouth latched around Tim's ankle. Tim lifts up his leg and kicks out to shake off the dog, but Doug hangs on, his jaws locked tight. From the side, Noah bundles into Tim. Doug drops away.

Tim loses his footing and lets go of me to right himself. I

shove him away from me with both hands. He stumbles, catches his foot in the guttering around the edge of the roof, and trips backwards.

His arms cartwheel as he's suspended in space. Then he falls. There's an ugly thump as he lands on the patio about eleven feet underneath.

I grab Noah to me and hug him. We both pant and cry. Doug winds around our legs.

"Hey!" a male voice shouts.

My head turns towards the sound. There's a man stood in the next-door garden. A neighbour.

He continues, "You're going to be all right. You stay right there. The missus is already calling the police and an ambulance."

He climbs up and over the fence and looks down at where Tim landed. He shakes his head and retches. Then he looks up at me. "He won't be hurting you again, love. You're safe now."

I collapse to my knees, and Noah falls with me. We hold each other tight.

35

Two days later, I sit at the dining table with a cup of coffee and a huge slab of homemade carrot cake that my neighbours brought over earlier when they checked in on me. They've been incredibly kind to me since witnessing the rooftop struggle. I've also had a victim support officer assigned to me, and they came around yesterday and will pop in again tomorrow.

My laptop is open, and I'm reading all the bonkers emails that Ashley sent to my clients.

I'd trusted her to send emails to them to say I was unwell and off work, but she'd emailed rants or nonsense or confessions that I'd overcharged them or that I loathed working with them.

The full extent of what they did is still coming to light, and how they'd thought of everything to make me appear insane to everyone around me.

They knew how it would've looked when I visited Toni and Marcus, and then Blake, when I was drugged up and delusional. They were building a case so that when they faked my suicide, all the evidence would suggest I was mentally unstable and it was to be expected.

I take a bite of cake and look through the Sent Items at the other emails she'd sent.

Ashley had also kept up regular weekly emails to my aunt and uncle with photos of Doug in the garden or on the beach that claimed that I was doing great and that everything was fine. It ensured my aunt and uncle didn't return from their trip early if I'd stopped emailing them because they were worried. She sounded so much like me in how she wrote and the words she used. They were none the wiser.

The doorbell rings. It makes me jump. I think it always will, but I know it's nothing to be worried about. It's Detective Adam Mealy, and he messaged me earlier to say he'd be dropping by to update me on the case.

I open the door, and we head into the lounge.

"Do you want a coffee?" I ask.

"No, thanks." He holds up a flask of water. "Trying to cut down on the caffeine and drink more H_2O. Doctor's orders to save my poor kidneys."

It reminds me of Kevin's obsession with staying hydrated, and once again, I'm reminded how they almost had me by making me believe getting power of attorney was all my idea. How their plan to rob and murder me by faking my suicide had come so close to success.

Detective Mealy settles himself on the sofa and pulls out a notepad. He has a kind face and a warm smile. He's overweight with a large belly, and he has a steady and efficient manner about him that I appreciate. "How are you doing?"

"I'm doing okay. I think all the drugs are finally working their way out of my system." They'd plied me with all sorts, my blood tests showed. And probably even more that didn't show up in my system, based on the police's analysis of

Kevin's stash of illegal and legal drugs, which they'd found hidden under the bed.

"That's good to hear. Well, I thought you'd like the latest."

I nod. On Sunday, the police and an ambulance had arrived within ten minutes. Ashley and Kevin were both found in the upstairs hallway. Ashley was still unconscious from Tim's headbutt, and Kevin had been beaten to within an inch of his life.

They found Tim on the patio in the back garden. He was already dead, having hit his head when he fell on a low brick wall that surrounded a raised flowerbed.

Noah and I were discovered still clutching one another on the flat roof, and it took a lot of coaxing by some very patient police officers to convince us we were now safe. We'd been taken to hospital for various tests while Doug had been looked after by my neighbours.

Noah and I had caused a scene about being separated, but it was the only appropriate course of action, according to the police. Noah had been taken into care, and I'd been kept in overnight and discharged on Monday morning.

The detective continues, "Ashley and Kevin have been charged with fraud and conspiracy to murder and a few other charges related to possession of illegal drugs and so on. They are wanted on charges in a few other counties too. It appears they were quite prolific at conning people. They'll be going to jail for a long time."

My skin crawls at the thought I was just another mark. "Good. They won't be able to swindle anyone again. What about Kevin's treatment of Noah?"

He takes a swig of water, grimacing slightly as if he'd much rather be drinking coffee. "Kevin has also been charged with child abuse. He's being assessed by psychologists, but it's likely he'll be diagnosed with a mental health disorder called 'Munchausen syndrome by proxy'. It's where a caregiver makes up an illness in a person under their care. It's clear that Ashley was completely oblivious that Noah was healthy and trusted Kevin implicitly. Noah's pretend illness was Kevin's way to manipulate Ashley."

I think of the skinny, pale boy in his stripey dressing gown, so desperate for a friend. "Poor Noah."

"Yes. Noah was manipulated by Kevin, and at first, Noah believed he was ill. But then he caught on. Kevin used Ashley's fear of hospitals against her. Noah was kept inside for years because of his fake condition, and Kevin home-schooled him."

"That's so awful. Why would Kevin do that to his son?"

"Well, this is where it gets interesting. Kevin and Ashley have a *complex* history. They met at school. He was her teacher. She was fourteen and he was twenty-nine when they started a relationship. They ran off together to France when she was fifteen because she was being severely bullied and sexually abused by one of the guardians she went to live with when her parents died. She was suicidal. Kevin thought he was her saviour. And she thought he was saving her."

"Wow. So her being an orphan was true, then."

"She told you that? Then yes, that bit was true. Anyway, they were caught, of course, and brought back to the UK. Kevin went to prison for two years for child abduction but served one and a half. They stayed in touch. And when he was released, they restarted their relationship. But he'd been kicked out of the teaching profession, and both had been ostracised by their families, so they turned to conning people for money. Kevin had been a physics teacher, but after prison, the only jobs available to him were hard labour, which he failed miserably at. And Ashley had left school with no quali-fications. Both were very bright and avoided police notice for many years by targeting wealthy widows, rich philandering married men and lone elderly people. But it all started to go wrong when Noah was born. Kevin didn't want a child. He was obsessed with Ashley, but Ashley was desperate to be a mother."

"Sounds really messed up."

"Under interview, Ashley is turning on Kevin. But he's remaining loyal to her. But they've both said that Tim was the mastermind of the plan to manipulate you into giving power of attorney to Tim so he could oversee your financial affairs, access your bank accounts and steal your money."

"I just can't believe it almost worked. They almost had me convinced that I was losing my mind."

"Well, they preyed on your weaknesses. They knew making you believe you had a stalker would trigger your mental health issues. And Ashley's faking a miscarriage was bound to bring you two closer due to your personal experiences."

They'd found fake blood in Ashley's possessions. The stuff used for fancy dress, easy to buy online. She'd put it on her jeans so I'd see it. I push my fingers into my hair and lift it off my scalp. "Everything was a lie. I really thought she was my friend."

"I'm sorry about that, Jess."

I stare into space. I never thought something like this would ever happen to me. Who does?

After a couple of seconds, he continues, "There's been a few more things come to light."

"Such as?"

Detective Mealy looks at his notepad and flicks a few pages until he finds the notes he's looking for. "There was a man, Jamal Little, who was hired to seduce you and then dump you to cause emotional distress."

"Jamal? Oh my God." I'd thought he was potentially *The One*. How fooled I'd been.

"He also played the part of an estate agent too, I believe,

when they attempted to trick you into thinking you'd almost purchased a house."

"That was fake too?"

"And there was a"—he checks his notes—"Dr Clegg."

"He wasn't a real doctor?"

"Not exactly. He's actually a real doctor, from Leeds, who is wanted for some fraudulent dealings with gangs. He and Jamal were promised payment by Tim for playing their parts in your swindle. A warrant is out for their arrest."

"I believed it all. I feel so stupid."

"Don't. These are professional con artists. It's what they do. Looking at their history, they were very experienced. There's a couple more things." The detective checks his notes again and continues, "We found a receipt in Kevin's possessions that indicated the car seats of your Honda had been repaired after they slashed them. And according to Ashley, Tim hired an actor who looked similar to your ex-husband."

I groan. In this past month or so, absolutely nothing had been real. They'd had their fingers in all of it.

The detective continues, "And we've confirmed that Tim was the one who attacked you down that alleyway and that your aunt mentioned in passing you'd be going to a co-working place when she met with him. The Hive is the only one in town."

I wish I'd listened to my gut that Friday night. It had told me it was Tim, loud and clear. And I'd ignored it. "Was Tim a grifter too?"

"No, Tim was a small-time criminal in Leeds. Suspected of drug dealing, mostly, and some illegal dogfighting activity, according to West Yorkshire Police. There was also a domestic abuse charge that got dropped. It's safe to say he had connections in the shady underworld. He found Ashley and Kevin through friends of friends. That BMW he drove was stolen, and his business website was all faked."

I shake my head. "He seemed so genuine." I indicate the seahorse blanket. "Do you mind?"

"You go right ahead," the detective replies.

I pick it up and wrap it around me. "I seem to go from cold to hot to cold again."

"It's likely the drugs still working their way out of your system. On that note, toxicology results indicated Tim was a regular cocaine user."

"So he'd kicked the heroin but moved on to cocaine."

"He was a heroin addict? Then yes, there were no traces of that. It appears he was a high-functioning drug user."

I think of his face in the split second before he fell. He hadn't looked scared, he'd looked... surprised, so gobsmacked that he'd not won. The police told me they'd cleaned up the patio as much as possible when I got back from the hospital, but I still haven't gone out there. I can't bring myself to look at that spot just yet. "What's going to happen about him?"

"There'll be an inquest into how he died, and you might need to attend. But you've not been charged with his death. Your testimony, that of Noah's, and the neighbour witnesses all corroborate that it was an accident and that you acted in self-defence. Plus, Ashley and Kevin are chirping like hungry chicks about his involvement and his obsession with getting revenge on you."

I'd honestly thought I'd got my brother back. Although I know I shouldn't grieve for a man who'd planned to drive me insane and then fake my suicide, I can't help it. We'd been so close as children. He'd been such a sweet, funny boy.

"What will happen to Noah?" I ask.

"Well, he's with a foster family at the moment. There's no chance he'll ever go back to his parents. I imagine he'll be put up for adoption. But as he's ten, it might be hard to place him."

"You know, I thought he wasn't real when I first saw him. I thought I was hallucinating him."

"The psychological torture they inflicted on you was truly awful. But we'll make sure justice is served."

"Thank you."

He stands and tucks the water bottle under one arm. "Right, well, I think we're all caught up, so I'll be off. Do you have anyone who can come and stay with you for a while?"

"Yes, my aunt and uncle are on their way home from their cruise. I tried to tell them not to come, but they insisted. They were fooled by Tim too and feel awful about it."

"When do they get home?"

"Tomorrow."

"Good. This is going to take some time to get over. And I think you need them here to support you."

I see the detective out and pick up Doug for a cuddle. I know it will take a long time for me to heal. Trusting people and being betrayed cuts deeply. But I'm not the only one who's been betrayed by those they trusted.

I walk along the beach at Weston-super-Mare. The tide is in for a change. It's a crisp, sunny, spring day. Every breath of clean air feels refreshing and rejuvenating. I walk the dog two to three times a day now. Even during the week, I put my thriving business on hold to get out of the house. The exercise is good for me, always lifting my mood.

My new house is only a short stroll from the seafront. I decided to make this town my own, close to my aunt and uncle and perfect for the quiet, settled, drama-free life I longed for.

The house is big, but I don't feel anxious in it. I'm not alone.

Noah whoops and cheers, chasing after Lexi, a border collie cross we adopted from the rescue shelter. She loves her ball to be thrown, and she loves to run. Just like Noah. I'm pretty sure he'll be a sprinter when he grows up.

Every now and then, Noah looks around in wonder, and I remember that he was shut away for years of his life. Running in a wide-open space is still novel for him. He had a horrific childhood, the son of con artist parents, and never went to school, but I have a lot of love to give and all the time in the world to help him get through it.

He's adjusted quickly, though. Children are so resilient. It's incredible, really. He loves his new school. He's very clever, excelling at sciences. And although it took a little time, he now has a great group of friends – and a best friend he tells all his secrets to, I'm sure.

And he's helped me heal too. I'm a mum now, and I love my adopted son. We're in this together, and I'll never let him down. I fought hard to adopt him. I couldn't let him stay in the care system, in and out of foster homes and knowing he wasn't as 'adoptable' as the younger ones. He's the one who saved me. If it hadn't been for Noah, Tim's plan would've succeeded, and I wouldn't be here.

I know it'll take time for me to learn to trust anyone again. My new counsellor tells me that I'm naturally very trusting of people, that I want to believe they are genuine and see the good in them. She says that's not something to feel ashamed about. It's a superpower. Who wants to go through life doubting everything anyone ever tells them and suspecting everyone's intentions are dishonourable? It's no way to live. It's just unfortunate that other people have taken advantage of my trusting nature. She's encouraging me not to fight against it but to embrace it and instead teaching me to recognise the red flags that indicate when others are taking advantage.

It's a work in progress, but I'm getting there. I have a second date tonight with the son of my aunt and uncle's neighbours, the ones who called the police and ambulance and who were so kind to me after. We're taking it very, very slowly. But so far, he seems like a really nice guy.

All in all, life couldn't be better.

AUTHOR'S NOTE

Did you enjoy reading *Here For You*? Please could you leave a review on Amazon? Your review will help other readers to discover the novel and I hugely appreciate your help in spreading the word.

Massive thanks to Brian, Garret and Claire at Inkubator Books. I really enjoy working with you all to bring my stories to life.

Big love to my parents, Ann and Brian, and to my wonderful sister, Kath, for all their endless support, honest feedback and patience.

I'd also like to say a huge thank you to my best mate, Becky, who lets me regularly come to stay at her house in Weston-super-Mare and showed me the sights for 'research'. Also to all the fab people I've met at co-working spaces around the world – thank goodness none of you have ever turned out to be an Ashley.

My gratitude to my uncle who often lets me look after his awesome border terrier, Reggie. And also to my friends, family, unsuspecting acquaintances and random strangers who supply me with so many ideas for back-stories, events and weird character quirks.

And a shout-out to all my readers – thank you for taking a chance on me and my novels and for taking the time to read *Here For You* – I'm very grateful for your support.

Nora Valters
December 2021

ABOUT THE AUTHOR

Nora Valters grew up in the New Forest in the south of England and has lived in London, Manchester, Bournemouth, Oxford and Dubai.

She studied English Literature and Language at Oxford Brookes University before embarking on a career in marketing and copywriting.

Her debut psychological thriller was published in 2020 and she's been writing ever since.

Nora loves to travel and has journeyed around the world. She enjoys exploring new places, painting, hiking, and is an avid reader. She's also a bit obsessed with dogs...

Find Nora on her website www.noravalters.com or connect with her on her social media.

ALSO BY NORA VALTERS

Inkubator Books Titles

NOW YOU KNOW

HERE FOR YOU

THE PARTY

Other Titles

HER BIGGEST FAN

Printed in Great Britain
by Amazon

41420948R00169